W9-AWE-179

AN UNUSUAL COLLECTION

The Ripper smiled at the face of Jennifer Kress, floating in a jar of preservative, the long hair fanning out around the face. Such a lovely face.

The Ripper loved all the dead faces in the collection—and it was *quite* a collection. The Ripper did not always take the faces. Sometimes the faces would be ugly—and the Ripper did not like ugliness—so sometimes something else would have to be taken. Some other beautiful part of some lucky boy or girl's body would go into a jar, and join the Ripper's lovely collection.

Most of the Ripper's victims' bodies hadn't been found, having been carefully buried over the years and several thousand miles. The Ripper thought, *where is the challenge?*

Sighing, the Ripper carried each large jar back to its place, placing a long, wet kiss against the glass. *Oh, wouldn't it be lovely to kiss those dead lips!* But once sealed in the fluid, living lips would have to touch only the coolness of the glass and play pretend.

This is beginning to get boring . . . what can I do to make this game more interesting?

What the Ripper Did Next Was Unbelievable . . .

NOW THERE'S NO NEED TO WAIT UNTIL DARK!
DAY OR NIGHT, ZEBRA'S VAMPIRE NOVELS
HAVE QUITE A BITE!

THE VAMPIRE JOURNALS (4133, $4.50)
by Traci Briery

Maria Theresa Allogiamento is a vampire ahead of her time. As she travels from 18th-century Italy to present-day Los Angeles, Theresa sets the record straight. From how she chose immortality to her transformation into a seductive temptress, Theresa shares all of her dark secrets and quenches her insatiable thirst for all the world has to offer!

NIGHT BLOOD (4063, $4.50)
by Eric Flanders

Each day when the sun goes down, Val Romero feeds upon the living. This NIGHT BLOOD is the ultimate aphrodisiac. Driving from state to state in his '69 Cadillac, he leaves a trail of bloodless corpses behind. Some call him a serial killer, but those in the know call him Vampire. Now, three tormented souls driven by revenge and dark desires are tracking Val down—and only Val's death will satisfy their own raging thirst for blood!

THE UNDEAD (4068, $5.50)
by Roxanne Longstreet

Most people avoid the cold and sterile halls of the morgue. But for Adam Radburn working as a morgue attendant is a perfect job. He is a vampire. Though Adam has killed for blood, there is another who kills for pleasure and he wants to destroy Adam. And in the world of the undead, the winner is not the one who lives the longest, it's the one who lives forever!

PRECIOUS BLOOD (4293, $4.50)
by Pat Graversen

Adragon Hart, leader of the Society of Vampires, loves his daughter dearly. So does Quinn, a vampire renegade who has lured Beth to the savage streets of New York and into his obscene world of unquenchable desire. Every minute Quinn's hunger is growing. Every hour Adragon's rage is mounting. And both will do anything to satisfy their horrific appetites!

THE SUMMONING (4221, $4.50)
by Bentley Little

The first body was found completely purged of all blood. The authorities thought it was the work of a serial killer. But Sue Wing's grandmother knew the truth. She'd seen the deadly creature decades ago in China. Now it had come to the dusty Arizona town of Rio Verde . . . and it would not leave until it had drunk its fill.

Available wherever paperbacks are sold, or order direct from the Publisher. Send cover price plus 50¢ per copy for mailing and handling to Penguin USA, P.O. Box 999, c/o Dept. 17109, Bergenfield, NJ 07621. Residents of New York and Tennessee must include sales tax. DO NOT SEND CASH.

WILLIAM W. JOHNSTONE

ZEBRA BOOKS
KENSINGTON PUBLISHING CORP.

ZEBRA BOOKS are published by

Kensington Publishing Corp.
850 Third Avenue
New York, NY 10022

Copyright © 1994 by William W. Johnstone

This novel is a work of fiction. Names, characters, places, and incidents are either the product of the author's imagination or are used fictitiously, and any resemblance to actual persons, living or dead, events, or locales, is entirely coincidental. The town of La Barca, California is fictional, and to the best of my knowledge, so is radio and TV station KSIN.

All rights reserved. No part of this book may be reproduced in any form or by any means without the prior written consent of the Publisher, excepting brief quotes used in reviews.

If you purchased this book without a cover you should be aware that this book is stolen property. It was reported as "unsold and destroyed" to the Publisher and neither the Author nor the Publisher has received any payment for this "stripped book."

Zebra and the Z logo Reg. U.S. Pat. & TM Off.

First Printing: November, 1994

Printed in the United States of America

Somewhere—in desolate windswept space—
In Twilight land—in No-man's land—
Two hurrying Shapes met face-to-face,
And bade each other stand.

"And who are you?" cried one agape,
Shuddering in the gloaming light.
"I know not," said the second shape,
"I only died last night!"

—Thomas Bailey Aldrich

Chapter 1

"If God created anything better than pussy," Wind-jammer said, "He damn sure kept it for Himself."

"Oh, my God!" Dick Hale said, glancing wildly around him, his eyes wide. "You fool! Is your mike closed?"

Windjammer stared at the station manager, open contempt in the gaze. After working in broadcasting for more than twenty years, from New Jersey to California, with stops both north and south of that famous Mason/Dixon line, Windjammer had reached at least one firm conclusion about most station managers; they all shared one thing in common: they were totally ignorant about control rooms.

Before Windjammer could tell Dick where to take his asinine question, and in what part of his anatomy he could shove it once he got it there—which would have been very uncomfortable for the man, not to mention unsightly—the chief engineer stepped in and once again Windjammer's job was secure; at least for another day.

"Dick," the engineer said patiently, in the tone one uses when attempting to converse with a very small child or a cocker spaniel. "As long as you can hear the music coming out of that speaker," he pointed, "the mike is closed."

"Oh!" Dick said. "Well. Good." He walked out of the control room.

"As if that puke-brain hasn't been told that at least twenty thousand times in the past," Windjammer said, shaking his head. His recording was winding down. Automatically, from years of experience, he put his brain into gear a split second before his mouth opened, and introed the original Charlie Barnett recording of "Cherokee," then turned back to the engineer.

The engineer cut him off short. "Don't start with me, Jammer. You got it made here, and you know it. You also know that Trickie-Dickie doesn't like you at all. But all you have to do to keep your job, is keep your mouth shut around him. Look, you got good pay, great hours, a gorgeous P.D. to work under—"

Windjammer grinned lewdly. "I'd like to work under her, and around her, and beside her, and—"

"All right, boys," Stacy Ryan announced her presence, as she pushed open the door to the control room. She knew DJs very well. "Knock off the locker-room talk." The program director of radio station KSIN stepped into the control room, the door automatically closing behind her. The scent of her perfume was an invisible fragrant touch.

Windjammer groaned and began panting.

The engineer shook his head, even though he knew Stacy did not take the slightest bit of offense at the Jammer's actions. "I'm leaving," he said, looking at Stacy and pointing at Windjammer. "If you feel safe around that animal, that is."

She laughed, a sexy, throaty laugh. "His bark is worse than his bite, Cal."

"I'll bite you anywhere you like, Stacy," Windjammer said. "And right now I can think of—"

"Shut up, Jammer!" she told him flatly. "Now you listen to me. You can get away with that kind of talk with me. But if you ever leave this station—and the odds of that are pretty damn good right now—there are a lot of women who would slap a sexual harassment suit on your butt in a heartbeat. And win it. So you just shut up and listen for a minute. See you, Cal."

"I'm gone."

The control-room door hissed silently open and closed as Windjammer took note of Stacy's serious expression. "All right, Stacy. Lay it on me."

She sat down on a stool. "This war between you and Dick has to stop, Jammer."

"There is no war, Tally." Stacy's on-air name was Tally-Ho. "The man is ignorant, obnoxious, overbearing, and a total jackass."

"I agree, Jammer. All that is true. But he is the boss." She paused. She did not have to tell him his recording was ending. Any DJ worth his or her salt had invisible monitors and clocks in their heads. She waited while Jammer ad-libbed right to the mark for thirty seconds, wondering aloud whether Dolly Parton had ever in her life been able to look down and see her feet. Jammer ID'd the station, then hit network news.

He swiveled in his chair to look at her.

"I mean it, Jammer. Try to avoid Dick as much as possible. When you have to be around him, be civil and not smart-assed. I'm not asking you to give him a great big, sloppy kiss. Just be civil to the man."

Jammer smiled ruefully. "Man? If that prissy bastard is a man, I'm an aardvark. Okay, okay, Tally. What you're saying is: I either kiss his ass, or I'm out on my ear, right?"

"It would be over some very loud objections from me; but that *is* the bottom line, buddy. High rating or no."

He nodded his head, all the while thinking some pretty bloody thoughts. He mentally shoved those away. They'd been occurring with alarming regularity of late. "Level with me, Tally: is Mister Prissy out to get me?"

Without hesitation, she said, "Yeah, Jammer. He sure is. Ever since those things you said about his kids got back to him."

Jammer laughed. "Hell, Tally. I *wanted* them to get back to him. I said his daughter was a spoiled brat and a snooty bitch, and his son a total nerd. Am I wrong in that assessment? Am I not entitled to a personal opinion?"

The program director of KSIN FM sighed. Jammer was right about Dick's kids; both of them *were* insufferable brats, for a fact. And Stacy despised Dick Hale just as much as anybody. And that was very nearly everybody that ever came in contact with the bastard. "Jammer . . . you just chill out with the remarks. Free speech ends at the employer's door. Sad, but true." She stood up and walked out of the control room.

Not even the sight of Tally-Ho's marvelously shaped derriere could overcome the sudden realization that his time with KSIN was coming to a close. DJs have a sixth sense about that, too. Windjammer leaned back in his chair, wondering how long he had left. Did he have enough time to accomplish what he'd set out to do? He hoped so. He'd worked long and hard at setting it up. God, he hated Dick Hale.

La Barca, California sat almost exactly between San Francisco and Los Angeles. A bay town, the bay named Puno Bay because it was shaped like a fist, the city built around the knuckles. La Barca was a factory and tourist city of almost half a million. The number one radio station in the area was, of course, thanks to the kids, a rock-and-roll station. But number two was KSIN; a very comfortable and very profitable number two.

During the day, from six in the morning until six in the evening, KSIN played adult music for mature people. Not the department store/elevator, saccharine type of music that has been known to drive listeners mad, but original recordings from the Ink Spots to any contemporary music the PD felt would flow with the sound she wanted. A little Ronstadt, Manilow, Milsap type of sound; some very soft rock. Programming was the only area in which Dick kept his mouth out of matters, and that was due in no small part to the fact that a Mrs. Carla Upton owned fifty-five percent of KSIN AM, FM, and TV, to Dick Hale's forty-five percent. And Mrs. Upton and Tally-Ho were good friends. *Very* close. Intimate, one might say.

Carla Upton was on the long list of people who positively loathed Dick Hale. She also was a very smart businesswoman who knew that Tally-Ho was a fine program director who worked well with people and kept KSIN FM solidly in the black, despite the excesses of Dick Hale.

While KSIN held a good share of listeners during the day, it was at night that the station showed its stuff. At night, KSIN played night music for night people. Music to tune into if you're having a cocktail party for adults; music to work and relax and make love to. Sexy saxes and smooth trumpets, the classic beat of Brubeck and Davis. The pipes of Sinatra and Bennett. KSIN grabbed the adult audience of La Barca and surrounding areas in a velvet fist and held it.

"SIN radio," was the call. "It's nighttime in the city."

William "Bill" Jarry, known on the air as BJ,

shoved off at six in the evenings and stroked it until ten at night. Ah . . . but at ten. That was when Jennifer Lomax, known to a quarter of a million people as Jenny Caesar (just like the salad, good to eat), took the mike at SIN and no less than a thousand males on any given night ejaculated to her voice. Jenny was the top DJ at KSIN. She allowed only twelve minutes of commercial time per hour, and the sponsors paid dearly and willingly for that time. Jenny's voice was a soft, wet kiss in the night, with lots of tongue action and foreplay.

At two o'clock in the morning, Jimmy Turcotte, known as The Turk, took over and carried it until six in the morning. Hal Fortier, known as Frenchy, grabbed the mike for wake-up time in La Barca. He ran the board until ten, when Tally-Ho took over. From two until six in the evenings—known as drive time—Windjammer ran the ship.

The part-timers, while not as good as the regulars, were very nearly as professional, with no change in format, ever.

Of course, the regulars had their voices heard seven days and nights a week, on tape, on TV, and on KSIN AM, as well as on FM. Some of the music heard over KSIN was on tape. Since much of the music played on FM was not available on CD, putting it on cart was a smart move. A very smart move on one person's part.

That person understood overdubbing and tracking. That person had spent years studying the subtleties of subliminal perception and suggestion. That person was a genius. And that person had the patience to wait while the subject's subconscious mind absorbed the subliminal messages cleverly hidden behind the music.

That person had worked hard to cover any back trail that might expose the real identity. Had worked very hard to conceal all the years spent in locked rooms in private mental institutions, while the most skilled doctors available tried to heal the brilliantly tortured mind.

The doctors had failed.

Of course, what was being done at KSIN was all in fun.

Fun being relative to that individual's state of mind.

Chapter 2

"It's gonna be a gorgeous day in Fist City," Frenchy said, knowing how the term Fist City irritated the elected and appointed hierarchy of La Barca. "We've got a current temp of fifty-nine and a high today of sixty-nine. And sixty-nine is a good high . . . in more ways than one."

"Don't take it any further, Frenchy," Tally-Ho muttered, as she stretched and yawned and kicked the covers from her five-foot seven-inch frame. She lay naked on the satin sheets. As far as she was concerned, clothes were a necessary encumbrance during the day, but she'd be damned if she'd wear them to bed.

Frenchy introed Frankie Laine's "River Saint Marie" and let the matter of sixty-nine remain only a thought in the minds of the listeners.

As Tally had known he would.

She had a staff of solid professionals at KSIN. Everybody knew their jobs and knew to keep their noses out of other people's departments.

Everybody except Dick Hale.

God! how she hated that bastard. When the time was right, he would get his. She promised herself that every day. Several times a day. When the time was right. She ached for the day when she could hear Dick Hale scream . . .

She shook that thought away and headed for her bath.

Frenchy loved the shift he worked. Like most good DJs, it had not taken him long to find where he worked best in any on-air schedule. He was a morning man, and a damned good one. Frenchy could get out of bed announcing, and in a good mood—at least once he hit the air. Until Dick Hale came into the control room. Even if he kept his mouth shut, Dick still screwed things up just by standing there.

God! Frenchy hated that bastard. He'd do anything to get Hale's license jerked by the FCC. *Anything!*

He calmed himself and opened his mike. "Good mornin', folks. We're gonna have traffic for you shortly, and while I get the whirly bird on the horn, here's Brubeck and 'Blue Rondo A La Turk.' "

Dick Hale would not leave his mind. Frenchy hated him more than any person he could name. Hated him even more than he'd hated his father. And that rotten, abusive obscenity had been the absolute scum of the earth.

Until Frenchy had taken matters into his own hands and . . .

Brubeck was hitting the last notes. "Hey, folks!" Frenchy leaped back into his morning-man role. "Gonna be warm today out from Fist City and away from the coast. Look for a high of about 88 in the outlying communities. Yep. Just like a politician: out lying."

Seconds later, Frenchy's phone light began flashing. He looked at it, knowing in all probability who it was. With a sigh, he picked it up. "KSIN."

Dick Hale. "Goddamnit, Frenchy!" Dick's grating voice ground into Frenchy's ear. "I am sick and tired of your off-color remarks, and your constant use of Fist City on the air. Either shape up and do what I tell you to do, or draw your check and get the hell out! Do you understand all that, you childish fool?"

And Frenchy's show went flat.

Tally picked it up immediately. She was just stepping out of the shower when she heard Frenchy introing Sarah Vaughan. He had about as much enthusiasm in his voice as a person waiting for a double root canal.

She called the station, knowing full well what had just happened. "What's wrong, Frenchy?"

"Pricky-Dickie, what else? Tally, I don't mind being chewed on, but not on the air. Can't that stupid bastard understand it's hard enough to stay up on a good day. But after a lecture from that—" He bit back the words.

Tally knew a DJ could not stay up after a chewing. Just like a singer or actor or anyone else in the performing arts. She'd personally been there too many times. "I'll take care of it, Frenchy. You go get yourself a cup of coffee and try to work it back up. Okay?"

"All right, Tally. I'll do it. You know I will. But I hate that son of a bitch. I really do." He hung up.

Tally-Ho called Carla Upton.

"I guess, by god, I told him who's boss around here," Dick said to his wife, June, and his kids, all seated at the breakfast table.

"Uh-huh," his wife said sweetly. She *knew* who ran the show, and it wasn't her husband.

His kids gushed all over their father.

Like father, like son, and daughter. Sort of.

"Those on-air people are like children," Dick launched into dime-store psychology, which was the only type of psychology he knew anything about . . . and little enough of that. "They have to be disciplined periodically."

"Oh, Daddy, you're so smart," daughter Sue said, nibbling on a piece of toast.

"Well," Dick's ego ballooned. "I have been in broadcasting a number of years."

True. But never behind a mike. Dick, like so many others in his position, could never hope to understand that professional DJs and announcers—and there is a difference—are as much actor and actress as those who appear on the stage or in front of a camera, with just as much temperament.

There were a great many things that Dick Hale seemed not to understand; including the members of his loving family.

He seemed unaware that his son was having a homosexual affair with his suite-mate at collage. He seemed unaware that his daughter was single-handedly— or single-mouthedly—attempting to blow the entire male student body of La Barca Central High School.

He seemed unaware that his wife was involved in some rather bizarre affairs that took place several times a month in the hills above La Barca.

And he did not know that his mistress was tape-recording everything that went on when Dick visited her—in and out of bed.

In short, Dick Hale appeared to be a classic space cadet.

*　*　*

Tuesday morning began as usual for Jessica Kress. Nothing out of the ordinary during her bath, drying her hair, putting on her makeup, drinking her coffee, and eating a bowl of cereal. With lots of fiber. All this was done while listening to her favorite radio station: KSIN. There was that funny commercial that made her laugh. She reached across the breakfast bar and turned up the volume. Then, without consciously realizing she was doing it, she picked up the phone and called KSIN, requesting "September Song"—the version popular years ago, not the latest nasal congestion.

She had no conscious memory of doing that.

She heard the song, heard something slightly different this time, smiled, and said, "All right." Then she locked up the house and went to work.

"Dick," Tally-Ho sat down in his office. "I thought we had cleared the air as to who runs what in this station?"

"Didn't take long for that prima donna to call you," Dick replied, leaning back in his expensive chair; where he kept his butt most of the day. That is, when he wasn't going home to take naps or visiting his mistress.

"Frenchy isn't a prima donna, and he didn't call me. I called *him* after I heard his show go flat. Dick, if you had the common sense to know horseshit from peanut butter, you'd have understood long ago that there is a time and a place to chew on DJs."

Dick flushed deeply and pointed a finger at her. "Little girlie, *you* do not talk to *me* in that manner."

Tally smiled. "I have a legal, binding contract with this station," she stood her ground. "That document spells out, very clearly, my duties at this operation. It further states that it is my responsibility, and mine solely, to hire and fire and discipline on-air personalities. Now, if you want to argue that, Mrs. Upton is awaiting your call." She met his gaze without wavering.

Dick tried to meet her steady gaze. But like most very insecure people, he could not maintain the eye-to-eye contact. He dropped his gaze and cursed. "You goddamn libbers really think you have us men by the balls, don't you, little girlie?"

"You call me Little Girlie again, and that's exactly where I will have you, Little Dickie."

Dick jumped to his feet. "By God, this is *my* station, Stacy! I run it."

Tally stood up, meeting him eyeball to eyeball. "Run it? That's a joke. You can't even splice a tape or cue up a record, before we went to CD and cart, that is. You don't know anything about a control room. You don't know anything about on-air personalities. You've never sat behind a mike in your life. You wouldn't last five minutes, if you really had to work in radio or TV. If your daddy hadn't given you the stock in this operation, you'd be out on the street panhandling. We've got the best salespeople in this city here at KSIN, Dick. They're the ones selling the time, not you. You couldn't sell a heater to an Eskimo. The only thing you do around here is draw a check . . . and a damn good check, thanks to the efforts of those who work here. Now we have a contract, Dick, and by god, I'm going to hold you to that contract. Now, if that is not agreeable, you can buy out my contract. Right now. I take my format with me, and every DJ you've got here will walk out with me."

Dick paled. Her contract had just been renegotiated. "That's a three-year contract, Stacy."

"That's right, Dickie," she said with a smile. "So the next move is yours."

Dick did some quick math. As usual, he got it wrong, but he came close enough. He swallowed hard. "There will come a day of reckoning, litt—Stacy. Bet on it."

Tally's smile changed, becoming hard and mean. "I'm looking forward to it, Dick. I can't tell you how much I'm looking forward to it."

"Get out of my office, you—cunt!"

She laughed and flipped him the rigid digit, then walked out, slamming the door behind her.

"You bitch!" Dick fumed at the closed door. Then he took his anger out on his secretary. "Bring me a cup of coffee!" he shouted over the intercom. "And do it right now!"

"Sorry, Paula," Tally said to the receptionist. "I got him all stirred up."

Paula Darling smiled her understanding as she stood up and moved to the coffeepot. "One of these days I'm going to work up the courage to pour this on his head."

"Get it good and hot and dump the whole pot on his crotch," Tally suggested. "That'll really get his attention."

Gil Brown, the Windjammer, called in sick that day. Said he had a sore throat. Everybody extended their air time one hour and covered for him.

Instead of driving straight back to her apartment, as was her custom Monday through Friday, Jessica Kress pointed the nose of her Toyota north, toward the northernmost knuckle of Puno Bay, up in the hills. Before leaving work, she had called KSIN and asked the DJ to play a song for her at precisely five-thirty that afternoon. At five thirty, right after the ID, one of her favorite oldies pushed through the speakers in her car.

"Yes," she said several times while the music drifted all around her. "Yes. That's right."

She turned off onto a blacktop road, followed that for a few miles, then turned onto a gravel road. She parked by a field and sat for a time. Then she got out of the car and walked over to a stand of trees.

"Hello," the voice came from behind her.

Jessica turned around, a smile on her lips. The smile faded as her eyes took in the horror standing before her. Reality returned in a wild rush. She looked around her. She did not know where she was or how she got there. Then she began screaming.

"Up and at 'em," Leo Franks told his partner. It was a warm and pleasant morning. "Time to go to work."

Lani Prejean looked over the rim of her coffee cup. "So early in the morning?"

"We've got another disappearance."

"Damn!" Lani sat her cup down on the desk.

"City wants some county help on this one. Same MO as the others. Woman leaves work and vanishes. This one is a Jessica Kress. Left work yesterday afternoon, and drops off the face of the earth. She was supposed to see her fiance last evening, both of them to meet with the priest, to go over marriage plans. She never showed up."

"Cold feet, maybe. It happens, Leo."

"Not this one. Bet on it. Very devout Catholic. Homebody. Real good kid—"

The intercom on Lani's desk buzzed. "Yeah?"

"CHP just found the car belonging to the Kress

woman. Just off One North on County 45. You two get up there. And don't do it on a full stomach."

Lani looked at the remnants of a sweet roll on her desk. She'd already had two that morning. "Why, Captain?"

"Because Jessica Kress is scattered all over a field. Her heart was cut out of her chest and nailed to a fence post."

Chapter 3

Neither detective had ever seen anything like what greeted them in the meadow. They were both seasoned cops, with years of witnessing the worst in human behavior. But this topped it all.

After recovering from her shock, Lani said, "Where the hell is her *face?*"

"We can't find it," the CHP man said. "We've found and staked out most of the other body parts, but no sign of her face. Whoever did this skinned her head."

"Jesus Christ!" Leo blurted. "This guy just keeps getting worse and worse."

"If it's a guy," Lani amended that.

"We're pretty sure it is," the highway cop said. "We found some footprints . . . shoe prints, rather. If it's a woman, she's got a hell of a foot on her."

The county cops squatted down and looked at the shoe prints. " 'Bout an eleven," Lani guessed. "That would be a big-footed woman, for sure."

"Take a look at that stride," Leo pointed. "That's a good twenty-eight to thirty-inch step."

They backed off as the forensic crew went to work.

"We have a real nut on our hands," Leo said softly.

"Certifiable," Lani agreed.

"And here comes the crew from KSIN TV," Leo said, watching the dust kick up behind the wheels of the mobile van. "We have them to thank for naming this bastard. The Ripper. Not very original of them."

"Well, you're senior to me," Lani said with a smile. "You handle it."

"Thanks so much."

"That's what friends are for," Lani said sweetly.

The Ripper brushed the wig carefully, then replaced it on its mount. The bloody jeans and shirt had been burned the previous evening, when the night chill of the bay drifted into the coastal town and people lit their fireplaces. The Ripper smiled at the face of Jessica Kress, floating in a jar of preservative, the long hair fanning out around the face. Such a lovely face; so expressive even in death.

The Ripper glanced at the clock on the dresser. Time to go to work, and after work, the next love affair would be selected. The Ripper loved all the dead faces in the collection; it was quite a collection. The Ripper did not always take the faces. Sometimes the faces were ugly, and the Ripper did not like ugliness. The Ripper liked beautiful things. Most of the Ripper's victims' bodies had not yet been found, having been carefully buried over the long years and several thousand miles. But after awhile, that had turned boring. If the bodies could not be found, where was the challenge?

The Ripper lovingly carried each large jar back to its hiding place, placing a long and wet kiss against the glass. The Ripper longed to kiss the dead lips, but knew once sealed in the fluid, living lips would have to touch only the coolness of the glass and play pretend.

The Ripper had been playing pretend for years.

Ever since childhood. Oh, to be a child again, and gaze up into the faces of adults and lie so smoothly and convincingly after a disappearance of a playmate. That had been such fun!

After replacing all the jars, the Ripper consulted a leather-bound ledger and carefully wrote in another name. The Ripper never wrote in the latest love's real name, but a name that came to mind just at the moment of death. It never failed. It always came to mind. Jessica was renamed Swallow. Just like a lovely swallow. Oh, my yes.

And now Swallow belonged to the Ripper. Forever and ever.

Lani sat down wearily at her desk. The Ripper had been handed to Lani and Leo. Exclusively. All their other cases had been given to other detectives. Her feet hurt and she longed to go home, stretch out in a tub of hot soapy water, and just soak all the aches away. Leo had gone home and the room was deserted, the second shift having reported in and gone. She looked at the huge stack of reports from other departments around the country, and sighed. She opened the bottom left-hand drawer and took out a bottle of Crown Royal and a glass, pouring a good three fingers of the liquid. She took off her shoes, took a sip of Canadian whiskey, and began working her way through the stack. Thirty minutes and three phone calls later, her weariness vanished, the whiskey was forgotten, and Lani was rapidly jotting down notes on a long legal pad.

"You screwed up, my man," she muttered. "You made a mistake, and I caught it."

She reached over and turned on the radio. It stayed tuned to KSIN FM. Just like the radio in her car and the radios in her home. BJ the DJ was on. She smiled as BJ introed the old Floyd Cramer hit "Last Date." She vaguely recalled her parents dancing to that. They had just moved from Louisiana to California. Lani still remembered some of the Cajun French she'd spoken as a child. A few words.

Her parents, both factory workers, had retired and moved back to bayou country. Lani stayed in California and became a cop after graduating from college. She was thirty-five, divorced after five years of marriage. No kids. She was the stereotypical California girl, blond and blue-eyed, tanned and very attractive. She was also a very good cop. She and Leo had been partners for several years and worked well together. Leo was married with four kids, hopelessly in love with his wife, Virginia, and Virginia and Lani were good friends.

Lani hummed along with the old forties' hit, "Amapola," and straightened up her desk, placing the reports in the top right-hand drawer and locking it. Now she had a place to start, and she and Leo would start first thing in the morning. She headed for home.

After a long, hot soak in the tub, Lani piled up in bed and watched the late news. The anchor at KSIN played up the recent killing, inferring in not-too-subtle terms that the La Barca and Hancock County cops didn't have a clue as to the Ripper's identity and probably never would.

"Screw you," Lani said. She clicked off the set and went to sleep.

Three days later.

"Nineteen seventy-one?" Leo questioned. "Outside of Albany, New York. Christ, Lani, that's three thousand miles away and twenty-three years ago!"

"I'm just getting warmed up," she said with a smile. She unfolded a map of the United States and spread it out on the hood of the car. She and Leo had agreed not to discuss the case back at the station. Too many leaks were occurring. "Look here," Lani said, pointing. "In 1972, a kid's body was found here, his face missing."

"Albany, again," Leo said softly.

"In 1973, the body of a little girl was found, here," she said, pointing. "No face."

"Rochester."

"Two years later, the body of a teenage girl was found here." She pointed. "No face."

"Buffalo."

"In 1977, the body of a woman was found here." She jabbed at the map. "No face."

"Akron. He's moving west."

"More than that, Leo. Can't you see it?"

Leo frowned, then shook his head. "You're past me, Lani. I don't see what you're getting at."

"This monster started his killing as a *child*. He's been doing this since childhood. As he grew older, he progressed to killing adults."

"If it's the same person."

"It's the same person. Look. In 1978, another body was found. Right here. No face."

"Peoria, Illinois."

She pointed at the map. "Nineteen eighty-two. Another body."

"Des Moines. Why the four-year gap?"

"Several options, buddy. The bodies were not found. The person was in prison. Or more than likely, committed to some sort of mental institution."

"I buy the latter."

"Me, too. Look." She jabbed the map. "Nineteen

eighty-three. Two bodies found. A man and a woman. No faces."

"Wichita."

"Five years go by. It's 1988. A body found here, just outside of Denver. A nun. No face. She had been raped and sodomized repeatedly. Go back a decade, to 1977. To Akron. That woman was a nun. Go back to 1972. To Albany. Both those kids were reported missing from a Catholic school."

"What happened between '83 and '88?"

"Institutionalized, probably." She touched the map with a finger. "Nineteen eighty-nine, just outside of Albuquerque. A priest and a nun were found. They were naked and tests revealed both had sex before they were killed. They both had been tortured. No faces."

"This guy is twisted, Lani. You know the first thought that popped into my mind?"

"The priest and nun were tortured into having sex."

"You're a mind reader. How old was the first kid in Albany?"

"Six."

"The second kid in Albany?"

"Nine."

"Jesus."

"Nineteen ninety. A woman's body was discovered outside Phoenix. No face. Nineteen ninety-one. Salt Lake City. Two sisters, twins. No faces. Nothing between '91 and late '93. Then bodies started popping up in this area."

"Five bodies in five months. Now what?"

"We go see Dennis Potter."

"The father of the first girl killed in this area . . . that we know of. Why?"

"Because he's offered a quarter-of-a-million-dollar reward for the capture of the killer, and we don't have the budget to go traipsing all over the country chasing down these leads."

Leo stared at her. "You're really going to ask Mister Potter for the money to do that? Lani, you've got more brass on your ass than Batman!"

She smiled sweetly. "Bat*woman,* Leo. Let's go."

Dennis Potter listened as Lani laid it all out for him. She left nothing out. Dennis Potter was one of the wealthiest men in the state, and an avowed conservative. He was a self-made man, the son of itinerant fruit-pickers. He hated criminals and thought that the judicial system—the way it was presently being administered—sucked. After Lani had finished, Dennis walked to the phone and called one of the banks he owned. "I want MasterCards and Visa Cards in the name of Lani Prejean and Leo Franks. No limits. I want them tomorrow; have the statements sent to my office." He called American Express and told them the same thing. Then he called the sheriff. "Lani Prejean and Leo Franks will be working the Ripper case exclusively, right?"

"Yes, sir," the sheriff was very respectful. Dennis Potter *owned* Hancock County.

"Fine. You probably won't be seeing much of them for the next couple of months. They'll be flying around the country, chasing down leads. You have any objections to that?"

"No, sir."

"Fine. And not one word about this, Sheriff. Not one word." He hung up and turned to the cops. "Be out here tomorrow afternoon for your credit cards. Where will you go first?"

"Albany," Lani said.

"Good hunting," Dennis Potter said.

* * *

Cal Denning was reading a manual on a piece of equipment when something in a commercial caught his ear. He listened until the commercial was over. Cal had started out as a DJ, and still did the occasional voice-over just to keep his hand in it. What the hell was wrong with that commercial?

He started to get up, to go into the control room to pull that cart and listen to it more closely, then he paused and sat back down. No, he thought, he'd wait until shift change.

Now why would I want to do that? he questioned. He could come up with no answer, but he still decided to wait. Something was sure odd about that commercial.

"Ah, hell," he muttered. "You're just getting old, Cal. Imagining things."

But he knew he wasn't imagining anything. Something was out of sync with that commercial. He'd check it later.

Sheriff Brownwood, Brownie to his friends, leaned back in his chair and thought about his brief conversation with Dennis Potter. He had known Dennis for nearly forty years. They both were the sons of itinerant workers, had met in labor camps, and both had risen to some degree of prominence in the county . . . Dennis far and away more than Brownie in terms of wealth. And Brownie knew something else about Dennis: he was utterly, totally, relentlessly ruthless when it came to his family, his horses, or his dogs. He loved them all, in that order. Ruthie had been the youngest, and was the apple of Dennis's eye. The man had very nearly lost it when the Ripper had killed his daughter. If Lani and Leo didn't find the Ripper, Dennis would hire someone who would, and Dennis would not give one damn about the legality of it all.

The illegality part of it didn't particularly worry Brownie either, for someone like the Ripper had no rights as far as he was concerned. And the same went for child molesters and the like. But he was a good lawman and followed the rules, despite his personal feelings. Dennis Potter would not.

And he knew why Dennis wanted him to stay mum about Lani and Leo and whatever they might uncover . . . the Ripper could be anybody. Even one of his own people. It happens; cops crack. They go bad. It doesn't happen often, but it happens.

"Get this thing wrapped up, people," Brownie muttered. "And let's do it legally."

Leo and Lani were beat when they rented a car at the Albany airport and drove to the Holiday Inn. They checked in and agreed to meet in the lobby in an hour, have an early dinner, and then hit the sack. It's a long way from California to New York, even by jet. With one stop.

At eight o'clock the next morning they were talking with a Det. Bill Zanetis of the Albany PD.

"Well, that was before my time," Zanetis said. "But I dug out the file for you to look at. But you're going to be very disappointed."

"What do you mean?" Leo asked.

"There was a suspect, but he was a juvenile."

"Shit!" Lani said. She knew what that meant. Sealed records. It would take a court order to open them, and that wasn't very damn likely to happen.

"You got it," Zanetis said, eyeballing the rise and fall of Lani's breasts.

"Any chance of opening them?" Leo asked.

"Not a prayer. Wouldn't do you any good, even if a judge gave the order. They've been destroyed."

"Why?"

"Well, I found out after you called that the suspect is dead. Died about a year after the first girl was murdered. I called, but you and your partner had already left."

"Do you have a name?"

Bill shook his head. "No."

"The second girl was a copycat murder?" Lani asked.

"I guess so. But no one was ever caught."

Lani had a sudden thought, but she would wait to share it with Leo. All Bill Zanetis had on his mind was looking at her tits.

"Dead end," Leo said glumly, as they sat in the rented car.

"Maybe not," Lani said. "I had a thought in there, while the good detective was eyeballing my tits . . ."

"Jesus, Lani. You have a dirty mouth, you know that?"

She laughed at the expression on her partner's face. "Just suppose, for the sake of argument, that our killer is a really bright fellow. Genius I.Q. Even as a child, a devious, cunning, and very careful planner . . ."

"I'm with you. He plants evidence on some poor kid, and then kills him to throw off the scent."

"Right."

Leo shook his head. "We're reaching, but I'm game." He dropped the car into gear. "Where to?"

"Ever been to a Catholic school, Leo?"

"For the first eight long, miserable years of my academic life," he said glumly. "We called one of our teachers the Nun from Hell."

Chapter 4

The California cops struck out at the school. None of the nuns had been there when the two murders had occurred, and none of the priests at the adjoining church knew anything about any murders.

"You might try Father Daniel," a young priest told them, walking the cops out of the church and back to their car. "I know he was here during that time frame."

"He's retired?" Lani asked.

"In a manner of speaking," the young priest said with a smile. He wrote an address on a slip of paper and handed it to her. "You'll find him working there. He owns the business."

Lani looked at the paper. "Dan's Flowers?"

"Yes. Good day."

Father Daniel was a very pleasant man in his late fifties. "Not Father anymore," he told them. "I got married and kicked out on my butt. My wife works downtown. What can I do for you folks?"

Leo took it and explained.

"Ah, yes. I remember those murders well. I'll go to my grave believing that little shit Jack Longwood killed them both."

Lani perked up. "Jack Longwood?"

"He was nine years old when the first murder happened, ten when the second one occurred. The devil's own child, that one."

"You don't mean that in the Biblical sense, do you?" Lani asked.

"Indeed, I do," the ex-priest said flatly. "The boy was born with the mark of Satan on him. Just being around him caused the hair on the back of my neck to rise up, and created chill bumps on my flesh. He was a born liar, thief, sadist, pervert, and God alone knows what else. Oh, and a murderer, too. At least in my opinion."

"Where is he now?" Leo asked.

"In Hell, I hope. How about some coffee? I just made a fresh pot."

Lani and Leo waited while Dan took two phone orders and then the three of them sat down on stools behind the counter, mugs of coffee before them.

"Jack and Jim Longwood. Rich boys. Their parents were very very wealthy."

Were? Leo thought. "From around here?"

"Yes. Jack was a twin. His brother, Jim, left here right after their parents were murdered. That was back in, oh, let's see, '79, I think it was. You can find all the details on microfilm at the newspaper offices."

"The murderer ever caught?" Lani asked, a sick feeling growing in the pit of her stomach.

"No. Of course, it was Jack. Or maybe Jim. I always had doubts about him, too."

"The officials at the school weren't too helpful in this matter," Leo said. "I can't believe some of them didn't know about this."

"Oh, they knew. They all know. Even the newest additions know. I think it's required study. But you couldn't get them to talk about it under torture. All records of the twins were ordered destroyed years ago."

"By whom?"

"Church officials, I presume. I really don't know. I had been, ah, seduced by the pleasures of the flesh and booted out when that happened." He laughed, and it was a good laugh, full of humor. "But that's another story. Jack and Jim Longwood. They'd be . . . well, about thirty-two or thirty-three now. And no, I do not have any idea where either of them might be."

"Their parents' wealth?"

"After their murders?" Dan shrugged. "I guess the boys got it. The mansion is still standing, unoccupied. The story I hear is that it cannot be sold, ever."

"Why?"

"The boys ordered it, I suppose. It's one of the town's mysteries. Longwood's lawyers were, and still are, I suppose, in New York City. Good luck in trying to find them. No one around here can. Or if they can, they're not talking."

"So the boys would be wealthy?" Leo asked.

"Oh, my God, yes. Worth millions of dollars. Longwood was just as peculiar as his offspring, so he set things up in such a way that neither of them could ever touch the bulk of the estate. They would receive a check each month for the rest of their lives. A very substantial check, I'm told."

"That'll be easy to trace," Lani said.

"Wrong," Dan said bluntly. "Police around here gave up on that years ago. You see, the boys changed their names. They just vanished. But they're alive. Bet on that. They're too evil to die. You're here because of what the newspapers are calling the Ripper case, right?"

Lani nodded her head.

"Jack and Jim. I'd bet a place in Heaven it's them."

"But Jim—"

"Was the careful one," Dan cut him off. "The cautious one. The charmer. They were good-looking boys. They would be very handsome men . . . in an effeminate way. But not big men. The Longwood family was short, traditionally. They would be five-seven, maybe. Maybe less."

Dan looked up as the door opened. "Ah, Sally. Right on time. Sally, handle things here for a time. I have to run some errands."

"Glad to, Mr. Jennings," she said.

"Let's go," Dan said to the cops.

"Where are we going?" Leo asked.

"I'll show you," he replied mysteriously. "We'll take my car."

They drove out of town and turned down a winding county road, finally stopping in front of a locked wrought-iron gate. Inside the walled estate, stood the house.

"The Longwood mansion," Leo said.

"Correct," Dan said. "To the best of my knowledge, not a living soul has set foot in that place in fifteen years."

"Where are the Longwoods buried?" Lani asked.

"No one knows. And I'm not kidding. No one knows where they are buried. If they're buried."

"And you think Jack Longwood killed his parents?" Leo asked.

"Or Jim. Jim is just as capable of doing that as Jack."

"The boys are mentally ill, then?" Lani asked.

The ex-priest shook his head. "No, they're not. They're just evil."

* * *

Back at the motel, over lunch, Lani said, "I want to go inside that mansion, Leo."

"You're reading my mind. We'll have to break in."

"That bother you?"

He grinned.

The two California cops parked behind the estate, in a clump of trees and thick brush, and went over the walls, making their way to the rear of the huge mansion. They carried flashlights—but would not use them until they were in the building—and had extra batteries in their pockets. There was enough moonlight for them to avoid falling into the long-emptied swimming pool, and to dodge the many statues that were placed about the grounds.

The ex-priest had told them that no one had ever broken into the mansion, for the security system was an elaborate one. It took Leo about sixty seconds to bypass the alarm box, and then Lani jimmied a back door, and they were inside.

Sheets covered the furniture and a thin layer of dust lay everywhere. Cobwebs hung in corners. Rat and mice droppings were very much in evidence. Lani cast the small beam of her flashlight along the walls. They both could see where the valuable paintings had been removed—either to be sold or stored; they had no way of knowing.

"Do we split up?" Lani asked.

"No," Leo said quickly. "I don't like this place. And I have a hunch those two weirdos just might have left some unpleasant surprises behind. Be very careful in moving about."

"I'm with you on that."

As they began their search of the huge old home, the

word that popped into the minds of both cops was: Spooky.

They expected to find nothing on the first floor, and that is exactly what they found.

Lani and Leo stood at the base of the stairway and looked up into the darkness.

"Dan said the parents were axed to death while they slept," Lani broke the silence.

"Yeah. And that Jim Longwood left right after the murders."

"I wonder if the bedroom . . . ?" She trailed that off.

"You know as well as I do it's just as the cops left it."

"Wonderful," she said drily. "Who goes first?"

Leo smiled. "Ladies first, dear."

"You're such a gentleman."

"I do try."

She started up the dark stairway, and Leo closed a hand around her forearm and stepped in front of her. "No way, kid. Stay three steps behind me and to my left. You know the drill."

"What the hell do you think is up there, Leo?"

"I don't know. Probably nothing. But this place is giving me the creeps."

"You're not alone."

They made their way cautiously up to the second floor of the home, and stood for a moment on the thick and dusty carpet.

"This stuff must have cost seventy-five dollars a square foot," Lani remarked.

"And speaking of feet," Leo said, lowering his beam of light to the carpet.

After all the years, the stains left by bloody feet were plain in the carpet. Lani used her narrow beam of light to backtrack the stains. They led to a room at the end of the hall. The yellow tape with the black lettering was still in place. CRIME SCENE—DO NOT CROSS.

"My God," Leo said. "To leave that much blood . . ."

"Yeah," Lani agreed. "He must have wallowed in the gore. Look." She lifted the light to the hall wall. Bloody handprints were still staining the wallpaper. Huge handprints.

"He wore gloves," Leo said, kneeling down to more closely inspect the stains on the carpet. "Five will get you ten he wore rubber boots. Interesting. The prints stop right here." He stood up.

"He took off his boots right where we're standing, and probably walked off in his stocking feet."

"Yeah. This is one cold bastard."

Together, they walked down the hall to the bedroom and stood for a moment, shining their lights into the room. As the beams touched the walls, both of them were thankful that they had not been the ones to work this when it was fresh.

It was carnage.

Bloodstains spattered the walls, and there were even bloodstains on the ten-foot-high ceiling. The sheets had been stripped from the bed as evidence, but long before the local cops had arrived, the blood had seeped through and stained the entire top of the king-sized mattress. There were handprints all over the walls, matching those in the hall.

"He played in the blood," Lani whispered.

"Yeah. Look over there." Leo shone the light.

"What is *that?*"

"I don't know. Some sort of a symbol. Did you remember to load the camera?"

She gave him a dirty look, and before shooting some film of the strange symbols, checked to see if the drapes in the room were all closed. They were. The flash would not be seen outside. Lani took several shots, then moved closer. "I know what these are. They're music notes."

"Is it a song?"

She shook her head. "I don't know. I've got a tin ear when it comes to music. You're looking at a kid who failed music appreciation."

"Back up and get the whole sequence, will you?"

That done, the cops moved out of the bedroom and opened the first door past the landing. It was like stepping back in time. The posters were all of musicians and songs of the nineteen thirties, forties, and fifties; movie stars of the same periods. Lani pointed to a stereo and records beside it. They were both wearing gloves, so she thumbed through the albums. There was no rock music. Everything was smooth ballads and big band.

"This was, *is* a very weird kid," Lani said.

"In more ways than one," Leo said, shining his light on a bookshelf filled with paperbacks and magazines. Cross-dressing, homosexuality, bi-loving, bondage, S and M, and worse.

"Jesus!" Lani whispered, her eyes taking in the titles and covers. "Talk about a twisted sister. The only thing that isn't here is bestiality."

"Thank God for small favors," Leo said. He picked a Bible off another shelf and opened it. "This was Jack's room. Inscription is made out to him." He fanned the pages and grunted in disbelief. "Look at this. Obscenities and filth of the worst kind written on every page."

"No sign of satanism, though," Lani said, peering over his shoulder. "He just hates religion. Close it, Leo. I feel funny reading crap like that in a Bible."

"Me, too." Leo put the Bible in the small bag he'd brought and they left that room, heading into the room across the hall. Jim's room. It was almost identical to the other brother's room: posters from the same time periods, and music from the same periods. And the same types of books and magazines.

"Does it strike you as odd that their parents would allow this type of perversion to be so prominently displayed, Leo?"

"Very. But some parents never go into their children's rooms. Remember that lawsuit back home, where the kid won the right to privacy?"

"Oh, yeah. But surely they peeked in when the kids were gone?"

Leo shrugged. "You never know about the rich. They're different from the rest of us."

She looked at him. "How so?"

Leo smiled. "They have more money!"

Chapter 5

The cops made a quick but careful search of the rest of the rooms in the great mansion, and found nothing of any particular interest.

"We have proof that the boys were twisted," Leo said. "At least sexually. Now all we have to do is find the boys."

"The Longwoods had to have relatives. Everybody is related to somebody. We'll start digging in the morning, but do it quietly."

Leo glanced at her. "You think somebody in this town is feeding information to the brothers?"

She shook her head. "I have no reason to think that. But if we assume that's true, we'll dig more carefully. Leo? There is a basement here."

"I know. But I've seen enough for one night. How about you?"

"Let's get out of this place. I feel . . . *unclean!*"

Leo reset the mansion alarm, and moments later they were back at the motel. Both of them showered under a spray as hot as they could stand it. Both were asleep minutes after their heads hit the pillow.

* * *

In La Barca, Tammy Larson locked the front door to her lounge and walked the short distance to her car. Settling in the bucket seat, she made certain her driver's side door was locked, then buckled her seat belt, started the car, and turned on the radio. Jenny Caesar was on the air, and Tony Bennett was singing "Because Of You." Tammy hummed along with Tony, and then smiled as that funny commercial came on.

"Yes," Tammy said, about midway into the commercial. "Oh, that's right. Yes. I'll certainly be there." She had no conscious memory of saying it. She hummed along with Eydie Gorme, until she turned into the parking area of her apartment complex. She looked forward to a hot bath and a good night's sleep. Soon, Tammy would sleep forever. Without her face.

Lani decided to get her hair done and gently pump the stylist for information. Leo found a seedy-looking bar that catered mainly to the older crowd, and decided to concentrate there. They would meet back at the motel early that afternoon to compare notes.

"That must have been the most hated family in all of New York State," Leo said, after sugaring his coffee and taking a sip. "Just the mention of their name brought a full hour of talk at the bar."

"Yeah," Lani agreed. "All the women at the salon had something to say about the Longwoods. You go first."

"The elder Longwoods had a chauffeur. He's retired and living just south of Glens Falls. Name is Karl—with a *K*—Muller. His wife, Anna, was the cook and boss of the household help. I want to talk to him."

"My stylist has an uncle, who retired from the police force here just after the Longwoods were murdered.

According to her, who got her information from him, both the Longwood boys should have been strangled at birth, and their bodies burned and the ashes sealed in concrete for all time."

"Nice boys."

"Oh, just delightful. Seems Jack and Jim were constantly in trouble. The parents bought them out every time. They would offer people enormous sums of money to drop the charges. Only a few people didn't accept, and a couple of them ended up dead."

Leo did some soft but highly passionate cussing. "It never fails, does it, Lani? No matter what side of the tracks they come from, it's always the same. Parents refuse to see their kids as anything other than sweet little angels. It's always somebody else's fault. Did the elder Longwood hire the killings done?"

She shook her head. "The townspeople think the boys did it."

"Good God! How young were they when the killings started?"

"Six."

Leo almost dropped his coffee cup. "You have got to be kidding!"

"No. We're dealing with a pair of real nuts here. Did you find out about the other brother and sister?"

"No. No one mentioned that."

"Actually they're *half* brother and sister. From an earlier marriage. Last address was Boston."

"So what do you think?"

"Let's drive up to interview this chauffeur, and then head for Boston. We can always come back here."

"When do you want to leave?"

"How about right now?"

* * *

Cal Denning checked the program log, found that the commercial that seemed odd to him would not be played again for several hours, and pulled the cart, taking it back to his office. He locked his door and sat down, sticking the cart into the playback unit. He put on earphones and hit the play button, leaning back in his chair. He listened to the commercial twice. There was something wrong with it. But damned if he could figure out what it was. Something was just not . . . well, *right* with it.

He transferred the commercial over to reel to reel and slowed it down. Still, he could not pick out exactly what was the matter. He slowed it down as far as he could and listened.

There! There it was. Behind the words and music were other words. What the hell was going on here? He played it again and again and again. Tam. Tam. Tam . . . no, Tammy. That was it. Tammy. Lar. Lar. Lar. Son. Tammy Larson.

Tammy Larson. Who the hell was Tammy Larson? And what was her name doing on an automobile commercial? He removed his earphones and stopped the tape. Cal took the cart back to the control room, waiting until the DJ had stepped out for a moment before he replaced the tape in the rack. He was unaware that another employee of KSIN had seen him enter the small room. The employee smiled at the furtiveness of Cal. He was so amateurish. Quite silly-looking actually. Looked like something out of a Peter Sellers movie.

Oh, well. No matter. This was of little consequence. Whatever Cal had discovered, could be taken care of easily. This was going to be fun.

The employee carefully unwrapped a small package and placed it in the far reaches of a drawer in Dick

Hale's desk. Along with another object that had been placed there the past week. Trickie-Dickie was going to be in for a shock before long. And no one was more deserving of a good shock to the system than that obnoxious, arrogant, pompous son of a bitch.

The employee was chuckling, furtively slipping out the side door of Dick Hale's office.

"You don't have to talk to us, Mr. Muller," Leo said to the man who stood on the porch. "I want to make that clear right from the beginning. We're California cops. We have no authority here in New York."

"It's about the twins, isn't it?" Karl asked. "Jack and Jim."

"Yes, sir," Lani told him.

"Come on in. I'll be glad to answer any questions I can."

Back in Albany, Det. Bill Zanetis slowly replaced the receiver in its cradle. The caller had refused to give his name, but the voice was young. Sounded like a teenager. Probably out parked and getting it on with his girlfriend. Said he had spotted a car parked in the woods behind the Longwood Estate late last night. He'd written down the license number. Zanetis ran it and got a response back quickly. Rented car. A local one, from the airport rental.

"Those California cops snooping around, I betcha," the detective muttered, reaching for his coat. He left the squad room without telling anyone where he was going.

* * *

Anna brought them coffee and fresh, hot, home-baked cinnamon rolls, and Karl asked her to sit and join them.

"Evil," Karl said. "Those boys. Evil through and through. The bad seed ran in the whole family. Mother, father, children. All the children. Even those from the first marriage."

"Do you know where the kids from the first marriage are living?" Lani asked.

"They were living in Boston. That's all I know. I pray to God every night that I never see any of them again."

Anna nodded her head in solemn agreement. "On our knees we do. The both of us. Together."

"If these people were so . . . evil, why did you continue working for them?" Leo asked.

"The money," Karl replied honestly. "The family was so despised they could not get people to work for them. They paid us enormous sums of money. Our health insurance is paid to this day from the estate. For life. Forever. Until we die. We had no expenses, so we could save every penny. Our food we ate there. Our uniforms were furnished. Our living quarters were wonderful. For enough money, one will ignore the screams in the night."

"Screams?" Lani leaned forward.

"Yes," Karl said. "Occasionally, from the basement. I don't know what went on down there. There are several large rooms. All with steel doors. All locked. Not even the police know about them."

"Why not?"

"A panel must be moved to get to the rooms. The lever is on the right side, facing the panel. If the power is off, they can be opened by hand. Remove the two knots in the wood in the center of the wall. The panels slide open, left and right, with a bit of force."

"Have you ever been in those rooms?" Leo asked.

"*Gott, nein!*" Karl slipped into his mother tongue. "I would never go in there. It must be a chamber of horrors."

"Tell us everything you know that the boys have done," Leo urged.

Halfway through the telling, Lani excused herself and went into the bathroom and vomited up her coffee and cinnamon rolls. Two minutes later, Leo matched her output in another bathroom.

When they returned, Anna was crying and Karl was ashen-faced. "I am dreadfully sorry," he said. "But you wanted to know it all."

"But the police . . . !" Lani said.

"What can be done, if no one brings charges or the people drop them?" Anna said. "Do you have any idea of the power that can be bought with half a billion dollars in the hands of a ruthless man?"

Both Leo and Lani thought of Dennis Potter and nodded their heads.

"Do either of you know, if the boys were ever committed to a mental institution?" Lani asked.

"I don't believe so," Karl said. "We worked for the Longwoods from the time the boys were six or seven, until the murders. After that, we would have no knowledge."

"How did you happen to go to work for the Longwoods?" Leo asked.

"They interviewed us in Dresden, then brought us over from Germany. Arranged for our citizenship . . . everything. We . . . had no idea what we were getting into."

"You both went into the house, didn't you?" Anna asked.

"Yes," Lani admitted. "Last night. We broke in."

"Don't go back," Anna warned them. "Don't. That

house is just as evil as those who once lived in it. It lives."

"It . . . *lives?*" Leo asked.

"Believe it," Karl backed up his wife. "It can't be destroyed. It won't let you destroy it."

"Mr. Muller—" Lani said patiently.

The old man held up a big hand. "Listen to me. Do you know how old that mansion is?"

"Oh . . . forty years old, I suppose," Leo guessed.

Anna smiled. "It was built in 1801. Check the county records, if you doubt me."

"After the murders, and the police had finished their investigation, I tried to burn it down," Karl said. "I set fire to the drapes. The other drape put out the flames. I poured gasoline on the carpet. It wouldn't burn. It just wouldn't burn. I thought I had bad gasoline. I went into town and bought more. Nothing in the house would burn. Then the house tried to kill us, both Anna and me. Drape cords became as snakes, whipping around, tangling in our feet, wrapping around our necks. Knives from the kitchen flew through the air. Show them, Anna."

The woman stood up and pulled up her blouse. Lani and Leo could see the long scar on her stomach. "I almost died from that wound."

"I can believe that," Leo said.

Karl pointed a finger at the cops. "You hunt them down. Every member of that family. You drive a stake through their hearts. Jack and Jim, their half brother and sister. Those are the four remaining with the bad blood. Kill them, and the house will die."

Outside the Muller house, the detectives sat in their rented car for a few moments, both of them shaken by the words they'd heard. Lani finally broke the silence.

"The house is alive? It can't be destroyed? Kill the four remaining Longwood children, and drive stakes through their hearts? Jesus Christ, Leo!"

"What the hell are we dealing with here, Lani?"

"Do you believe in the supernatural, Leo?"

Leo was silent for a time. "Drive," he finally said, as dusk settled around them. When they were on the road back to Albany, for they had decided to spend at least one more day in the city, Leo said, "Lani, I was raised a Catholic. If a person believes in God, the devil, angels, Heaven, Hell, then one believes to a certain extent in the supernatural. Some theologians might disagree with that, but that's their option. Do I believe in werewolves and vampires? No."

"I'm not sure you answered my question."

"That's all you're going to get."

They rode for a few miles in silence. Lani said, "Drapes coming to life and putting out the flames. Carpet that won't burn after being saturated with gasoline. Secret rooms in the basement that the local cops couldn't find. Drape cords that suddenly turn into snakes, or something like that." She shook her head. "It's getting a bit much, Leo."

"I want to check out the age of that mansion."

"And then?"

"Cults, devil worship."

"I want to read what the newspapers have on file about the Longwood family . . . all the way back to the beginning. As far as the files go."

"I want to go into that basement. Push on those knots and see if the wall really slides back."

"I want to check on Karl Muller."

"We'll be busy tomorrow."

"You tired, Leo?"

"Yeah. Yeah, I am."

"Go to sleep. I'll wake you up when we get to the motel. Go on. I'm not a bit tired."

Leo was asleep in moments. Lani glanced over at him and smiled. Good, solid, prodding Leo. A cop's cop. Methodical, slow to anger. A bulldog on any case. Devoted family man. Everything about Leo was average. Average height, average build, neither handsome nor unattractive. He could go unnoticed in a crowd of three. But his courage was limitless. Lani and Leo made a good team, right from the beginning.

She shook him awake at the motel, and he staggered off to his room. Lani took a bath and went to bed. She had nightmares about drapes that came alive, monsters lurking in the carpets of the Longwood mansion, and ropes and cords that turned into writhing snakes. She awakened tired. She took an ice-cold shower and that woke her up.

Lani was reading the newspaper and working on her second cup of coffee in the dining room, when a story stopped her cold and caused her hand to tremble so badly she had to carefully put down the coffee cup. She read the story twice.

"Hey, kid!" Leo said, sitting down and picking up the menu. "What's up?"

White-faced, she handed him the paper. Leo read, THE BODY OF ALBANY POLICE DEPARTMENT DET. BILL ZANETIS WAS FOUND LAST EVENING IN THE EMPTY SWIMMING POOL OF THE OLD LONGWOOD ESTATE, JUST OUTSIDE OF TOWN. A SPOKESPERSON FOR THE DEPARTMENT SAID THE DETECTIVE'S FOOT BECAME ENTANGLED IN AN OLD ROPE AND HE TRIPPED, FALLING ONTO THE CONCRETE FLOOR OF THE POOL, BREAKING HIS NECK ON IMPACT. THE ROPE WAS TWISTED

SO INTRICATELY AROUND HIS ANKLES IT
HAD TO BE CUT AWAY.

Leo's face was impassive as he laid the paper aside
and thanked the waitress for the freshly poured cup of
coffee. He ordered breakfast. When the waitress had
left, he said, "Accidents happen, Lani."

"What rope, Leo? There was no rope by the pool."

"That we saw. It was dark."

"The moon was out, Leo! We both commented on
how much light it was affording us."

"Now, you just settle down, Lani," he whispered.
"We're dealing with some kooks here, not the devil."

"He was so tangled up in the rope it had to be cut
away from his ankles, Leo."

"I read it. So? He panicked, and that made matters
worse. You ever try to kick a garden hose from around
your feet or ankles? I have. It's a mess."

"We're in over our heads, Leo."

"No, we're not. Now you listen to me, Lani. I've
never seen you so spooked. You know as well as me
that everything has a logical explanation. We've
worked too many murders together, kid. Get your
cool back. We'll solve this one."

The waitress brought their food, and Leo dug in.
Lani picked at her breakfast. "Eat, eat!" Leo urged
her. "We've got a long day ahead of us."

"I got a bad feeling, Leo."

"You constipated or something?"

Lani laughed at the expression on his face and
started eating. Leo could always make her feel better.

Chapter 6

They met back at the motel restaurant for lunch, and Lani's mood had lifted considerably. Leo was in his usual good mood.

"Karl Muller has a history of mental problems, Leo. He had a major breakdown just before the murders. Anna was confined for more than six months due to mental problems. Both of them were treated for hallucinations."

"So much for flying knives and drapes that come alive, and ropes that turn into snakes."

"Right. What'd you find out?"

"The Longwood mansion is as old as the Mullers claim it to be. The original plans are on exhibit at a local museum. No hidden chambers or secret rooms to be found."

"Are we through here?"

"I think so. For the time being. Let's check out and head for Boston. I have an address for the half brother and sister."

The same late afternoon that Lani and Leo were interviewing Karl and Anna Muller, Cal Denning had stopped on the way home for milk and bread. For reasons he could not understand, he was jumpy. His stomach was all knotted up with tension. Once home, with a martini in his hand, all settled in the recliner to watch the news (not the news carried by KSIN), he began to feel better.

Cal lived alone, up in the hills, in an A-frame with a lovely view. His nearest neighbors were more than a mile away. They never socialized, and that's the way he liked it. He didn't even know their names.

Cal was not an especially unfriendly type of person, he just liked his privacy and his cats. Twice married and twice divorced, Cal had made up his mind a long time back that he was better off single. He settled down for the early news and took a sip of his martini. One of his cats suddenly yowled loudly and made a dash for the kitchen. Cal thought nothing of it. Mice were not an infrequent thing.

"Get 'im, Mr. Nixon," Cal said, and turned his attentions back to the TV.

The last thing he remembered was a terrible, painful roaring in his head, and Cal Denning's world turned black.

Since he had the next two days off, he would not be missed by anyone at the station complex.

The big male cat, Mr. Nixon, leaped at the intruder and landed on the trespasser's back, digging in with his hind claws and ripping at the person's face and neck with his front claws. With a scream of pain and rage, the cat was slung away and the bloodied individual stumbled for the back door, blood pouring from a deeply slashed face, the tire iron used to smash Cal's head firmly held in a gloved hand. The denim-clad person disappeared over a ridge.

In the house, Cal stirred once and moaned, then he was still.

* * *

Lani and Leo struck out cold in Boston. They checked out every Longwood on the tax records in Boston and surrounding communities, but none were the right ones. Then they went to the newspapers for help and accessed the microfilm and computers for anything that had the name Longwood in it. They found lots of Longwoods, but not the right ones. Then they went to the libraries to ask for help. Again, they found Longwoods, but not the right ones. It was a very frustrating four days. On the evening of the fourth day, after a hot soak in the tub, and then sprawled out on the bed, Lani decided to call the office just to see what was happening back in Hancock County.

"Engineer out at KSIN got the back of his head bashed in," she was told. "It's a strange one, too. Nothing was taken from his wallet or home."

"Ripper-related?"

"We're not treating it as such. We think something scared the burglar away."

"Is Cal dead?"

"No. But he's still in a coma. The doctors think he's going to make it."

"No more Ripper attacks?"

"Not that we know of."

Lani lay on the bed for a time, then dressed and walked down to Leo's room. He was relaxing on the bed and pointed to a bottle of Crown Royal on the dresser. She fixed a drink and sat down, telling him about Cal.

"I know Cal Denning," Leo said. "He's worked on our equipment for free. I'd be very much surprised to learn that he has an enemy in the world. He's a very laid-back guy. And a nice guy."

"Well, he was almost a dead guy." She looked down at her drink then lifted her eyes. "It's related, Leo."

He stared at her for a moment. "You're reaching, Lani."

"I can't help it. It's related. I know it is. I feel it."

Leo sighed and slowly nodded his head. "I think the half brother and sister are in California, Lani. In the La Barca area. Did we get anything back on our request to force the opening of the Longwood trust?"

"Denied. No reason to believe the boys have anything to do with the Ripper case."

"Shit!" Leo cussed, which was something he did not do very often. But this case was causing him to swear more than Lani had ever heard him do.

"The judge said it isn't against the law to change one's name. And after reviewing the files, he further stated that since the boys had committed no crimes prior to the name change, they have every right to expect privacy. Our people are appealing."

"That'll take two or three years!"

Lani shrugged her shoulders. "You know how it goes, Leo."

"Let's get out of here, Lani. Catch a plane to Rochester first thing in the morning."

She reached for the phone. "I'll make the reservations."

Damn cat! the Ripper thought, inspecting the face in the mirror. It would be days before the deep claw marks would finally fade. And Denning was still alive. Damn the man! And the Ripper had learned that two county pigs, Leo Franks and Lani Prejean, were now traveling all over the country, backtracking the movements of the Longwood boys. But that little matter was going to be taken care of, very soon. Permanently. No more oinkies.

The face in the mirror sighed in frustration. The urge to strike was building within. Strong now. Almost overpowering. It would have to be soon. If not, the Other would take control, and the Other was not nearly as cautious as conditions warranted.

The face in the mirror smiled. Pretty Tammy would soon be added to the collection of faces, and if everything went as planned, Dick Hale would find his butt in jail, and those bad boys in lockup knew what to do with a cherry-butt like Dick.

The face in the mirror laughed and laughed and laughed. This was such fun.

The Rochester detective dropped a thin file on the desk. "That's it," he said. "But since that happened, the remains of seven more have been found, and we think they're all connected."

"And there might be seven more undiscovered around here," Leo said.

"Or seventy," the detective said. "How's it going with you guys?"

"Slow and frustrating," Lani said, opening the file.

"Ain't it always? Take your time. Use my desk. I've punched up on computer what we know about the other nine. Coffee is over there." He pointed. "The one who drains the pot makes fresh. Have fun. I got to go work a rape that will probably turn out to be an unsatisfying scrape, and now she's got a grudge against his ass. No offense, Lani."

"None taken. I know what you mean." The detective walked away, and Lani and Leo looked down at the photos of the dead girl, before and after. Before was pretty and vibrant, after was awful.

"Leo," Lani said. "What does this guy *do* with the faces?"

Leo looked at his doughnut. "I don't know. You have a guess?"

"He saves some of them."

"Good God, Lani!" He laid the doughnut aside.

"He preserves them to take out and look at from time to time."

"I worry about you, Lani. I really do. You have a weird mind."

"It's the only explanation that makes any sense." She closed the file. "The cops would know the person is missing. There would be a full description: age, height, weight, hair coloring, scars, and marks. He's not trying to disguise the victim to prevent ID. He loves these faces, Leo."

Leo grimaced, burped, and put a paper napkin over the doughnut.

"Remember what Zanetis said? Since '72, they have discovered five more bodies in the Albany area. That's seven over there. Eight here. I'll bet you when we're through, we'll have a total of three or four *hundred* bodies over a twenty-year period."

Leo sighed and settled back in his chair. "He's been a busy boy."

"Let's go talk to the medical examiner."

"Yes," the man said the word slowly. "I remember the cases very well. Of the seven additional bodies found in this area, I can verify that four of them had their faces cut away."

"You have spare photos we could borrow?" Leo asked.

"Oh, yes. You can have them. Where do you go from here?"

"Buffalo."

* * *

"Yeah, we hated to let this one go," the Buffalo detective said. "She was the daughter of a cop." He shrugged his shoulders. "But after nineteen years . . . ?"

"And how many more bodies have been found since the first one?" Lani asked.

"Nine. Five of them with their faces cut away. That we can prove, that is."

"Do us a big favor?" Leo asked.

"Anything. Name it."

"Run the name Longwood. See if you have anything."

"It'll take some time. But I'll be glad to get it done. Come back in the morning?"

"We'll be here."

The detective was nervous. He motioned the California cops to follow him. They got in his car and drove away from the central station. "This is juvenile stuff," he said. "You didn't get it from me, and you can't use it in a court of law."

"We understand," Lani said. "We don't have to like it, but we understand. You ought to work in California."

"No, thanks. New York State is bad enough. It's absolutely unfair to the law-abiding public not to release the names of perverted little creeps." He pulled over to the curb. "Jack and Jim Longwood, twin brothers, attended a private school just outside of town. It's closed down now. Has been for years. They were both brought in for questioning after the disappearance of a boy from the school. The boy's body has never been found. The school is—was—located on the

Tonawanda River. The body was probably dumped in the river and ended up as fish bait in Erie. We had pictures of the little twin bastards, but for some reason unbeknownst to me, the pictures are gone from the file. You know their father was enormously wealthy?"

The California cop nodded their heads.

"Well, money can buy a lot of things. Including cops, I'm sorry to say." He handed them the file on Jack and Jim Longwood. "Read it in my presence and give it back."

It did not take Leo and Lani long to memorize the pertinent facts and return the file to the Buffalo cop. "Thanks," Lani said.

"I hope you catch them. Where do you go from here?"

"Akron."

"Busy little bastards, aren't they?" the Buffalo cop said. "I just wonder how many they've killed over the years."

"You sound convinced it's them," Leo said.

He smiled. "I was uniform then. Yesterday when we spoke, it all came rushing back. I was the first to interview the twins. Arrogant, profane, snooty, little crapheads. Smug. Ten, eleven years old, and they knew all the dirty words in the book. And called me everyone of them."

"Are the school buildings still standing?" Leo asked.

"Oh, yeah. The complex has been tied up in the courts for years. If you're thinking about going out there, I don't want to know about it." He smiled. "But there is a stand of thick timber behind the school. Be a dandy place to hide a car."

*   *   *

There was no security at the old private school, and getting in was a piece of cake. There were boxes and crates stacked all over the halls, and someone had been kind enough to mark the contents on the outside of every box and crate.

Luck was with them, and they found a crate marked: YEARBOOKS 1975. But in the space for Jim and Jack Longwood was printed: Photo Not Available.

"Shit!" Lani said.

"Now we start looking for records."

It took them more than two hours, and when they finally found the records section, they were covered with dust and grime and cobwebs. It took them another hour to find the files on Jim and Jack Longwood.

Neither of them realized it, but they were both holding their breath as Leo opened first one file, then the other. They exhaled as the pictures of the twins looked back at them.

"Gotcha, you little jerks!" Leo said.

"We can do a computer enhancement and pretty well know what they'll look like at age thirty," Lani said.

"We finally got a break."

They put fresh batteries in their flashlights and repacked as best they could. On the way out, Lani literally tripped over a small box and hit the floor. On the floor, her beam of light caught the printing on the side of the box. DISCIPLINARY RECORDS.

"Well, now," she said, standing up and brushing some of the dust off of herself. "This just might prove interesting reading." She opened the box and found the files on Jim and Jack Longwood, and shoved them into her large purse.

"You taking those?"

"You better believe I am. We can always say some-one mailed them to us."

Leo suddenly clicked off his light and shushed her. "Listen!" he whispered, as Lani instinctively cut the beam of her light.

They could clearly hear the sounds of footsteps on the concrete walk outside.

"More than one person," Lani whispered.

"I make it two people. And we're trapped."

"Jimmy the goddamn thing," a woman's voice reached them in the dark and dusty corridor. Let's get in here and get this over with."

"I got news, Sis. It's already been jimmied."

"The half brother and sister," Lani whispered.

"Yeah."

The California cops heard the jimmied door open and close.

"And here they come," Leo whispered.

Chapter 7

The man and woman stood still and used flashlights to search the long corridor. Lani and Leo were well aware that the beams of light were picking up their footprints in the decade's-old dust on the floor. There was nothing they could do about that. There was nothing they could do, period. The newly arrived man and woman were blocking the way out.

The flashlights were abruptly switched off, plunging the hall into darkness. Then the sounds of running feet reached the California cops. The man and woman were leaving . . . in one hell of a hurry.

"No way!" Lani muttered, throwing caution to the wind. She jumped to her feet and ran after the pair.

"No!" Leo yelled. When his warning had no effect, he leaped to his feet and took off after his partner.

The unknown man was fumbling with a stubborn door when Lani slammed into him. The old door shattered, and both Lani and the man went tumbling outside, landing on the concrete. The woman turned and faced Leo, stopping the cop for a few seconds.

Leo had never before in his life seen such hate and evil on a human face. But he was quite familiar with the gun in her hand.

She screamed at him, the fury in the shrieking echo-

ing throughout the empty building. Leo threw himself
to one side, just as she pulled the trigger. The booming
of the pistol was enormous in the emptiness. The slug
slammed into the glass of the trophy case and breaking
glass tinkled to the tile.

The man Lani had hurled against was addled, having bumped his head on the concrete. She jumped up
and threw herself at the woman's legs, knocking the
woman down. The pistol slid away into the darkness.
Lani got a second's glimpse at the woman's face, and
nearly recoiled at the hate and evil so vividly expressed
there. Then the woman was up and delivering a vicious
kick to Lani's belly, driving the wind from her. She
grabbed her pistol and ran out the door.

Leo fired, the slug from his 9mm missing the woman
and grooving a hot line in the half-open wooden door.
Then the woman was gone, her male companion staggering along with her. Lani lay gasping on the dirty
floor, both hands clutching her stomach.

"You all right, kid?" Leo panted, kneeling down
beside her.

"Yeah," Lani gasped. "That bitch can kick like a
mule."

Both of them heard a car crank up and drive off,
back tires spinning in the pea-gravel parking lot.

Lani sat up, her back to the wall. "Did you see the
face on that woman?"

"I sure did. Scared the crap out of me. No artist
could ever paint that much evil."

"I agree."

Leo spotted something lying just outside the shattered front doors. He left Lani and picked it up.

"So much for the half brother and sister being in
California," Lani said, getting to her feet. Her stomach hurt like hell.

"We'll soon know," Leo replied. "The man lost his wallet."

"George Prott?" Leo said aloud, looking at the driver's license. "Prott?"

They had returned to the motel, making certain they were not followed.

"The prott thickens," Lani said with a smile.

"Oh, Lani," Leo groaned, shaking his head. "That's bad, kid. Pull up your shirt. Let me look at your belly."

She was going to have one whale of a bruise, but there was no swelling to indicate anything ruptured.

"What's the address on the license?"

"P.O. Box in Binghamton. A hundred dollars. No credit cards, no business cards, nothing." He looked carefully at the license. Fingered it. "It's a phony." He handed it to her.

Whoever had done it, had done a good job. But the license was still a phony. She tossed it on the bed. "The boys know we're after them, Leo. They're cleaning up any paper trail that might be behind them."

"Yeah. But who's helping them do it? The half brother and sister?"

She shook her head. "I don't think so. The man and woman we tangled with tonight were older. I'd guess in their mid to late forties."

"But we heard the man call the woman *sis.*"

"Oh, I think it's still all in the family. I think this family is all nuts. Cousins, maybe. Hell, Leo. I don't know. Can we call the Bureau in on this?"

"If we could prove it was the boys, yeah. Crossing state lines would do it. Let's see them in the morning."

* * *

The agent in charge listened to the California cops. When they finished, he said, "You have no concrete proof linking the twins to the murders?"

"No," Lani said. "But isn't the cutting off of the faces enough to prove the killer, or killers, is crossing state lines?"

"It is in my opinion. I don't have the last word, though. I'll kick it upstairs and see what happens."

They did not, of course, tell the FBI man of their breaking into the school, or of being attacked by the man and woman.

Lani and Leo moved on to Akron. In addition to the original woman who had been killed and mutilated back in '77, authorities in and around the city had since discovered eight more bodies, most of them without faces. On a hunch, the California cops went to Columbus. There, in addition to the man who had been killed in '78, the police had since uncovered twelve more bodies, all of them, they believed, linked to the first murder.

It was in Akron that Leo suggested they rent a car and just drive the route the Ripper had—according to their theory—taken on his cross-country murdering spree. They would stop at each county seat along the way, and talk to the sheriff and chief of police, for both Leo and Lani had a hunch that the Ripper had not confined his murders to cities. They okayed their plan with Sheriff Brownwood and with Dennis Potter, and rented a car.

They cut down to Springfield and had a chat with a local detective. One more faceless body to add to the list. Two in Columbus, one outside of Lima. They stopped in Fort Wayne, Logansport, Lafayette. More bodies over the years.

"It can't be the twins doing it all," Leo said, as they rolled along through Indiana, nearing the Illinois border. "They're not old enough, and couldn't have covered this much ground."

"I agree. The older half brother and sister must be in on it."

"Or more."

"Elucidate, please."

"Elucidate? Don't go fancy on me, kid."

"You want to explain?"

"It's a club."

"A *club?*"

"A killing club."

She arched one eyebrow and waited. According to a road sign, Danville, Illinois was only a few miles away.

"I don't believe any of that crap Karl Muller told us about the house and the torture chambers and all that. I don't think Mr. and Mrs. Longwood were killers or kinky or anything like that. Just rich and arrogant and contemptuous of other people and overly protective of their twins. I think we're going to find that the older half brother and sister started the killings, and then saw the twisted minds of Jim and Jack and introduced them to the . . . well, call it a game for want of a better word. I also think that the twins were—contrary to what we've been told—confined at one time or the other, to mental institutions. And there, they recruited other people who were and are twisted in the same way."

They crossed over into Illinois before Lani spoke. "You've been working on that theory for several days, haven't you?"

"Yeah."

"All right. What about those recruited in the institutions? Are they still active? Are they still killing?"

"Maybe. Some of them. But not very many of them."

"The twins and their half brother and sister killed them, didn't they?"

"That's the way I see it."

"Why?"

"To permanently shut their mouths."

"All right. I'll go along with that. What's the total, so far?"

"To this point on the map?"

"Yeah."

"Forty-seven bodies."

"Now we're coming up on that four-year gap between '78 and '82."

"Yeah. So when we get to Peoria, we start checking for mental institutions around the state, and we visit every one of them."

"Those goddamn shrinks aren't going to tell us anything."

Leo smiled. "But disgruntled ex-employees will."

Leo and Lani got the names of mental institutions around the state, rented a P.O. Box in Peoria, and ran an ad in several of the state's larger newspapers. The ad claimed a class action lawsuit was about to be filed against certain (unnamed) mental institutions throughout Illinois, both state and private. Any interested parties should come to Room 103 at a local motel.

"Talk about illegal and not worth a damn in court," Lani groused, after reading the ad.

"This case will never come to court, Lani," her partner said bluntly. "These people will never allow themselves to be taken alive."

Lani had faxed the school pictures of Jim and Jack

Longwood back to California, and had received a computer enhancement of what the boys would look like at various ages. The pictures were thumbtacked up in the room. The cops would ask no direct questions about the boys. They were already breaking enough laws without adding possible harassment charges to the growing list. They hoped that someone would recognize the pictures and volunteer information.

Lani and Leo took down names and addresses and listened to dozens of complaints for two days, before a woman stared at the enhancements and blurted out, "My God! The twins from hell!"

"I beg your pardon?" Lani asked, trying to keep the excitement from her voice.

"Jim and Jack Silverman," the woman said. "Jack was released after being confined for about a year. Jim escaped from lock-down about three years later."

The woman was the last person waiting to be interviewed, and Leo quietly got up and removed the sign from the door.

"Well," Lani said, winging it, "to be perfectly honest, I think Jack is the one who is behind all of this. We don't know much about it. We were just hired to do the interviewing."

The woman stared at the cops for a moment, then shook her head. "You must be mistaken. Those two despised us all. Someone else must be behind the lawsuit."

"It's possible," Leo said, sitting down with a fresh pot of coffee and three cups. "Like Lani said, we don't know much about the particulars. The twins must have made quite an impression on you, ma'am."

"*Impression?* I would certainly say so. They were psychotic, delusionary, schizophrenic, and God only knows what else. Jack fooled the doctors into believing he was cured. Jim never denied what he was."

"Why were you discharged from the institution?" Lani asked.

"I knocked the piss out of Jim Silverman," she said bluntly. "He somehow got out of his room one night, and tried to rape me. When their father—he's some rich man from back East—heard about it, he put on the pressure and got me fired."

"Well, that's not fair!" Lani said, real indignation in her voice.

"Sure as hell wasn't. But," she sighed, "that was a long time ago, and I'm sure those twins are either dead or confined in some mental institution by now. I would sure hope so. They're both very, very dangerous men."

The cops gently led the woman deeper and deeper into conversation about Jim and Jack Longwood. Then they bought her a nice dinner at the motel restaurant and continued getting information from her. They learned that Jim and Jack were from New York State. The only visitors they had had was a half brother and sister. Their parents, to the best of her knowledge, never came to see the twins. The twins would be in their early to mid-thirties by now. But she was sure they were either dead, in prison, or confined in some mental institution.

The next morning, early, Lani and Leo had checked out and were on the road, heading west.

Chapter 8

"We leave the Bureau out of this," Leo said, as they drove. "We've broken and bent too many laws. If we went to court with what we've gathered thus far, the judge would take one look at it, throw it all out, and put us in jail."

The California cops stopped in Davenport and Cedar Rapids, before touching base with the PD in Des Moines. Eight more bodies along the bloody route from New York State. In Des Moines, in addition to the three bodies discovered back in '82, they could now add ten more to the list, all with their faces cut away.

"That's either sixty-nine or seventy," Lani said. "I'm losing count."

"Where the hell are they picking up their money?" Leo said that night, sitting in Lani's room after dinner. "Or are they? Are they working along the way? If so, what are they doing? What are they qualified to do?"

"We haven't found where they even graduated the eighth grade," Lani said.

"But we have found, thanks to those records you swiped back at that private school, that their I.Q.'s are astronomically high. Far and away above genius level. So let's assume they're self-taught."

"We know they both like old movies and old music. Along with several million other people. Or more," Lani said glumly. "Including me."

"And me. My radio stays tuned to KSIN."

The cops looked at each other for a moment, then both of them shook their heads. Leo said, "I know all the people out at KSIN FM. Remember all those public service announcements I did last year? I got to know them all pretty well. But I guess we could check them out, when we get back."

She nodded her agreement and said wearily, "Wichita, here we come."

Counting the man and woman who were found in '83, eight more bodies had been uncovered over the years. That brought the Wichita count to ten . . . at least. There were no radio stations in Wichita that played music from the '30's and '40's, and no theaters that showed classic movies. They angled up to Denver and found the count was now sixteen in and around the city.

"Counting all the smaller towns and cities we didn't check," Leo said, "the death count is probably well over five hundred nationwide. We'll never know."

The cops drove down to Albuquerque and then over to Phoenix. Then they headed north to Salt Lake City. In Leo's room at the downtown Holiday Inn, the road-weary cops tallied up the count.

"I make it one hundred and thirty," Lani said. "Give or take a couple. And that's not counting those in our own backyard."

Leo nodded and called into the station. He listened for a moment, then hung up. "Add one more," he said grimly. "A Tammy Larson was just found."

"Minus her face?"

Leo shuddered. "Minus more than that, kid. The Ripper has added a new twist. She had been completely skinned."

The cops had been on the road for weeks, and they were worn out. After arriving back in La Barca, they checked in with Sheriff Brownwood and then drove out to the Potter mansion.

The multimillionaire was clearly shocked at the news. "A hundred and thirty-one dead?" he managed a whisper.

"That we know of," Leo said. "We figure the total is probably over five hundred."

"Good God!" the man blurted. "This is . . . monstrous!"

"The problem is—" Lani said, "one of many—is that most of the evidence we've managed to piece together, we did illegally. It would never stand up in a court of law. It would never reach a court of law."

Dennis Potter looked first at Lani, then at Leo. His eyes were very, very bleak. When he spoke, his voice was clear and cold and flat, utterly devoid of emotion. "It is my opinion, that in some cases, justice is much more important than adhering to the strict letter of the law." He turned his back to them for a moment, staring out a window. "Keep and use the credit cards whenever you need them. These . . . monsters must be stopped. I don't expect you two to do that tomorrow, next week, or even next month. But you'll find them, eventually, and you'll stop them. One way or the other. You have proven yourselves to be very fine police officers. I compliment you both." He turned and picked up a picture from the fireplace mantel. A color eight by ten of his dead daughter. Dennis went to the cemetery every Sunday afternoon and placed a

dozen roses on his daughter's grave. He had lost his
wife only a couple of years back. His other children
were all married and gone. Dennis Potter was a very
rich, very lonely man, in a lovely mansion. "You two
both know your way out," he said softly, not taking
his eyes from the picture of his daughter. "Thank you
for all you've done. Please keep me informed."

Lani and Leo left the study and let themselves out.
They stood for a moment on the wide porch. Lani
said, "I counted about five different messages in that
little talk of his."

"At least. Let's go look at what's left of Tammy
Larson."

"I was afraid you'd say that."

Both cops were badly shaken as they left the morgue
late that afternoon. The M.E. had said, that in his
opinion, it had taken the Ripper many hours to carefully and completely skin the victim. And there was no
dirt imbedded in the tissue, so it was, again in his
opinion, done in a fairly sterile environment. In a
home, probably. And whoever had done the skinning
had used very sharp knives, and knew something
about the human anatomy. Might have had some
medical training.

"I'm going home to get reacquainted with my wife,"
Leo said. "Providing she hasn't changed the locks on
the doors."

"I'll see you in the morning, Leo."

Instead of going home, Lani went back to the station, got the key from the personal effects room, and
drove out to Cal Denning's place. She carefully tossed
the den first and found nothing. She went into the
master bedroom and looked at the small pile of per-

sonal effects on the bed. A money clip containing twenty-eight dollars. A wallet filled with the usual stuff. Some change, a key ring, and a folded slip of paper.

She unfolded the paper and felt the blood rush from her face. Printed on the page were the words: Tammy Larson.

Since Cal was still in the hospital in a coma and sure as hell wasn't going anyplace, Lani waited until the next morning to drop it in Leo's lap.

"No way," her partner said. "Not Cal."

"You can't be sure of that."

"Yeah, I can. When Ruthie Potter was killed, Cal was attending an engineers' convention in Las Vegas. When the third girl was killed, Cal was in San Diego on a three-day weekend. He was shacked up with George Benson's wife."

Lani's mouth dropped open. "The Episcopal priest's wife!"

"Yeah. She and Cal have been a quiet item for several years." He grinned. "See? There are goings-on around here you don't know about."

"Smart-ass," she muttered.

"Cal may have been bumpin' uglies with Tammy, too. Cal likes the ladies."

Lani grimaced. "You have such a quaint way of describing the sex act, Leo."

"That's what Virginia said last night. Twice."

"Now you're bragging. It isn't becoming," she chided him. "Come on. Let's go talk to Tammy's friends."

* * *

The lounge door was locked, but they could see people moving about, cleaning up. The door was opened at Lani's knocking.

The waitress shook her head at Leo's question. "No. I don't think Tammy even knew Cal Denning. He wasn't a customer that I know of. And I've been here ever since Tammy opened for business."

They drove over to Tammy's apartment. Cal's name was not in Tammy's address book. Leo sighed as only a cop can. "Well, we check out every name listed here."

Lani thumbed through the pages. "Ho-ho," she said.

"What?"

"Dick Hale and William Jarry. Look here."

Leo looked. "Dick Hale couldn't be Jim or Jack Longwood. He's too old, and he's lived here all his life."

"BJ the DJ hasn't."

"True. Jesus, I can't believe Tammy was humpin' Dick Hale. Talk about a jerk-off. That's the most obnoxious prick in the county."

"He came on to me one time," Lani said, making a terrible face at the memory.

"You should have shot him!"

"I thought about it."

They ran a check on William Jarry. In 1990 he'd been working in Phoenix. But nothing else about him fit what they knew of the Ripper. William was thirty-eight years old, and a native of Texas. They couldn't find that he'd ever been east of the Mississippi River.

"Oh, sure," William said to the cops. "Tammy and I dated lots of times. We stopped seeing each other about six months ago. We were still good friends and all that, but strictly on a social basis. She was dating some guy from Morro Bay."

"Henry Sparks?" Lani prompted.

"Yeah. I think that's the guy." William smiled. "You don't think I'm the Ripper, do you?"

"Tammy was killed between the hours of 6:00 and 10:00 P.M. on a Wednesday night," Leo said. "Where were you?"

"On the air. Check the logs and the engineer on duty."

Lani smiled. "We already have. Thanks for your cooperation, BJ. I enjoy your show."

Back in the car, Leo said, "We handle Dick Hale with kid gloves. He doesn't wield as much stroke as he thinks he does, but he's got enough to make things uncomfortable if we work it wrong."

Dick was all winks and good-ol'-boy talk and gestures. "Oh, sure. Tammy and I got it on a few times. You know how it is, Leo. Man's got to have some strange from time to time."

"No," Leo said, his dislike for the man extremely difficult for him to conceal. "I don't know. But you understand that we have to check out every name in her address book?"

"Oh, I suppose so. Stupid broad shouldn't have had my name in that damn book. This could be embarrassing."

"We'll be discreet," Lani said drily.

Dick picked up on her dislike and flushed. Bitch! he thought. Ought to be home taking care of babies and leave the police work to men. He smiled at her, but it was forced.

Under questioning, Dick finally admitted that he could not prove where he was between six and ten the night Tammy was killed and skinned. "I was just driving around," he said. "No law against that, is there?"

"No, sir," Leo said, and the two cops then left Dick's office.

Back in the car, Lani said, "God, how I dislike that creep!"

"I don't think he had anything to do with Tammy's death, Lani, but let's run him."

It didn't take long and both cops looked at the printout with renewed interest. "Premed in college," Lani said. "Studying to be a surgeon. Wonder why he didn't finish?"

"He had to come back here to take over the radio and TV stations," Sheriff Brownwood answered that question, standing in the office door. "After his parents died. You two actually think Dick Hale is the Ripper?"

"No," Leo said quickly. "But this could be a bad copycat. It's the first time in more than one hundred victims that the entire body was skinned."

Brownie came in and sat down on the edge of the desk. "Lay it all out, gang. Tell me what's on your mind."

"How did Tammy get the money to buy that lounge?" Lani asked. "She went from a cocktail waitress to a club owner overnight."

"Did Dick give or loan it to her?" Leo asked. "Was she blackmailing him?"

"Neither one of us think Dick killed her," Lani said. "But there are some questions that need answering."

"Then find out," the sheriff said. "I know how you both work. You're not going to ride rough over Dick. I—"

He stopped at the ringing of the phone and motioned for one of them to take it. Lani did and listened for a moment. "Look, give me your name. I . . . " She fell silent and began scribbling on a note pad. "Wait a minute, sir! Wait. Don't hang up." She grimaced and hung up the phone.

"What'd you got?" Leo asked.

"A citizen who wouldn't give his name. Said he saw Dick Hale and Tammy Larson together about seven o'clock on the evening she was killed. Said they appeared to be arguing. Said they were in Dick's Cadillac and heading north out of town, up into the hills. Said he was sorry, but he didn't want to get involved. Then he hung up."

Before Brownie could speak, another detective walked in. "Tammy's bank records. I just got them. For the last two years, a thousand dollars every month from Dick Hale's personal account."

"Thanks, Ernie," Leo said, taking the statements. To Lani: "Before we pull Dick in for another chat. Let's have one more go at William Jarry. I want his reaction to Dick screwing Tammy." To Brownie: "Get us an order to impound and let forensics go over Dick's car?"

"You got it," the sheriff said, and left the office.

Lani stood up. "Let's go see BJ the DJ."

Chapter 9

William Jarry was clearly shocked. He sat down hard on the couch in his apartment. "Tammy was having an affair with Dick Hale? God, that's too gross to even think about."

"William, does anybody like Dick Hale?" Leo asked.

The DJ shook his head. "I don't believe so. I can't think of a single person who would spit on him if he was on fire. Now I can figure out where Tammy got the money to buy that lounge. From Trickie-Dickie."

An idea was forming in Lani's head. She'd work on it before speaking to Leo about it.

But Leo was on the same track. In the car, heading for the broadcast complex, he said, "This may be a frame-up, Lani."

"I was thinking the same thing. For sure, Dick Hale is not the original Ripper."

"This is too absurd for words," Dick said. "Both of you get out of my office, I have work to do."

Leo tossed the verified bank statements onto his desk.

Dick paled and started to sweat. He opened his mouth to speak.

Lani held up her hand and said, "You have the right to remain silent. If you give up that right, anything you say can and will be used against you in a court of law. You have the right to an attorney. If you cannot afford one, one will be appointed . . . "

But Dick wasn't hearing a word. He had fainted.

"I tell you, I did not kill Tammy Larson!" Dick shouted at the cops in the interrogation room. "Tammy was a high-class hooker. I paid her a thousand dollars a month for . . . services. And she rendered them well."

"Dick," his attorney said.

"No," Dick said. "I want my name cleared in this mess."

Brownie entered the room and whispered for a moment into Lani's ear. She nodded and said, "Dick, you are under arrest for the murder of Tammy Larson." She waggled her finger at a uniform. "Book him."

It took three cops to drag the screaming, kicking, struggling, and fighting Dick Hale out of the interrogation room.

"He's a vain, arrogant man," Leo said, after Brownie told him what he'd whispered to Lani. "But he's not stupid. He's really a very bright person. He's being set up."

"I agree."

Bloody clothing had been found in the trunk of Dick's car. The blood was a match with Tammy's type. Her fingerprints were on the dash. Hair found in the car matched hers. She had been taperecording their visits together, and the tapes were very explicit, although Dick was not very inventive with his love-making. And two very sharp and very bloody knives were found in a drawer in Dick's desk in his office.

Things did not look good for Dick Hale.

Carla Upton pulled Stacy in to take over as general manager of KSIN FM and Cathy Young—Frenchy's live-in girlfriend—was brought up from the part-timers to fill Stacy's on-air slot. Cathy was very good, with a husky, sexy voice and an easy, on-air demeanor.

With Dick in the bucket (bail had not yet been set), conditions eased up at KSIN. Oddly enough, ratings went up for the broadcasting complex—AM, FM, and TV.

Lani and Leo ran every employee of the complex, and they all checked out. DJs are a nomadic bunch, tending to move around quite a bit. The cops carefully checked past employment history. Everything proved out to the good.

"Well, that's it for the employees," Lani said, hanging up the phone, after speaking with the general manager of a radio station in New Orleans. "They're in the clear. We're right back to square one."

"I was sure it was one of them," Leo said.

"So was I. But, no. By the way, Dick passed the polygraph and the PSE." Psychological Stress Evaluator. Many believe it far more effective and accurate than the polygraph. "The judge is going to set bail today."

"I don't feel sorry for the man, but he's had a rough time of it in jail."

"Is he still in isolation?"

Leo nodded his head. "Ever since he got raped. First day in lockup. He'll be out this afternoon."

"First we arrest the man for murder, and now I feel an obligation to prove he didn't do it."

"Is he going to sue?"

"Yeah," Lani said. "Papers already in the works. And that's not the only thing in the works." Leo looked up at her. "Dick's wife left him. Threw all his clothes out in the front yard. His lawyer has rented him a house up in the hills."

"Like the little girl on the salt box: when it rains, it pours."

Dick was told by his attorney—the best in California and one of the best in the nation—to go home and stay home. Don't leave the house. Have groceries delivered.

One week after Dick was released from jail, a man who had been out of town on an overseas business trip returned, read the paper, and immediately drove to the sheriff's office and asked who was working the Dick Hale case. He was pointed to Leo and Lani.

"Dick Hale didn't kill that girl," he told them. "I saw Tammy in the parking lot of her apartment complex about seven thirty that night. I know them both. I like—*liked*—Tammy; I couldn't tolerate Dick Hale. He's the world's greatest craphead. My girlfriend lives at that apartment. I had just visited her to say good-bye—I was going out of town for a couple of weeks—and was walking to my car, when I saw Tammy. Some fool had blocked me in—parked behind my car—and I had to wait for them to return before I could leave. I spoke to Tammy. She didn't reply; acted like she was in some sort of trance. She was just standing there, a blank expression on her face. Kind of scared me; like she was on drugs or something. I got in my car and waited. A dark-colored car pulled up beside her, and she got in. It was a woman driving. They, ah, embraced and kissed and drove off. I waited and waited for the jerk to come move his car. After about thirty minutes, I started back into the apartment building. Dick Hale drove up in his Cadillac and rode up in the elevator with me. I spoke, but he didn't. He acted like he was in a trance; just like Tammy. Like he was hypnotized. I didn't think much about his not speaking. He doesn't like me and I don't like him. I was curious about what he was doing there. I got off on the same floor as he did and stalled around on the floor. I'd heard that Tammy had been doing some hooking. I'd heard she had four or five fairly well-to-do clients. Dick had a key to Tammy's apartment and unlocked it and went in. He came back out in about a minute and just stood there in the hall. He looked . . . dazed. Looked right at me and didn't seem to see me. It was really weird. Sort of scared me. He got into the elevator and I got into the other one and rode down to the ground floor. I watched him walk back to his car and drive away. In the opposite direction Tammy and the woman had taken."

Leo had the citizen's statement typed up, and the man signed it. Said he would be in town and would be willing to be called as a witness.

"This is getting strange," Brownie said, after reading the statement. "Could one—or more—of Tammy's clients have been a woman?"

"Or is the Ripper a woman?" Lani added.

"Or is the Ripper actually two people?" Leo said. "Like Jim and Jack Longwood. Or four or more people? One or more of them a transvestite?"

"Jesus!" the sheriff said. "Why didn't these New York State weirdos stay home? We have more than our share without adding to it." He got up and walked out.

"He does have a point," Lani muttered.

* * *

Cal Denning awakened from his coma with a bad headache. The first thing he asked about were his cats. The doctors assured him his pets were being taken care of, and that they were all fine and healthy. They also assured Cal that he would make a fast and complete recovery.

The problem was, Cal had lost a lot of memory. There were many things he simply could not recall.

"That's common with this type of injury," the doctors told Leo and Lani.

"Will his memory return?" Lani asked.

The doctor shrugged. "Maybe, maybe not. No way of telling. We don't know if he *wants* to remember. That plays a big part in memory return."

"Can we see him?" Leo asked.

"Oh, sure. But only for a few minutes."

Cal greeted Leo warmly and gave Lani a visual inspection. He liked what he saw. Nearly everyone did.

"The doctor says you don't remember the attack," Leo said. "Is anything coming back to you?"

"The doc is full of shit," Cal said. "I never told him that. I remember getting bashed on the noggin. I just can't remember anything for several days *before* the attack."

"Did you get a look at your attacker?" Lani asked.

"No. I remember one of my cats making a dash for the kitchen. Then everything went black."

Lani showed him the slip of paper found in his personal effects.

"That's my handwriting, all right," Cal said. "But I never heard of anyone named Tammy Larson. I mean . . . I guess I have, I wrote it down, I just can't remember it. What about her?"

Leo looked at the doctor standing near the bed, and the doctor nodded his head.

"She's dead. Looks like the Ripper—or a copycat—got her. Dick Hale was arrested for her murder."

"Trickie-Dickie?" Cal was clearly startled. "I find that very hard to believe. Dick's a jerk, but he faints at the sight of blood. I mean that. I've seen him hit the boards there at the station. Just ask anyone there."

Leo and Lani exchanged glances. Lani said, "Are you telling us that everyone employed at the broadcasting complex knew this about Dick, and yet no one came forward to tell us about it?"

"Hey, no one there gives a shit what happens to Dick Hale," Cal said. "Or his wife, or his kids. If you're asking whether any employee would stand by and let Dick Hale go to prison or the gas chamber for a crime he didn't commit . . . I would say yes."

"The man is that hated?" Leo asked.

"He's that hated," Cal said flatly.

Linda Arkin left work at the expensive boutique in the mall and was seen driving off. At seven that evening her father called the police and the sheriff's office to report his daughter missing. At nine o'clock the next morning, a very hysterical teenage girl called the sheriff's office.

"I beg your pardon?" the deputy asked.

The girl repeated her statement.

"Stay on the line," the girl was told. The deputy handed the phone to a female. "Talk to her. Calm her down." He ran up the hall toward the offices of Lani and Leo.

"You're not serious?" Lani blurted.

"I'm as serious as a crutch," the deputy said. "The girl's on the line now." He shouted the last, for Leo and Lani were already running for the front door of the station.

CHRIST IS COMING! the billboard proclaimed. ARE YOU READY?

"I hope she was," the CHP man muttered, looking at the billboard.

Linda Arkin's nude body, minus her face, was nailed to the billboard.

"It's like a . . . crucifixion," Leo said.

Sheriff Brownwood drove up. He got out of the car and stared pale-faced at the bloody sight. "Get your pictures taken and get her down from there, goddamnit!" he shouted.

"Too late," the CHP man said. "Here comes the press."

"Shit!" Brownie said.

MONSTER ON THE LOOSE silently screamed the town's daily newspaper. The only reason they didn't print the picture of Linda's naked and crucified body was fear of a lawsuit. But the event was printed in graphic detail.

"Sells newspapers, I suppose," Lani said.

Leo snorted in disgust and threw the newspaper in the wastebasket.

Brownie appeared in the doorway. "ME fixed the time of death between eight and ten last night. The girl had been raped and, ah, sodomized. Among other things. And we have a witness who places Dick Hale near the scene at nine o'clock last night. Driving around alone. Go pick the stupid son of a bitch up, and bring him in."

* * *

In the basement of the home, the Ripper looked at the face of Linda Arkin, floating in clear preservative, and smiled. The face was just too lovely for words. It was exquisite. The loveliest of them all. The Ripper kissed the coolness of the glass jar and sighed. "Mine forever," the Ripper said. "Forever and ever."

"You go to hell!" Dick shouted at Leo and Lani from behind the closed front door. "I'm not going anywhere with you."

"Dick—" Leo said patiently.

"No!" he shouted. "You know what was done to me in jail! Those goddamn nigger savages used me like a woman. I'll kill you, before I let you take me back to that place. I've got a gun. I mean it." A few members of the press were beginning to gather.

"Let's back off and call for a unit," Lani suggested. "They can park out front and make sure he doesn't run, until we talk to Brownie."

The sheriff was at the scene in twenty minutes, and so were the press, print and broadcast. "Dick," Brownie called from outside the front door. "I promise you we won't put you in general population. But you've got to come in with us."

"I'll die first!" Dick shouted.

"You were seen near where the girl's body was found nailed to that billboard, Dick," the sheriff persisted.

"That was a setup and I can prove it!"

"How, Dick?"

Brownie, Lani, and Leo heard the dead bolt click open. "You three can come inside. But I've got a gun in my hand, and I won't hesitate to use it. You better believe that."

"Hell, I don't blame him," Brownie whispered.

"Not after getting gang-shagged by that pack of scum in jail."

"Sheriff, I heard him call those poor unfortunates you have locked up niggers!" a reporter yelled from the road. "I'm going to see that the FCC hears about this."

"Yeah, you do that, you son of a bitch!" Brownie muttered.

"I bet he'd change his song and dance routine if we put *his* cherry ass in lock-up," Leo uncharacteristically said, glancing at the oh-so-politically-correct reporter.

"I'd give a hundred dollars to see it," Lani added.

Brownie and Leo looked at her and smiled. Like so many cops, they had very little use for the nation's liberal press.

"Dick," Brownie called. "We'll come in. But we're armed, and we intend to remain armed."

"That's fine. Just remember, so am I."

The front door opened.

Chapter 10

Dick stood in the foyer with a pistol in each hand. "Come on in," he said. "Over by the phone in the den." He stepped back and followed the trio of cops into the den.

"I received the call last evening," he said. "At the advice of my lawyer, I had that tape recorder installed. It's a good one. Punch the play button."

It was a young woman's voice on the tape, somewhat muffled. She said she had information that would clear Dick, and would he meet her at the crossroads near that old, abandoned service station. They heard Dick ask her what time she had, and the woman give the time. They heard Dick agree to meet her, and she hung up. Dick said, "This is a setup, and I know it. But I have to go."

Dick laid a small, portable cassette-recorder on the coffee table. "I talked the entire time I was gone," he said. "I had KSIN FM on the entire time. BJ gave the time and temperature several times and played commercials. All this can be checked on the logs."

"You're wising up, Dick," Brownie said. "But if this happens again, call us first. I've told you repeatedly, I don't believe you committed any of the murders. Now,

I'm going to let slide the fact that you're armed and you threatened us. But don't you ever do it again."

"Goddamnit, Sheriff! Somebody is out to get me. To frame me. To frame me for something I didn't do!"

"That is our thinking, too, Dick. But the fact remains that you cannot threaten police officers with a gun and expect to get away with it."

"How about those goddamn savages who raped me in *your* jail, Brownie? Do they get punished?"

Sheriff Brownwood faced the red-faced man. "Let me tell you something, Dick. You want to know what you can do about gang-rape in jails and prisons? I'll tell you what you can do? And you can be the first to do it. It'll make you a hero among the conservative voters and boost your ratings."

"You tell me; I'll do it."

"You can editorialize. You can take a hard law and order stance and work the citizens up into a frenzy. Shake them out of their complacency. Interview kids and adults alike who have been tossed in the bucket and gang-raped. Get brutal with it. Get down dirty and raw with it. When enough of you broadcasters do that, the public will demand action. And the government will be forced to act. Get some of these federal judges off our backs and let us enforce the law. You know what I mean."

Dick shook his head. "I can't do that. The government would pull my license."

"What?" Leo asked, startled by that remark. "What do you mean by that? Pull your license?"

"It's been tried by others," Dick said, sitting down and wiping his sweaty face with a handkerchief. "You want to know what happens to broadcasters who come down too hard on the IRS? Hammer away at them? Demand change and less Gestapo-like power for the IRS? Funny things happen. Like they get audited, year after year after year. The government claims it doesn't happen. But it happens. You want to know what happens when small independents like me start talking tough about crime, and why don't we take a hard-line stance? Let's put it this way: the major networks are all run by liberals. The news anchors are all sobbing-sisters. The commentators are all hanky-stompers. I defy any one of you to find me a true conservative with power on any network news program or talk show . . . " He paused for breath and for a drink of water.

This was a side of Dick Hale that none of the three cops even knew existed, and they were fascinated. The man was actually making sense without being obnoxious or demeaning to anybody.

"Are you all right in there, Sheriff!" the voice boomed over a bullhorn.

"Handle that, Lani," Brownie said.

Lani walked to the door. "We're all right! Everything is okay."

Brownie sat down and unloaded the pistols on the coffee table. "Go on, Dick. I never heard this side of you before."

"I know what people think of me," Dick said, leaning back and closing his eyes. "And I know what I've turned into. And I don't like it. I came back here and tried to run a real broadcasting complex. I tried for several years. I tried everything I knew to do. But that bitch Carla Upton blocked me at every turn. Believe me, gentlemen and lady, when your teenage daughter is fucking and sucking everything that wears pants, your only son is a queer, your wife is involved in some sort of a bizarre cult doing God only knows what, and your program director and major stockholder are both a couple of dykes, having an affair, you soon realize that the odds are stacked against you." Dick tore open a pack of cigarettes and lit up. "Try living with all that for a while and see what *you* become . . . before you judge me too harshly."

The trio of cops were silent for a moment. "I didn't know you smoked, Dick," Brownie said.

"I hadn't in twenty years. I started up again in jail."

"You were going to be a surgeon, weren't you, Mr. Hale?" Lani asked, surprisingly gentle.

"Yeah. But I suddenly developed an aversion to blood." He laughed sourly. "Isn't that something? I was twenty-two years old, making top grades in medical school, and suddenly the sight of blood caused me to get light-headed, nauseous, and sometimes pass out on the floor. Still does. The doctors say it happens. Sure happened to me. When my wife has her period, I can't even sleep in the same bed with her." He laughed again. "Of course, we haven't slept together in ten years anyway."

"What is your personal physician's name, Dick?" Brownie asked.

"Henson. Over at the center. But he's on vacation in Hawaii. Be back next week. He can verify what the sight of blood does to me. And so can a dozen other people who've seen me hit the floor and barf and anything else you can imagine. No way I could have killed and done those things to those women. I'd have been passed out right beside the body."

Brownie stood up. "Dick, I know you're a reasonably wealthy man. My suggestion is that you hire off-duty deputies to stay with you twenty-four hours a day. Don't move without them. That way you can have a credible witness as to your every movement. I'll set it up, if you like."

"Do that, Brownie. I'd appreciate it. I'll pay them well." He looked at Leo and Lani. "Please find out who is killing these women. Get me off the hook."

"We'll do our best," Lani said. "But you never finished what you were saying about why broadcasters won't take a hard-line stance against crime and criminals."

"Oh, boycotts, for one thing. They're a very effective tool in shutting people up. And you're powerless to prevent them. There is no law against a boycott . . . not that I know of. And you can set off minority groups without ever knowing—until it's too late—how you did it." He sighed, then smiled sadly. "The age of political correctness. What do you call a fat person now? This is no joke. A calorically adventurous person. You think I'm kidding? I guarantee you that my stations are going to be boycotted because I let slip the word 'nigger.' Bet on it. And you know what else? I don't care. I'm coming out from under this cloud of suspicion fighting. For as long as the government lets me, that is. Which won't be very long. For if they don't stop me, some goddamn minority group will. Bet on that, too."

"This is going to get interesting," Brownie said, standing by the road, leaning against his car.

"How much of what Dick said in there do you buy?" Lani asked the sheriff.

"Oh . . . fifty/sixty percent of it. Dick was a horse's butt as a kid, a young man, and a grown man. He just blames his family for all of it. But he came by it naturally. His father was a horse's butt, too."

"So if Dick Hale didn't kill those women—and I don't believe he did—then who did?" Leo asked.

Brownie smiled. "That's what the county is paying you two to find out."

* * *

Dr. Henson had a good laugh when he found out that Dick was under suspicion for killing and mutilating two women. "No way!" he said firmly. "Dick faints at the sight of blood. A classic and quite severe case of hemophobia."

That and all the other evidence that pointed away from Dick, caused the DA to quietly drop the charges.

But Dick was anything but quiet about his lockup and his experiences while in jail. He moved Stacy back to program director, moved Cathy Young back to part-time, and over loud objections from Carla and Stacy, he began editorializing. He warned Carla that if she tried to interfere, he would fight her and use every dirty trick he could dredge up. "And," he added, grim-faced. "I can get plenty damn dirty if I have to, Carla."

Carla backed down. She knew exactly what he meant, and did not want any personal dirty linen flapping out in public.

To his credit, Dick openly and on-air admitted to being gang-raped while in jail, and urged others to come forward with their jail or prison experiences. He ended his first editorial thusly: "The good, decent members of the Black community will support me in calling for jail and prison reform. The niggers will boycott the station."

"Oh, shit!" Lani said.

Carla Upton and Stacy "Tally-Ho" Ryan almost had simultaneous heart attacks; while the Ripper was highly amused at the content of the editorial.

This was even better than Dick in jail, the Ripper thought. Let him destroy himself financially.

The Federal Communications Commission, whose members (many people think), are no more than notoriously self-righteous "Morality Police" of broadcasters, threatened to pull the license of KSIN. Dick

Hale told the FCC to go to hell. All he was doing was exercising his right of free speech.

"You can't offend others and call it free speech," Dick was told.

That gave Dick what he thought was a fine idea, and he retired to write another editorial. Since all charges against him had been dropped by the DA, Dick no longer employed off-duty deputies and city police officers. Bad mistake on his part.

Certain minority groups gathered and voted to boycott the KSIN complex. The leader of the boycott was a very pretty young Black woman who really did have the best interests of the Black community at heart. But like so many other groups who wave placards and march around demanding this and that, Tina Gamble had never learned that there are a great many people who don't like to be forced into doing something . . . whether they support that particular cause or not. Freedom of choice must be a door that swings both ways.

The Ripper watched Tina Gamble on TV and smiled.

Cal Denning was getting quick mental flashes of his lost memory. Flashes that were returning so fast he could not pin any of them down.

Dick Hale drove down to Los Angeles to meet with his attorney. But his attorney had been called to New York City, and Dick decided to make a day of it in the city . . . alone.

Gil Brown, the Windjammer, called in sick and a part-timer, George "Gunda" Dan, was pulled in to work the Windjammer's shift.

Lani Prejean and Leo Franks sat at a desk in the station, surrounded by mounds of material they had gathered on the Ripper, and looked at each other. They were stumped.

At four o'clock that afternoon, Tina Gamble vanished.

Lani listened to the ringing of the telephone and sighed. It was seven o'clock. She had been looking forward to a quiet evening at home, an early dinner, and bed by ten o'clock. She jerked up the receiver.

"Yeah?"

"Lani? Brownie here. I've got people crawling all over me down at the office. Get cracking. Tina Gamble's disappeared, and Dick Hale is nowhere to be found."

"Where is his escort?"

"He stopped using them. I warned him, but he just wouldn't listen to me."

"On my way."

Tina Gamble was surrounded by faces. There appeared to be hundreds of them, but that was an illusion created by the careful placement of many mirrors of various sizes and extremely bright lights. Tina had been raped repeatedly, and beaten in between the sexual assaults. But she was alive, and determined to get away from this awful place. She forced herself to ignore the faces floating in clear liquid in what appeared to be gallon jars.

She knew she didn't have much time, for she had felt the sting of a needle in her arm and already was becoming very light-headed. But she had been left alone for a few minutes, strapped naked to the floor. For her small size, Tina was an incredibly strong woman, physically and mentally. Mentally, she fought the drugs in her system, and physically, she strained against the leather straps that were fastened around her wrists and ankles. She was beginning to hallucinate mildly, wild colors exploding in her brain. She wondered what kind of a drug had been injected into her system?

The leather straps around her wrists became slick with her blood, as the straps lacerated her flesh. She slipped one small hand through the strap and quickly unbuckled the other strap. Both hands freed, she worked frantically freeing her ankles. Then she was on her feet, looking wildly around her for a way out. She carefully picked her way through the lights and mirrors and floating faces, until she stood in darkness.

She was beginning to hallucinate badly now, and realized she had perhaps only minutes before she lost all control of her mind. She could hear footsteps above her. Tina found a small window, covered with the dust and grime of years, and pushed it open, crawling out into the coolness of night. She pushed the window closed just as the drugs began to take effect, colors and wild shapes mingling and bursting in her brain. She began to run. Rocks cut her bare feet, and brush tore at the flesh of her legs. She fell down a dozen times, bruising and cutting her knees. She ignored the pain and ran.

She did not know where she was. The darkness of the night and the drugs in her system were confusing her. She did not know how long she ran. Minutes, hours, days, years. She could not remember her name. Floating faces appeared before her. They came alive, taunting her. She saw lights ahead of her, but did not know if they were real or imagined.

She staggered and stumbled along, until she came to a small bluff. She did not see the earth end, and stepped out into nothing. She rolled down the embankment and hit the gravel road, oblivious to the pain in her body. She saw twin lights coming straight

at her, but could not move. She heard the sliding of
tires on dirt and gravel, and tried to cry out. Animal
sounds came from her throat.

"Jesus Christ!" the voice reached her ears.

"What the hell is it?" another voice asked. "A
deer?"

"Oh, dear God!" another voice added. "It's a
woman. Somebody call the police."

Tina passed out.

Chapter 11

"Sexually assaulted in just about any way you would care to name," the doctor said to Lani, Leo, and Sheriff Brownwood. Half a dozen CHP officers were standing in the hospital corridor, along with half a dozen more La Barca city police officers. "And tortured very skillfully. I think they planned to keep her alive for as long as possible, in order for the torture to last longer."

"And give them more pleasure," Lani ventured a guess with a sour look on her face.

"Yes. That would be my guess," the doctor agreed.

"Is she conscious?" Brownie asked.

"She's drifting in and out. She keeps muttering something about drugs and faces."

Lani and Leo exchanged glances.

"I'd think morning before she's coherent."

"I'm going home," Brownie said. "Why don't you two do the same?"

"We'll stick around for a while," Leo said.

They took chairs in the hall, after finding a coffee machine that dispensed coffee whose flavor was remarkably like what camel spit must taste like. Both the cops took one sip and sat the cups down on the floor and tried to forget them.

"You remember those musical notes on the wall of the boy's room back in New York?" Lani said.

"Yeah. I'd forgotten all about that. You figure it out?"

"No. But a friend of mine did. It's 'Mary Had A Little Lamb.' "

"Say what? 'Mary Had A Little Lamb'?"

"Weird, huh?"

"What else would it be in dealing with the Ripper?"

Tina's doctor passed by the cops. He slowed down and said, "Now she's muttering about mirrors and lights." He walked on, then stopped and turned around. "You mentioned something about having dogs out backtracking Miss Gamble's scent."

"That's right," Leo said. "Did you hear something?"

"No. But I think you can forget about that." He pointed toward the door, which looked like it was about a half a mile away down the polished hallway. "It's pouring rain and expected to last for a couple of days."

Leo and Lani looked at one another. "Shit!" they said together.

They were at the hospital at seven the next morning. A nurse built much like a Mack truck blocked the door to Tina's room. "You can't go in there. She's being bathed, and then she'll be examined by Dr. Kander, and then she'll have breakfast. Come back in an hour."

"Is the hospital cafeteria open?" Lani asked.

"Only if you have a death wish," the nurse said without cracking a smile.

"It couldn't possibly be any worse than the coffee we got out of the machine last night." Leo said.

"You wanna bet? Try the cafe down on the corner."

The county deputies, rather than brave the down-pour again, elected to have coffee, juice, and toast in the hospital cafeteria. "It's kinda hard to screw up toast," Leo said.

"What was that you said about not screwing up toast?" Lani said, scraping the burn off the toast.

"I'm wrong occasionally."

Back upstairs, the same nurse looked at them and said, "You ate in the cafeteria, didn't you?"

"Only toast," Lani told her.

"Was it burned?"

"Yeah," Leo said, a disgusted look on his face.

The stocky nurse suddenly laughed and held out a small paper sack. "I swiped a couple of sweet rolls from the nurses's lounge. Enjoy."

They got in to see Tina a few minutes later. She was in some pain, but willing to talk. Her feet were heavily bandaged, and thorns and branches had torn her legs from ankles to upper thigh. Her hands were bandaged, a result of many falls.

"Before you say it," Tina managed a small smile. "I know I'm lucky to be alive."

"What can you tell us about the Ripper?" Tina asked. "The place where you were held, and how the man snatched you?"

"I have no idea how I came to be . . . wherever it was they had me."

"They?" Leo asked. "More than one person?"

"A man and a woman."

There goes Jack and Jim right out the window, both cops thought.

"What do you mean, you have no idea how you got there?"

"Just that," Tina said. "I remember being outside the KSIN buildings. I remember telling Marge—

Marge Stillman—I was going to get us some coffee. I went to my car, got in, started the engine, and turned on the radio. I remember driving away. I remember pulling onto the parking lot of the Quick-Pack store. The next thing I remember was being raped and beaten. I know it sounds crazy. It *is* crazy! But it's the truth."

"We believe you," Lani said. "And we're having a guard posted outside your door, twenty-four hours a day. What can you tell us about the man and woman."

"Both of them slender, average height. The man was quite strong, and the woman was very shapely. I never got a look at their faces because they, they . . . " She shuddered and swallowed hard. "They were wearing faces."

"Faces?" Leo asked, his stomach doing a slow roll-over. He looked at the stocky nurse, standing by the bed. Her face was impassive.

"Human faces," Tina said. "Real human faces. Like the ones they had floating in those glass containers." She turned her head to one side and vomited.

"That's it!" the nurse said, shooing the cops outside. "Come back in a few hours. Move."

The cops knew better than to argue. They left the room and took seats in the corridor.

"A man and a woman," Leo said softly. "Who would have figured that?"

Lani shook her head. "Certainly not me. One of the trackers said he feels Tina probably ran for miles. And in her confused state, some of the time probably in circles. But this rain stopped them cold."

"It sure wasn't Dick Hale. Dick's built like a bear. So where does this leave us?"

"With Tina Gamble. She'll start remembering things. They always do."

" 'Mary Had A Little Lamb'?" Leo asked.

"I think we may as well forget Jim and Jack Longwood for the time being. They're running their horror show somewhere else. We've got our own feature attraction. Homegrown. Presented in living color."

"It's been a long movie."

"Yeah. But I don't think we've even reached the intermission yet."

Dick apologized for using a racial slur on the air, toned down his editorials, and the boycott of KSIN was called off. For two weeks the Ripper did not strike. Tina was released from the hospital and went back to work. She could remember nothing more about her ordeal. Cal Denning returned to his duties as chief engineer of KSIN. His office/workroom had been cleaned, and everything put away. The tapes where he had slowed down the commercial had been erased. The weather turned hot and dry.

Lani and Leo found themselves with a long weekend, and Leo had a suggestion.

"You want to go hiking?"

Lani looked at him as if he had lost his mind. "Leo, you know I am not the outdoors type. My idea of roughing it is the Sheraton with clean, crisp sheets, room service, and a good piano bar."

"We start where Tina was found on the highway and work in a circle."

"It's already been done."

"Not by us."

Lani thought about that for a moment. "When do we leave?"

"Right now."

* * *

Leo had a Ford four-wheel drive pickup, and it was packed with camping gear and food. Sheriff Brownwood had told them, "I don't care how long you two stay out there in the boondocks. Just find something. Anything."

Tina had been found on a county road in some pretty rough country. The road was not often used, and the only reason for the traffic that night was because a group of fishermen had been returning from a weekend of fishing at a lake on the west side of the Los Padres National Forest.

"She tumbled down the embankment here," Leo said, pointing. "The dogs backtracked her for two miles. In that direction." Again, he pointed. "Then the rain stopped them. The spot where they lost her scent is marked. Come on. Let's go."

The cops both wore comfortable but tough clothing and good hiking boots. They each carried two canteens of water.

They walked for about twenty minutes, and Lani said, "I'm lost, Leo."

He chuckled. "I showed you how to use a compass and how I shot our azimuth. We are not lost."

"Leo, I wouldn't know an azimuth if it hit me in the mouth. I'm a city girl. I *hate* the great outdoors. There are bugs and crawly things out here. Snakes. And bears."

"Mountain lions, too."

She moved closer to him.

"And coyotes and wolves."

"Awright already, Leo. Enough."

"And it's in this area where that madman with the axe used to chop up kids who came out to park and smooch."

She sighed. "That tale is told in every state in the Union. Smooch, Leo? Smooch? God, you're old, Leo.

Old. What the hell are we looking for, anyway? She was naked, for Christ's sake. Any bloodstains have been long washed away."

"I'm like that Supreme Court Justice when asked about pornography. He said, 'I can't define it, but I know it when I see it.' I don't know what we're looking for, Lani. But I'll know it when I see it. Keep walking."

"Yes, bwana. Right, sahib. Whatever you say." She pointed. "Is that stake where the trail was lost?"

"That's it. Let's take a breather."

"Thank you." Lani sat down and drank about half a canteen of water.

Leo pulled the canteen away from her mouth. "Go easy on that stuff, Lani. You'll make yourself sick."

"I'm thirsty!"

"Lani, make the water last. Put a pebble in your mouth and suck on it. It'll create saliva and make you feel better."

"A pebble? Wonderful. Eat a rock and feel better. Where'd you learn all this survival crap, Leo?"

"Vietnam, Lani."

"What were you, a Green Beret?"

"A green beret is a hat, Lani. No. I was a LRRP. That rhymes with burp. Stands for Long Range Recon Patrol. I was a Ranger."

"No kidding? I never knew that about you, Leo. You jump out of airplanes?"

"Yes. And climbed mountains and skied and learned to scuba, and all sorts of other neat stuff that I've been trying for twenty years to forget."

"You must have been young."

"Seventeen when I went in, and eighteen when I became a Ranger. Two months later I was in Vietnam."

"In country?"

Leo smiled. "Some people call it that."

"But you don't?"

Leo smiled and shook his head. "No. Lani, we're going to work in a big circle. We're going to stay within sight of each other and circle, an ever-widening circle."

"I saw John Wayne do this in a cowboys and Indians movie one time."

"Hush up. Are you rested?"

Leo wasn't going to talk about Vietnam. Now or ever, Lani realized. She nodded her head. "I'm rested."

"Let's go."

They rested several times and finally broke for lunch, which consisted of smushed peanut butter and jelly sandwiches and tepid water from their canteens. They had discovered nothing. At three o'clock, they still had found nothing, and Leo was just about ready to call it a day and trudge on back to where they'd left the pickup.

"Leo!" Lani called. "I found something. But I don't know what it might mean."

The handprint had been spared from the elements by a small overhang, and by some type of small animal that had taken shelter under the overhang. Probably a rabbit judging by the color and texture of the fur Leo fingered. He looked around carefully and saw a small broken branch from some scrub brush.

"She came from that direction and stumbled and fell here," he said, opening his compass and taking a heading. He took out a map and marked their location. He stood for a moment, filled with indecision. He couldn't send Lani back for the truck. She'd be lost as a goose in fifteen minutes. Taking a small camera from his pack, Leo took pictures of the scene and turned to his partner.

She had somehow picked up on his vibes. She sat

down. "I'll wait right here, Leo. I saw the dust kicked up by a vehicle on that gravel road over there. I can find that. You go back and get the truck, and when you get over there, honk the horn or fire off a round. I can make it."

"You're sure?"

She smiled. "Move, boy!"

Leo walked as swiftly as he dared. But he knew not to push himself in this intense heat. He wasn't all that worried about Lani. She could be tough as nails when she had to be, but she *was* out of her element. She was as good a street cop as anyone Leo had ever known. But this wasn't the street. This was rattlesnake country.

When Leo reached the truck, to save time he cut across country. While they had walked, Leo had mentally noted a way for the four-wheel-drive vehicle to make it back to where he had left Lani. The Ford pickup was high off the ground, and he'd taken it over much rougher terrain. When he was about halfway to where Lani waited, he blew a tire.

He knew cussing would be a waste of breath, so he just sighed and got out and changed the tire.

But when he reached the spot where he'd told Lani to wait, she was gone, and from all the churned-up earth, it looked like there had been one hell of a struggle.

Chapter 12

He cut his engine to hear better, and stood for a moment. He heard only the silence. He looked around and spotted Lani's shirt lying on the ground. "Oh, no!" he said. "Jesus Christ!"

He picked up the shirt. His thoughts were dark and very, very primitive.

"Lani!" he yelled. "Lani!"

No human sound greeted his words.

Leo had left his 9mm behind for this run, choosing instead to carry a .45 caliber autoloader. In his opinion (one shared by many others in the field of law-enforcement), the .45 caliber autoloader was the finest combat pistol ever developed. The big slug was a man-stopper that was unequaled in conventional calibers.

"Lani!" Leo shouted once more.

Nothing. Leo thumbed open the snap on his holster. Then he heard the faint sounds of cussing. The sound became clearer and Leo smiled. Lani was really letting the words fly.

"Lani!" he yelled.

"I'm right here!" she returned the yell.

He lifted the shirt. "What are you doing, Lani, sunbathing?"

"Hell, no!" she came into view, buckling her belt. "Why didn't you warn me, Leo?"

"Warn you about what?"

"Ants, goddamnit!"

Before Leo could answer, several dozen of the little insects chomped down on Leo's legs, and he started doing some fancy stepping of his own, slapping at himself and jumping around.

Lani stood and laughed at his antics. She had done virtually the same movements minutes before.

"Shit!" Leo hollered, and that doubled Lani over with laughter.

"The rain left a good-sized pool right down there," Lani called, pointing. "You better hit the water, Leo. It's the only thing that'll get them off of you."

As Leo passed Lani, he tossed her the shirt and gave her a dirty look as she laughed at him. "I'll move the truck away from those big ant mounds," she said.

"You do that," Leo spoke through gritted teeth, calling the words over his shoulder as he exited his pants.

Lani whistled at him.

"Very funny, Lani. Cute!"

Leo carried a well-stocked first aid kit, and they doctored themselves before moving out, both of them agreeing not to ever mention the ant attack to fellow officers back at the station.

They drove to the gravel/dirt road and stopped. "I don't believe Tina crossed this road," Lani said. "Even in her confused state of mind, she would have stayed on the road, following it for help."

"I agree. But I'll bet you the house where she was held is on this road. When she escaped, she exited the rear of the house and just ran, getting away the only thing on her mind. Left or right?"

"Turn right."

They drove for over a mile before coming to the first home. They got out and knocked on the front door. An elderly man answered the knock, and after they identified themselves, he waved them inside.

"No," he said, in response to the question. "There are only three more houses on this road 'fore it ends, and you got to turn either left or right. Left will take you nowhere. There is a stone house down to the right that was rented or bought by a young couple several years ago."

"Late '91," his wife added. "But we never see them. I think they live in the city and only come out here on the weekends. Maybe once a month. Sometimes less than that."

The old couple did not know the name of the young couple and could not describe them. Neither one had ever gotten a good look at them. They only came out at night, they said. Never during the daylight hours.

When was the last time they'd noticed the young couple's car?

Two weeks back, they thought.

The cops drove up the road, turned right, and slowly drove past the stone house. The home sat well off the road and was surrounded by a heavy chain-link fence. The gate was closed and locked.

"Let's do this legal, Leo," Lani said. "Right by the book."

"I agree." Leo reached for his radio mike, then hesitated.

"They'll never come back here," Lani said. "We could stake this place out forever, and come up with nothing."

He nodded and called in.

Two hours later, with about an hour of daylight left and armed with a search warrant, the cops used heavy bolt-cutters to snap the chain from the gate. Bill Bourne, from the La Barca city police, Sheriff Brownwood, members of the CHP, and a forensic crew waited as Leo and Lani walked up the sidewalk and hammered on the front door.

"You getting the same feeling I am?" Lani asked.

"Yeah. This place is deserted." Leo reached for the handle on the screen door, and stopped just as his fingers touched the handle.

"What's the matter?"

He shook his head. "I don't know. A feeling. It's too easy. Something is wrong. Back off the porch and don't touch anything doing so. Bring me a rope or some heavy cord."

"What the hell are you doing, Leo?" Brownie yelled from the gate.

"Staying alive," Leo shouted. He very carefully tied one end of the cord on the pull-handle of the screen door, and then backed off the porch, trailing out the cord.

"You smell a booby trap?" a CHP man asked.

"Yeah. I think the whole damn house is wired to go. I did some tunnel-ratting in Vietnam. I learned to trust my instincts."

"Everybody get down!" Brownie yelled. "But back up first. Get behind your vehicles. Tie some more cord on that thing, Leo. Give yourself plenty of slack to move."

Everybody got behind their vehicles and crouched. "Ready?" Leo yelled.

"Pull it," Brownie said.

Leo pulled and the screen door flew open. Nothing happened. "So much for your instincts," a CHP man said, standing up.

The house blew apart. The force of the blast knocked the California Highway Patrolman flat on his ass in the road. The roof was pushed twenty or so feet into the air; the stone walls mushroomed and disintegrated, hurling stones in all directions. The stones bounced off the cars and those crouched behind them.

"Goddamn!" Brownie yelled, as a rock clunked him on the forehead, bringing blood.

Lani and Leo scrambled under Leo's truck and were safe from the falling debris. Shattered wood and busted stones and other building materials rained down for what seemed like several minutes. Actually it was only a few seconds. A huge cloud of dust completely enveloped the explosion area. When the cops again peeped out over the hoods of cars and trucks, the house was gone. Leveled to the ground.

"Get floodlights and portable generators out here," Brownie said, holding a handkerchief to his bleeding head. "Pull everybody in. No one is off. I want this area sealed so tight a mouse couldn't get through. I don't want anybody inside that chain-link fence until I say so. As to opening the records, I don't care who you have to irritate, pull out of bars, or off of golf courses, or away from dinner tables. I want the names of the people who rented or bought this house. And I want it right now."

"Yes, sir," a young deputy said. He stood looking at the sheriff.

"Get it on the air, boy," Brownie growled. "Move."

The young deputy went quick-stepping to his unit, grabbed up his mike, and got dispatch.

"Must have been five hundred pounds of dynamite planted in that house," the CHP man whose butt had recently hit the gravel said.

* * *

"Plastic," the forensics man said, a few hours later. "C-4. These people don't fool around. This was over-kill all the way. One tenth of what they used would have been sufficient to do the job."

"The house was rented from a Mr. Ned Robbins over near Bakersfield," a deputy said. "He never met the people he rented it to. Said they paid the rent a year at a time, and he never had the first complaint about them from anybody living along this road."

"Well, hell!" Lani blurted. "No one else *lives* along this road."

"Did they tell him what they did for a living?" Leo asked.

"Said they were writers, and needed a place where they wouldn't be disturbed."

"There just might be more than a modicum of truth to that," a plainclothes CBI man said, walking up, holding up an evidence bag with several sheets of paper in it. "This is pretty dark stuff here."

Lani took the clear bag and turned to the light so she could read it. She shuddered and shook her head. "They're chronicling all the actions of their victims. This is about a nun who was raped and sodomized. Like that one in Albuquerque."

"I want every scrap of paper saved," Brownie said, more to himself than to any of the officers. He knew that when his people were through, every stone, stick, and brick would have been carefully gone over, and anything pertinent to the case would be tagged and saved.

Brownie turned to Leo and Lani. "Go home and get some sleep. That's an order. I'll see you both out here in the morning. Now, beat it."

* * *

The loss of the country house meant nothing to the Ripper. He and his Other had several homes rented throughout the county. He and his Other also owned several pieces of property, both in the city and county. And now those who followed the Ripper and his Other were gathering in California. It was going to be a very enjoyable time for the Ripper and his Other, and a very confusing time for the cops.

More than that—it was going to be *fun!*

The California Bureau of Investigation, CBI, a part of the state's Justice Department, met Leo and Lani when they arrived back at the explosion site the next morning. For now, there were two agents of the CBI assigned to this case, Brenda Yee and Ted Murray. Both of them in their early thirties.

"You guys did some great legwork on this," Brenda Yee complimented the county cops. Then she smiled. "How much of it can be used in a court of law?"

Leo chuckled softly. "Some of it."

"Look," Lani said. "It's the weekend. Why don't we all get together at my place this evening? Leo's wife and kids have gone up to Santa Cruz for a vacation. He's bouncing around alone in his house. We can have a few drinks, I'll do my impersonation of a chef, and we'll tell you guys just how we collected all this info."

"Sounds great," Ted said. "Brenda?"

"Hey, it's fine with me."

Brenda whistled softly and cocked her head to one side. "You guys were right when you said 'some of it' could be used in court. Breaking and entering, trespassing, impersonation . . . to name a few minor points. But what the hey? None of those little items ever have to be brought out."

"We hope," Ted said. "So you've put the Longwood twins out of this picture?"

"Tina said it was a man and a woman. She was adamant on that. The house that blew up is where she was held. We established that today. The house was rented to a man and woman. That pretty much puts the twins out of the picture. At least as primary suspects."

"The people who attacked you back at the closed-down private school?" Brenda asked.

Leo and Lani shrugged their shoulders. "No idea," Leo replied.

"But the both of you believe this might be the work of a cult. A cult that somehow revolves around the Longwood twins, Jim and Jack?" Ted asked.

"I think it's certainly something that has to be taken into consideration."

"I agree," Brenda said. "I think we're talking about a serial killer, or killers, with a string of bodies behind them that's going to set a world's record. I agree with your figure of over five hundred victims coast to coast. The FBI's got nearly every agent working on this string of terrorist bombings around the country, so we can't expect much help from them. There are only three hundred of us, statewide, and we're stretched pretty thin ourselves."

"Hancock County and La Barca city cops are up to their necks in robberies, murders, rapes, car-jackings, gangs, domestic crap, and all the other normal day-to-day work that takes up so much of a cop's time," Leo said. "So it's up to the four of us. How long can you people stay here?"

"Our marching orders were to stay until it's over," Ted said.

Lani stood up. "Well, we've got a green salad, spaghetti, Leo's famous—or infamous—meat sauce, garlic bread, and a pretty good bottle of California red. Let's eat."

Leo reached over and stilled the ringing of the phone. "Oh, shit!" he said, and that stopped everybody's movement to the dining area. "Okay, Sheriff. We're on the way."

"I gather dinner is delayed," Brenda said.

Leo stood up. "Yeah. Now it gets real ugly. A girl is missing. She vanished this afternoon. Mother says she's been acting trancelike for several days."

"Like the way that citizen said Dick and Tammy were behaving?" Lani asked.

"Yeah."

"How old is the girl?" Brenda asked.

"Ten," Leo said grimly.

Chapter 13

The girl, Theresa Lopeno, was found four days later. Her body had been dumped at the southernmost part of the county. Using tactical frequencies that the press, so far, had not discovered, the cops gathered at the scene. It was the ugliest rape and mutilation any of the four cops had ever seen.

Brenda Yee excused herself, walked off into the bushes, and barfed.

"Nothing like seeing it up close, is there?" Ted asked, a strain to his words.

"Especially when it's a child," Lani said. She stood with the others, waiting until the lab people finished.

The child had been sexually assaulted, tortured, and then her face had been cut away. The silent wish was that the last at least had been done after she had died, and not before.

"Parents been notified?" Leo asked, squatting down where the body had been. What was left of Theresa was now on the way to the ME's lab.

"Brownie's going himself," a uniform said.

"Tire impressions?" Brenda asked, walking up.

The uniform shook his head. "This is a favorite turning-around place. Must be fifty different sets here."

Leo stood up. "This is the most frustrating damn case I have ever worked on."

Back at the office, Leo had just sat down at his desk when his phone rang.

"Cal Denning, Leo. Look, some of my memory is returning. I'm calling from a pay phone, because I'm afraid to use the phones at the station. Can you meet me at my place this evening?"

"Sure. You think our people work at the station?"

"Maybe. I'm not sure. But what I've found is intriguing. See you about five?"

"We'll be there."

"I don't hear anything," Ted bitched.

The four of them were standing in Cal's home workshop. Cal had made dubs of the commercials and a few songs with hidden messages behind them before he'd been conked on the head. The memory had returned to him only that day.

Cal slowed the tape down further. "Now listen."

They all heard it that time. Tammy Larson.

"Jesus!" Lani said. "Subliminal suggestion."

"What?" Leo looked at her.

"I looked it up," Cal said. "What it means is this: repetition that is inserted into a particular person's subconscious without that person knowing it. It's below the threshold of consciousness."

"And it works, too," Brenda said. "I took some courses on it. One of the courses involved half the class going to a movie with only the standard advertising for soft drinks and popcorn and candy, and the other half being subjected to split-second advertising on the screen, coming so fast your conscious mind doesn't register it. But the eye picks it up and sends it to your subconscious. Gang, when the intermission came, it was a stampede; and we bought out the concession stand."

"Subtle brain-washing," Leo said.

"You could call it that, sure."

"Where was this commercial made, Cal?" Lani asked.

"Well, the original tape was made in San Francisco, for a local car dealership. But with the sophisticated equipment we have now—eight, twelve, sixteen, twenty-four tracks and up—inserting whatever you want behind words and music is easy. Anybody with a third-class engineer's license could do it. But it would take some time."

"Mr. Denning," Ted said. "Considering the fact that you've been attacked, and this," he pointed to the tape, "is probably the reason for it—your life is in danger. I'll okay a gun permit for you, if you want to carry one."

Leo laughed. "He's been carrying one as long as I've known him."

"Did your department issue him a concealed weapons permit?" Brenda asked.

"Hell, no!" Leo told her. "Law-abiding citizens have a right to keep and bear arms, if they so desire. As a matter of fact, I encourage them to do so."

"That's against the law, Leo," Ted said, a disapproving look on his face.

"It isn't against my law," Leo replied, his tone suggesting to all that the subject was closed. "Goddamn street gangs and thugs and punks stealing and raping and assaulting and killing with damn near impunity."

"I'll get you a permit, so you can be legal," Brenda verbally stepped in.

Cal shrugged his total indifference to whether he was legal or not. That is an attitude that many Californians have adopted over the past few years.

"Needless to say, but it bears repeating, you keep your mouth shut about this, Cal," Leo told him. "And you start being extra careful."

"Don't you worry about that. I'll have my own security system in place by this time tomorrow." He grinned, and it took years off his age. "I was a spook in the military. Worked with some real bright CIA boys."

"If it's dangerous to anyone entering your place of residence," Ted said, "it's probably illegal."

"Ted," Brenda said, an exasperated look on her face. "Did you know that your fly is open, and your dick is hanging out?"

Ted's mouth dropped open, he grabbed at himself, and the room rocked in laughter.

The two Hancock County deputies and the two members of the CBI met with Sheriff Brownwood, and then began exhaustive background checking on every employee of KSIN TV and radio. Dick Hale was finally and forever taken off the list of suspects, because he could prove without a doubt where he was when the Lopeno child was taken. But Stacy Ryan could not, and was reluctant to talk with the cops. They zeroed in on Tally-Ho.

But their investigation of the program director and disc jockey did not last long. Sheriff Brownwood called it off abruptly.

"What the hell, Sheriff?" Leo demanded.

"She was with Carla Upton," Brownie said. "Mrs. Upton called me a few hours ago. Not only that, but a couple of other women were there as well. Ladies whose names we all know quite well. They would prefer that their husbands not know of their, ah, outside interests."

"Doesn't anyone enjoy a plain ol' man/woman relationship anymore?" Leo bitched.

Lani laughed at the expression on her partner's face.

"Well, I sure as hell do!" Brownie quickly stated.

Lani held up a hand. "Sheriff, I believe the altered tapes can only play a part in luring the victims," she said. "Physical contact has to be made first. Whoever it is doing this, has to know the victims, has to know what songs they like, what commercials make them laugh. I've spoken with Dick Hale, and he's agreed to allow us to secretly tape record every incoming phone call to KSIN. The CBI has agreed to send in technicians to do just that. Now we need a judge's approval."

"I can get that," Brownie said.

The door to Brownie's office was pushed open, and a uniform stuck her head in. "Sheriff, we've got another one missing. The call just came in."

"Son of a bitch!" Brownie cursed.

"Lady out in the county says she sent her daughter to the supermarket hours ago. The car's just been found in the parking lot of the supermarket. No sign of the girl. And, Sheriff? The family lives about three miles from the house that blew up."

The girl's mother had been sedated and put to bed. The father was holding up, but just barely.

"No," he said, responding to Leo's question. "Ginny never listened to KSIN. And my wife and I don't either. We have a satellite system—you saw the dish outside—and don't watch much local TV. What's this about KSIN?"

"Just a hunch that didn't work out," Brenda said quickly. "We're playing all the angles, Mr. Atkins."

"We'd like a list of all Ginny's friends," Lani said.

"We want to know who she dates, where she hangs out in town, everything you can think of that might help us."

"She's dead, isn't she?" the father said numbly.

"We don't know that, Mr. Atkins," Ted said.

"Ginny wasn't the type to get in a car with someone she didn't know," the father said, after taking a long sigh. "You'll discover that when you talk with her friends. And she's brown-belt karate. She's tough. A boy she used to date tried to get too familiar with her last year. She broke his arm."

"I remember that," Leo said. "Try to keep your spirits up, Mr. Atkins." He looked down at the eight by ten picture of Ginny Atkins. Hang in there, kid, he thought.

The girl dangled about six inches off the floor, hanging by her wrists at the end of a rope. She was naked except for the hood over her head. The rape had been brutal, painful, and degrading. After the man had taken her, the woman had strapped on some sort of rubber penis and used her like an animal. She knew it was a woman, because Ginny could feel her breasts against her naked back. The more Ginny had screamed, the more the woman became aroused. Ginny finally endured the assault in silence.

Then the two of them had beaten her with whips. They had left only moments ago, saying they would be back in a few hours. Then the fun would really start. They told her to hang in there. They both thought that was really, really funny.

Just before they left, one of them had given her a shot of something. She'd heard all about what had happened to Tina Gamble, and figured the shot had been to knock her out. She didn't know how much time she had before the drug took effect, but she was determined to use every minute of it.

Ginny was agile and strong, and fear and anger made her even stronger. She began working her legs, swaying back and forth, gaining a few more inches with each effort, working like a trapeze artist. She finally was able to touch her toes against the overhead, and on the fifth try, hooked her ankles around a pipe of some sort. That released the tension on the rope around her wrists. Working calmly considering what she had just gone through, and the predicament she was in, Ginny got one hand loose and then the other. She dropped to the floor and jerked the hood from her head.

"Oh, my God!" she whispered, looking around her.

All dispatchers had standing orders about what to do if any of the Ripper's victims managed to escape and were picked up by units from the city or county: stay off the radio, and keep the press the hell away for as long as possible.

A sheriff's department unit spotted Ginny frantically waving for help and whisked her to a hospital. There, the deputy called in by phone.

Working very quickly and very furtively, the homes immediately surrounding the suspect house were cleared of residents, and city and county sharpshooters were stationed on all sides of the house. Ginny was being questioned by female cops even as she was being treated, over the strong objections of the doctors.

"It's a copycat," Leo said, crouching behind the shrubs on the north side of the home where Ginny had been raped and beaten. "Got to be."

"I agree," Lani said. "But, Jesus! Who would have ever suspected these two?"

The two people Ginny had very adamantly named—between some pretty fancy cuss words—were a very successful high school football coach and a French teacher. Both from the same school.

Leo grunted and Lani smiled at him. She knew that Leo was not a football fan. He couldn't even tell you who won last year's Super Bowl or where it was held. "Weirdos in every profession, Lani. And here they are."

The car pulled into the drive, and the man and woman got out. Leo, Lani, Brenda, and Ted all rose from behind the bushes, cocked pistols held in a two-handed shooting grip pointed at the couple.

"Sheriff's department!" Lani said. "Just freeze right there. Both of you!"

For a moment, it looked as though the couple was going to obey the orders. Then the coach screamed an obscenity at the cops and jerked out a pistol.

Four slugs hit the man. Two .357's, one 9mm, and one .45 caliber . . . Hydra-Shok(TM). The coach was flung backward by the impact and was dead before he hit the ground. The woman began screaming and jumping up and down.

Lani was across the drive and tackled the woman, sitting on her while Brenda cuffed her. The French teacher was doing some rather heated cussing, in English.

"Get off me, you goddamn, murdering pig bitch!" she yelled at Lani.

Lani resisted an impulse to hammer the woman's face in with her pistol. She read the woman her rights, and not too gently jerked her to her feet and shoved her at a couple of uniforms.

"Police brutality!" the French teacher screamed. "I'll sue you."

Lani smiled at the woman. Leo knew that smile and

grabbed his partner by the arm. "Let's check out the house, Lani."

The French teacher had switched to French and was really calling Lani some choice names, as she was stuffed into the backseat of a unit.

"I wonder what she's calling me?" Lani asked.

"She said she hopes you get the clap and your tits rot off," Leo said matter-of-factly.

Lani blinked a couple of times. "Well . . . the nerve of that bitch! I didn't know you spoke French, Leo."

Leo smiled. "I don't."

Chapter 14

They found the basement of the house exactly as the girl had described it. The rope was dangling from a rafter. Ginny's tennis shoes were still there, as were her bra and panties. Then the lab people shooed them out while they went to work.

Lani and Brenda were staring at a complicated-looking strap-on dildo. "Be sure and get some pictures of this . . . thing," Brenda said, disgust very plain behind her words.

Outside, they stepped over the body of the coach. The press was on the scene and making a nuisance of themselves. A line of city and county police were holding them behind a CRIME SCENE—DO NOT ENTER tape.

"Which one of you killed the coach?" a reporter yelled.

"We did have a good chance of winning state this year," a maggot-brain said. "But we can forget it now. Thanks to the cops." That statement even shocked some of the press present.

This time it was Lani who grabbed Leo. "Come on, Leo. It's not worth it. You know the mentality of some people."

Sheriff Brownwood walked up. "Settle down, Leo," he said.

"I hope the cameras got his face," Leo said darkly. "And the Ripper is watching."

"And I hope nobody else heard you say that," Brownie said.

"How can people get so worked up over a goddamn stupid game, that they lose all perspective of right and wrong and moral values?" Leo muttered.

"Get him in the car and out of here, Lani," Brownie said. "Please."

A few members of the press asked their usual stupid questions at the press conference later on that evening. "Why did the police have to kill him? Couldn't they have just shot him in the leg, or something?" And so on and so forth.

Luckily, Leo was not in attendance at the press conference. Leo, Lani, Brenda, and Ted were sweating the French teacher, and sweating her hard.

When she broke, she opened a spillgate of sexual perversion and told her tale of horrors. She and the coach had been sexually active with selected students for about a decade. But this was the first time they had ever kidnapped one. They had used coercion before; threats of grade failure and other methods. But never kidnapping. Until this time.

But she and the dead coach were not the team called the Ripper.

"What am I facing?" the French teacher asked.

"You'll be presented a list of all charges," Leo told her.

"I don't want to go to prison," she said. "They do terrible things to women in prison, and I'm not really a bad person. Really, I'm not."

Lani and Leo walked out of the interrogation room after hearing that.

"The problem is," Leo said, after building his third bourbon and water and knocking back half of it, "we're trying to deal with these characters logically and rationally. The killers do not have logical or rational minds."

"So what are you suggesting?" Ted asked.

"I don't know. I'm getting tight, I know that. And I know that we're missing something. It's right there in front of us, but we can't get a handle on it. And it's frustrating the hell out of me."

"You think you're alone in that?" Lani questioned. "Twin brothers, identical twins, with access to enormous wealth, just do not drop out of sight. We've plastered the entire West with pictures of how they probably look at age thirty-three, and we've had zip response. Nothing."

"We know they've left a trail of bodies all across this country," Leo picked it up. "Yet they've managed to elude the police for years. How?"

"We're closer than we've ever been," Ted tried to turn the conversation upbeat. "So far, the technicians have discovered ten doctored tapes at KSIN. Radio and TV. Those songs and commercials are played at the same time, every day or night. But so far no names of actual people have showed up. Just suggestions. 'Drink your morning coffee. Take your bath. I'm your friend. I won't hurt you. Trust me. Listen to KSIN.' But all the employees check out. They are who they say they are. Birth records, employment records, service records. Shit!" he concluded.

"And we can't tip our hand just yet," Brenda said. "You can't hold someone just because they flunk a polygraph. If we started that, the party, or parties, would just run again."

"And how much longer can we sit on what we're doing?" Lani questioned. "It's going to leak. Bet on that."

Leo hummed "Mary Had A Little Lamb," then frowned. "And what the hell does that mean?"

"Nothing," Lani said. "I've read the whole poem ten dozen times. I've memorized the damn thing. Nothing connects. But why, then, would he put the notes on his bedroom wall?"

Leo reached over and turned on the radio. KSIN. When the announcer came on between records, Leo straightened up, his drink forgotten. "That's not BJ the DJ."

Lani waited until another record was playing and dialed the studio number. "Where's Jarry?" she asked.

"Sick," the DJ told her. "They called me in at the last minute."

Thirty seconds later, the four cops had left the house and were running for their cars.

No one answered the knock on Bill Jarry's apartment door. Leo took several pieces of wire from his wallet and went to work on the lock.

"I'm not seeing this," Ted said. "I can't believe you're doing this, Leo! This is against the law. Any evidence we might find won't be admissible in court."

"Doing what?" Leo asked, pushing open the door. "Did you see me do anything, Brenda? Lani?"

"Not a thing," Brenda said. "The door was unlocked. We're just checking out an anonymous complaint that was called in."

Ted shook his head and muttered under his breath.

"No one here," Lani said, as the cops once more gathered in the hall. "Let's check the hospitals."

Bill Jarry had not checked into nor visited any of the area's hospitals.

"Stake it out," Leo told two uniforms outside the apartment complex. "When Jarry shows up, bring him in and call me."

"No matter the time?"

"No matter the time."

Shortly after ten that evening, the uniforms brought in a very angry Bill Jarry and set him down in a chair at Leo's desk.

"You don't look very sick to me," Leo told him. "Where have you been?"

"None of your goddamn business," BJ the DJ said. "If I want to lie to the boss to get a night off, that's between me and the boss."

Since there had been no reports of missing people that evening, and the cops had no evidence of any wrongdoing on Jarry's part, they could not hold him. But Bill would not tell them where he'd been that evening, or why he called in sick when he was not.

"I know what this is all about," Jarry said. "But you can check the logs and the engineers and other personnel at the station. I was on the air at the time the Kress woman was killed. I was right there in the station when Cal got bopped on the head. Hey, I read the papers. Some of what you two did back East has leaked out. Well, I've never even been in Indiana, much less in Fort Wayne. I've never been in Akron, Ohio. And I damn sure have never been in Buffalo, New York. Check it out."

"We have," Leo told him.

"And?" Jarry looked at him.

"You can go."

After the door to the interrogation room had closed, Leo and Lani and Brenda and Ted sat at the scarred table and looked at each other. Lani broke the silence.

"We've pretty well established that the Ripper either works at KSIN, or is a good friend of someone who does. That's firm. There is no other way they could gain access to so many of the commercials. We know for a fact that the Ripper is actually two people. We know for a fact that it is a man and a woman. All right. Try this: could one of the Longwood boys have had a sex-change operation?"

Leo blinked at that. Brenda's eyes widened. Ted said, "My word!"

"And they're living together as man and wife," Leo spoke the words slowly. "Yeah. It's possible. What did that ex-priest say? Both boys were effeminate-looking."

"That's right," Lani picked it up. "And we know for a fact that both of them are twisted sexually. It fits, people."

"This case is beginning to make me physically ill," Ted said with a grimace.

"All right," Leo said wearily. "Tomorrow we start checking out the DJs' spouses and/or girlfriends."

"It doesn't have to be a DJ," Brenda said. "It could be someone who works in a different capacity; not necessarily an on-air person."

"Not a word of this to anybody," Brenda said.

"Right," Leo agreed. "And we check out Stacy Ryan's sweetheart, Carla Upton. All the way back. If this is part of a killing club, with more than two people involved, or four—counting the half brother and sister of the Longwood boys—there will be a weak link in the chain. All we have to do is find it, and break it."

"Before they kill again," Ted added.

"I wish," Lani said softly.

*   *   *

The four cops quickly hit a dead end on the DJs and their spouses and girlfriends. Everybody checked out to the letter.

"Shit!" Lani said.

The foursome began the painstaking task of running everybody who worked at the TV/FM/AM complex. They found where Ed Jones, one of the engineers, had a warrant for his arrest back in North Dakota . . . five unpaid traffic tickets.

"Pay your damn tickets, Ed," Leo told the clearly embarrassed man.

Linda Price, a copywriter, had written a series of hot checks down in Tampa, Florida. But the statute of limitations had run out, and she was squeaky clean in California. They never mentioned it to her.

Jim Barrows, a reporter, had served time in South Carolina as a boy. He had gone joy-riding with some others in a stolen car. He had been released when it was proven that he did not know the car was stolen.

"Dozens of employees, and they all check out," Ted said. "We're right back to square one."

"Carla Upton is from an old California family," Leo said. "No evidence that she is a part of that group of weirdos swapping partners—which does include Dick Hale's estranged wife, June."

"And some other rather prominent citizens of La Barca," Lani added.

"What they're doing is bizarre," Leo said. "But not against the law."

"Just kinky," Brenda said.

"We have turned over some rocks and uncovered some dark secrets," Lani summed up. "But nothing that brings us any closer to the Rippers."

"Well, at least the Rippers haven't added anyone else to the list," Brenda said.

Wrong.

* * *

Mrs. Abigail Minniweather, president of the Hancock County Committee for Unified Nonexistence of Trash (no one in the group of well-intentioned ladies had yet to figure out that spelled CUNT), noticed a rather ugly lump of something that some cretinous individual had dumped in her backyard, right in the middle of her carefully tended and prize-winning flower garden.

"Come, Ulysses," she said to her poodle. Abigail marched right out there, back straight and jaw set in anger, Ulysses bouncing right along beside her. Abigail came to an abrupt halt about fifteen feet from the blob. So did Ulysses. Both stared. Abigail let out a squawk and snatched up Ulysses. She ran back to the house, making little mewing sounds as she heaved her bulk along. She managed to call the sheriff's department before she passed out cold on the recently mopped and waxed kitchen floor. It sounded like a walrus doing a double half-gainer off the high board. Luckily for Ulysses, she did not land on him. The poodle fainted, too.

"Jesus Christ!" Lani said.

Ted walked over to the bushes and puked.

Leo managed to keep his breakfast down.

Brenda fought back hot bile that threatened to explode from her throat.

Brownie looked at the half-eaten doughnut he carried in a napkin and gave it to Ulysses. Ulysses buried it among Abigail's begonias.

The blob was Dick Hale, Jr. He had been skinned. All but his face. From the expression on his face, frozen forever, the skinning had been done while he was alive and conscious.

Brownie wiped his sweaty face with a handkerchief.

"I'll go tell Dick." He turned to a uniform. "For god's sake, keep the press out of here."

Lani knelt down in front of the hideously tortured remains of the young man. She noticed his privates had been removed; pointed that out to Leo.

"Yeah," the older man said. "I see. Lani? Dick is going to blow his stack over this. I'll bet you he's going to get on the air and offer a reward . . . probably a very substantial reward. Brownie doesn't realize it, but there is no way—no *way*—we are going to keep this from the press."

"Citizens arming themselves and taking to the streets?" she questioned.

"Yeah. But would you blame them?"

She shook her head.

Detective Bill Bourne of the La Barca city police walked up and took a long look at the body. He turned a tad green around the mouth and fought the sickness back. He pointed to the body. "That's—" He couldn't finish it. He turned away and headed for the bushes, returning in a moment, his face pale and sweaty. "Dick Hale's kid," Bill said.

"Yeah," Leo said, standing up. "What's left of him. I didn't know you knew the kid."

"Vice had picked him up a couple of times for . . . well, you know."

"No," Lani said, a weary note to her voice. She stood up and faced the city cop. "Was he hanging with the rough trade?"

Bill nodded his head. "You better believe it, Lani. That kid was into it all."

Lani and Leo exchanged glances. "Might be a way to go, kid," Leo said.

"You read my mind."

"What are you two talking about?" Brenda asked.

"We start checking out gay bars," Leo told her.

"Sounds like fun to me," the Chinese girl said with a smile.

Ted was decidedly less enthusiastic.

Chapter 15

"You're not going to believe what he has in his jacket pocket," Brenda said, then doubled over in a fit of giggling.

"It's not funny, damnit!" Ted said.

Lani and Leo cut their eyes to each other. Brenda jammed a hand into Ted's pocket and came out dangling a surgical mask. Ted was beet-red and flustered.

Lani said, "You weren't really going to wear that, were you, Ted?"

"We're going to a bar called the Golden Tushie, aren't we?"

"Well . . . yes."

"I will definitely wear it for any close-up interrogation."

Brenda was giggling so hard she had to sit down on Lani's couch. She pointed to his other pocket. "He has rubber gloves in that one. I asked him if he was going to conduct body searches."

She fell over on the couch and exploded in laughter.

"Now, damnit, Brenda!" Ted said. "I don't find this amusing. What if one of those . . . people come on to me!"

Brenda's giggling was highly infectious, and soon

Lani and Leo were laughing at the expression on Ted's face.

"I'll wait in the car," Ted said stiffly, and left the apartment.

When Lani could again speak, she said, "Ted has this thing about gays, huh?"

Brenda wiped her eyes. "Ted is deeply religious. He's used more cuss words on this case than I've heard him use in all the time I've worked with him. And he's scared to death of catching AIDS."

"Well," Leo said, rising from the chair into which he had fallen while laughing. "We'll assure him that he doesn't have to date any of the people at the Golden Tushie. Just talk to them," he added with a serious expression.

That set Lani and Brenda off again. Leo looked at the hysterically giggling females and went outside to sit with Ted.

The bar was tastefully done and other than men dancing with men and women dancing with women, it was just like any other expensive watering hole.

"If any of them start kissing other members of the same sex, I'm gone," Ted said. "And I mean that."

Brenda had to stick one small fist into her mouth to stifle another burst of laughter, and Lani covered her mouth with a handkerchief.

"Just relax, Ted," Leo said. "And order us a Coke, or something."

"I will not drink or eat anything in this place!"

"Sit with him, Brenda," Leo said. "Just keep him quiet." He moved toward the bar and asked for the manager. A man was pointed out to him. Lani was talking with several women.

Leo ID'd himself and the man nodded his head. "I

know what it's about, Sergeant. I heard the news. Believe me when I say those of us in the gay community want this creep, or creeps, caught just as badly as straights. Maybe, for most of us, more so. Do I have to tell you why that is?"

"No. I know why. Can you help us catch them?"

"I don't know. We don't allow kinks and S & M types in here. Most of the people you see here are nine-to-five professionals. Hardworking, tax-paying, law-abiding people. We're just gay, and that's all the difference between you and me."

Leo most definitely had a retort to that, but kept it to himself. He said, "These people we're looking for are twisted. Real twisted. Where would I go to find those types you don't allow in here?"

The manager of the place, whose name was Hardy Stern (Leo had wondered about that), put serious eyes on Leo. "Why should any member of the gay community help the cops, Sergeant? You people roust us whenever you think you can get away with it. You don't dislike us, you *hate* us. We're not rated as high as second-class citizens; we're at the bottom of the ladder in your eyes. The gay-bashing has already started in the streets, Sergeant. And many of the cops stand around and smirk about it, while some gay is getting the shit kicked out of him, or her, and wait until the gay is down and bloody before doing anything about it. Don't deny it. You know it's true."

Leo said nothing. What Hardy was saying did hold some truth. Not even close to a hundred percent truth, but true to some degree. But if he thought gay-bashing was bad now, Hardy was in for a bad shock if the Rippers turned out to be gay.

"You know where the Cock 'n' Balls is, Sergeant?"

"Yeah," Leo said, unable to keep the disgust from his reply. "I know where it is."

Hardy laughed softly in the dim light of the saloon. "Disgusting and revolting, isn't it, Sergeant?"

"Yeah. It damn sure is."

"Might surprise you, but I agree with you. All right, Sergeant, here's what I know . . ."

Ted sat stiffly at the table, Brenda by his side. She was really concerned as to what Ted might do if approached by any of the men in the watering hole. Ted did not hate homosexuals, but he disliked their lifestyle intensely. What they practiced went against every religious and moral belief he had been taught since birth . . . and they were set in concrete.

Lani and Leo approached the table, and Ted stood up quickly. He's wound tight, Leo thought. Too tight. "Let's get out of here," Leo told the group.

On the sidewalk in front of the Golden Tushie, Leo faced Ted Murray. "You're out of this, Ted. You're wound up tight as a mainspring. You're liable to go off half-cocked"—Brenda giggled at Leo's choice of words, and Lani bit at her lip and suddenly had a desire to inspect the stars overhead.

" . . . and do something stupid," Leo finished with a patient sigh.

"I am in control, Leo," Ted said defensively.

"Barely," the county deputy said. "You ever seen two men jacking each other off, Ted?"

"Hell, no!"

"Well, you're *gonna* see it if you stay with us tonight. And a hell of a lot more. That is, providing we can even get in this private club without a search warrant . . . and I have my doubts about that. I can't give you orders, Ted, but I'll suggest that you go on back to the motel and take a shower and go to bed. We'll see you in the morning."

Some of the tension went out of Ted. He nodded his head. "Perhaps you're right, Leo." He shrugged his shoulders. "I know you're right. You'll ride with them, Brenda?" She nodded. "Then I'll see you all in the morning."

In the car, Lani said, "The women I spoke with said we'll probably get nothing out of the patrons who frequent the Cock 'n' Balls, but if there is anyone who knows anything about the killings, that's where we'll find them."

Leo signaled for a left turn. "Yeah. That's what Hardy Stern said, too."

"Hardy Stern?" Brenda shouted from the backseat. The women giggled all the way to the private club. Leo sighed. A lot.

Dick Hale had gone into a wild, shouting rage at the news of his son's mutilation. He had very nearly lost it when he insisted upon seeing his son's body. June Hale had completely flipped out, and had to be sedated and hospitalized. Dick had begun drinking early that afternoon, and by evening, he was out of control. Dick arrived at the Cock 'n' Balls just as Leo, Lani, and Brenda were pulling out of the parking lot of the Golden Tushie. He was armed with two pistols, a Colt Commander, .38 caliber, and a Colt .45 auto-loader. He had two spare clips for each pistol. He also had a 12-gauge shotgun, chambered for three-inch magnum loads. He had pulled the plug and loaded it full with double ought buckshot. Dick had stuffed his jacket pocket full of shells. He pulled around to the rear of the private club and parked.

A minor fender bender, no injuries or fatalities, held Leo up for several minutes, until the uniforms could get traffic moving again. Just after the rain begins is the most dangerous time to drive, because of the mixture of road oil and water, and a light mist had slicked the streets.

Dick got out of his car and shucked a round into the slot of the 12-gauge. He shoved in a shell to replace the one he'd chambered. Thunder rumbled just as the back door opened and a man walked out to dump a sack of beer cans. Just as lightning flickered across the sky and thunder crashed, Dick leveled the shotgun and very nearly blew the man in two. Leo pulled around the minor traffic jam-up and turned down the lane leading to the Cock 'n' Balls, several miles away.

Dick stepped into the storeroom of the private club. The rock and roll music was so loud, he could have been firing a cannon and it would not have been heard over the wild crash and thump of music. Dick shoved in a round to fill up the tube.

"Goddamn queers," Dick muttered. His eyes were wild and his face hard. Dick Hale had stepped over the line, and it was a passageway he would never cross again. Not in this life.

A man dressed all in black leather and chains, his crotch exposed, stepped into the storeroom and stared at Dick for a moment, not believing what he was seeing.

"Perverted son of a bitch!" Dick shouted, his words not audible over the music. Neither was the booming of the shotgun.

The face of the S & M lover disappeared in a splash of red and gray. Blood and brains splattered the walls of the storeroom. Headless now, the man slid down to the floor. Dick noticed the dead man had an erection.

Leo, Lani, and Brenda were about a mile away from the private club, driving slowly, for the mist had turned into a downpour.

Dick walked to the doorway and looked out at the scene. "Disgusting," he muttered. Naked men were

dancing on the stage. Some were fondling each other.
Two were engaged in some sort of bizarre sexual act.
Dick couldn't figure out exactly what they were doing.
He'd never seen anything like it. It looked like some
grotesque naked beast hunching on the floor. Dick
lifted the shotgun and emptied it at the men on the
stage.

It was carnage. The patrons, many of them in various stages of undress, went into a panic as blood and
brains splattered onto their nakedness. Those on the
stage who were wounded and still able to walk or
crawl, jumped and fell from the stage, landing on those
below them, slicking the men and women and the floor
and tables with blood.

Quickly reloading, Dick leveled the shotgun at a
leather-clad man who jumped at him. The heavy
charge knocked the man backward and under the bar,
where his falling body tore loose the hoses from kegs
of beer. Beer under pressure spewed out and into the
air, adding to the screaming confusion.

Leo turned the car onto the parking lot of the club.

Dick emptied the shotgun into the panicked crowd,
then pulled out his pistols, and started firing. One of
the wild slugs killed the DJ and he fell across his
control board, abruptly stilling the throbbing music.

Leo, Lani, and Brenda were just stepping out of the
car when the music died, the front door burst open,
disgorging dozens of panicked people in various styles
of dress and undress, and the sounds of gunfire could
be heard.

Inside the club, Dick had slammed home fresh clips
and was shooting at anything that moved, male or
female, and in many cases, it was impossible to tell.
Half a dozen people rushed him, and Dick emptied the
.45 into the knot of men. Two of the badly wounded
men staggered on and fell against Dick, almost knock-

ing him to the floor. Dick cursed them and threw them aside. He was bloody now, and spattered with the still spewing beer.

Leo, Lani, and Brenda could not get into the club because of the rush of people trying to get out. Leo grabbed a woman, who turned out to be a man, showed him his badge, and shouted, "What the hell's going on in there?"

"Dick Hale," the transvestite replied in a deep voice. "He's gone mad. Killing everybody in sight. So go do something, you pig motherfucker."

Leo shoved her/him away and ran toward the club, pistol drawn, Lani and Brenda right behind, pistols in hand. "I'll take the back!" Lani shouted.

"Go with her, Brenda!"

"Ten-four!" Brenda called and rounded the corner of the club, right behind Lani.

The club had just about emptied when Leo bulled his way to the front door. He had never seen so many strange-looking people in his life. And one of them was a senior sergeant on the La Barca PD. He was really quite stunning in a yellow dress and a large flowery hat. Sort of resembled that lady who used to do the banana commercial on TV.

"Sergeant Dixson," Leo greeted the . . . whatever it was.

"Screw you, Leo. I'm off."

"Certainly looks like it," Leo retorted, and ran through the doorway, staying low.

Dick spotted him and cracked off a round, the slug going wide of Leo.

"Drop the gun, Dick. Drop the goddamn gun!" Leo yelled.

"Hell with you, copper!" Dick said, doing a pretty good imitation of James Cagney.

Leo's finger tightened on the trigger, and Dick suddenly dropped to the body-littered floor, scooping up his shotgun.

"Oh, shit!" Leo muttered, diving behind a door that led to the coat and hat closet.

"Well, excuse me!" a voice said, just as Dick's shot-gun boomed and the slugs knocked a very large hole in the plaster.

Leo looked. It was a woman, crouched on the floor, her evening dress hiked up to her waist. He lowered his eyes. Wrong again.

"See anything you like," the man asked.

"You got to be kidding!"

Dick's shotgun boomed, and a scream came from the rear of the club.

"Brenda's down!" Lani yelled.

"Back up should be here any second," Leo called.

Dick started shooting out the lights.

"I have this huge erection," the man in the evening dress said. "Violence turns me on. Look, look!"

Leo would rather face the shotgun. He left the cloakroom in a rush and bellied down on the floor, worming his way toward several overturned tables. "Goddamn loony bin!" he muttered.

Ted Murray had heard the call and was the first officer to respond. He rushed inside, staying low. Dick spotted him and cut loose, the buckshot just missing Ted.

"Don't jump in the cloakroom!" Leo yelled.

Too late.

"Great god!" Ted hollered as Dick resumed his shooting out of the lights. Unfortunately, or perhaps fortunately for Ted, he couldn't shoot out the light in the cloakroom.

Ted left the small room a hell of a lot faster than he had entered, and that was pretty swift. He scooted across the floor, over to Leo.

"I tried to warn you," Leo said.

Ted was too shocked to reply.

"Brenda's down, Ted. I don't know how bad."

Dick shot out the last light in the normally poorly lit club, and the huge room was plunged into darkness.

Chapter 16

"Brenda's all right!" Lani called. "Just a small cut on her forehead. The bullet must have fragmented when it hit something, and she caught just a small piece of it."

The sounds of screaming sirens touched those inside the private club. The smell of smoke reached them at just about the same time.

"Get out, Lani, Brenda!" Leo called. "The fool has started a fire."

The man in the dress in the cloakroom let out a squawk, jumped up, and ran out the front door, the front of his dress all poked out.

"Go!" Leo said to Ted. "Move! I'm right behind you." Outside, Leo yelled to several uniforms, "Cover the back and both sides. Radio in for fire trucks."

Within seconds, the old building was a wall of flames. The smell of human flesh bubbling and sizzling was sickening. The heat was so intense, the police and fire fighters were forced to back up.

"No one will get out of that," the fire captain said, raising his voice over the roar of the flames and the crackling and collapsing of walls. "But this rain will keep it from spreading."

The press showed up and captured it all on film. But

nearly all of the patrons of the Cock 'n' Balls had left the scene immediately upon fleeing the building. Only the hard core remained, and they were vocal. Very vocal.

Leo had said nothing about running into Ms. Banana, otherwise known as Sergeant Dixson. He would share that information with Lani, later on. But he probably would not tell Ted.

Over Brenda's very loud protests, she had been loaded into an ambulance and taken to the hospital. The attending EMT had said her wound looked very slight, but she would probably be kept for twenty-four hours under observation. Just to be on the safe side.

The rain had stopped, the storm sweeping eastward very fast, and the night had turned clear and starry.

Ted had gone back to his motel room. Said he wanted to take a very long, very hot shower. His minute and a half in the cloakroom had unnerved him.

"You think Dick Hale was the Ripper?" a reporter asked Leo.

"No."

"Do you feel at all responsible for this terrible tragedy?" another asked.

Leo looked at the crap-for-brains reporter for a few seconds, and then walked off without dignifying the question with any sort of reply. "Idiot," he muttered to Lani.

Out of earshot of the press, Lani said, "I heard a window breaking just after we smelled the smoke. I think Dick got out. Or at least somebody did."

"Another nut on the loose," Leo replied. "Hell with this. Let's go make our reports and go home."

The pair known as the Ripper sat in their den and laughed at the news reports of the many deaths at the local nightclub. It was wonderful news. They had felt sure that Dick Hale would do something, but they had not dreamed it would be this delightful.

"I'm so excited," one said, taking the other's hand.

"Me, too," the other said, gently squeezing the hand.

"Shall we?"

"Let's."

They wandered off to the bedroom.

The official death count at the Cock 'n' Balls was twenty-two dead and thirty-five wounded. Some of the wounded were not expected to live. And some very prominent people from various communities all up and down the coast had been in attendance.

"Who all did you see in that loony bin?" Sheriff Brownwood asked Leo the next day. He closed the door and sat down, speaking to Ted and Brenda and Lani. Brenda had a small bandage over her right eye.

Leo looked at Ted, and said to hell with his original decision. "Sergeant Dixson for one."

"Al Dixson? The Bull?"

"Yeah. In a yellow evening gown with a big, floppy, flowery hat. Looked like Chiquita Banana. With a five o'clock shadow."

"Could he have been working undercover?" the sheriff asked.

Brenda giggled.

Leo looked over at Ted. "I don't know who that was in the cloakroom."

"What's this about a cloakroom?" Brenda asked, her eyes sparkling with mischief.

"Yeah," the sheriff said. "What about a cloak-room?"

Ted folded his arms across his chest and looked like a thundercloud.

"Ted had an encounter with a person in the cloakroom, while Dick was shooting at us," Leo said. "Did he show you his erection, Ted?"

"I'm leaving," Brownie said, standing up. He looked at Leo. "Question is: did he show *you* his erection?"

"Yeah," Leo said straight-faced.

Brownie shook his head. "I worry about you, Leo. Maybe you should call your wife and tell her to cut short her visit with her sister and come on back home." He walked out of the office.

Brenda was just about to bust wide open with laughter.

"I'm warning you, Brenda," Ted said, cutting his eyes at her. "You're pushing your luck."

"What'd I say?" she asked innocently. "What'd I say?"

The Ripper didn't let a little minor fire and twenty-two deaths put a damper on fun. Leo received a package at the office promptly at eight o'clock, and very nearly lost his breakfast when he opened it. Inside was the severed right arm of what appeared to be a white female, probably in her late teens, with no identifying marks or scars. About an hour later, a local delivery service brought another package to the sheriff's office, addressed to Lani. Inside was the left arm. Just before noon, two packages were placed at the rear door of the building and discovered by a motorcycle cop who'd come in the back way. They were addressed to Ted Murray and Brenda Yee. The boxes contained the left and right legs.

"I don't even want to think about where the torso

and head will show up," Brownie said, to the team at lunch. They were all brown-bagging it and sitting in the break room.

"Sheriff?" a deputy stuck his head into the room. "There's a big box sitting out in the parking lot. It's got your name on it."

Brownie looked at his half-eaten ham and cheese. "Shit!" he said.

The box contained the torso of the girl. But no head.

The torso was turned over to the lab people, and they quickly concluded that the girl had been sexually assaulted and savagely beaten.

The press played it up big, insinuating—not too subtly—that the police were so inept that they couldn't catch a cold. One newspaper reporter, Agnes Peters—who was so left-leaning many wondered how she managed to stand up straight—was particularly harsh with the city and county police. She had learned, somehow, about Dennis Potter's financing of Leo and Lani's trip East, and insinuated that the entire sheriff's department was in the pocket of the richest man in the county, there only to do his bidding. Agnes, it seemed, hated all rich people. She was a long and strong advocate of wealth redistribution (that's spelled S-O-C-I-A-L-I-S-T and occasionally D-E-M-O-C-R-A-T). Agnes concluded her venomous tirade by stating: Perhaps the police and sheriff's department doesn't really want to catch the Ripper, since his prey have been overwhelmingly the poor, the minorities, and those who practice an alternate lifestyle.

"I wasn't aware that Ruthie Potter was poor, a member of any minority group, or practiced an alternate lifestyle," Brownie said, after reading the column.

"I'll give Ms. Agnes Peters about seventy-two hours before she learns it's not nice to fool with one of the richest people in the state, and probably one of the richest persons in America," Lani remarked.

Brownie shook his head. "I doubt that Dennis will do anything. If she had defamed Ruthie, he would buy the paper and fire her."

"He bought LGH Industries two years ago, and fired the plant manager after the man made repeated slurs about Ruthie's character," Brenda said softly. "I know. We investigated that buy-out for possible violations of several laws."

"The outcome?" Lani asked.

"The case was suddenly ordered closed," Ted said. "Dennis Potter's power reaches very high."

"You don't know the whole story," Brownie said, glancing up. "The plant manager's son was trying to get Ruthie to go out with him. He became very persistent, and Dennis warned the man to put the brakes on his son's mouth and his stalking of Ruthie. The man cussed Dennis and said his son could do any damn thing he liked. The plant manager then started spreading rumors about Ruthie being a slut and a whore . . . and those were the nicest things he had to say. Dennis got tired of it. The only person to lose their job was the plant manager. Since Dennis's buy-out, the employees have all been given raises, and the company is doing better than it ever did before. Dennis *is* Hancock County. He's built parks and playgrounds for kids, given millions of dollars to local charities and schools. When the local police and this very sheriff's department got in a money crunch last year, it was Dennis who bailed us all out. All his plants have free day-care for the kids of working mothers. Dennis's good far outweighs whatever bad he might have. No, he'll let this foolish reporter slide . . . this time. But if she's got any sense at all, she'll never mention his name again. Dennis and I grew up together, in the migrant workers' camps. I know him better than anyone. And he can be ruthless."

"What's he really worth, Brownie?" Leo asked. "Do you know?"

The sheriff smiled. "About five billion dollars. Dennis was one of the pioneers in the computer business. He invented about a half a dozen of some sort of gadgets. Then he started buying factories and land. You know the rest." Brownie left the room just as a uniform walked in.

"Five billion dollars," Lani spoke the words softly. "I can't even visualize that much money."

"Well, visualize this, Lani," the uniform said. "They found the girl's head. Over at St. Anthony's on Elm Street. Just about freaked out the priest."

The four stood up and walked out silently.

"Jesus, Joseph, and Mary!" Leo muttered, staring up at the crucifixion on the wall behind the pulpit.

The Ripper had tied the head of the girl over the face of Jesus. The face of the girl was contorted by the last, hot moment of agony before death. Her tongue was blue/black, protruding out of swollen lips. Her eyes were bulging and horror-filled. She had been completely scalped, the whiteness of skull bone glistening in the dim light of the church.

Several priests and nuns were murmuring low prayers in the shadows next to a wall.

"Get pictures of it," Leo said to a uniform. "Did you call the lab people?"

"Right, and yes."

"We'll assemble the body parts in the lab and try to ID the kid."

"What kind of person would do something like this, detective?" the older of the priests asked.

Leo remembered the words of the ex-priest back in New York State. "A very evil person, Father. Evil through and through."

"There is good in everybody, my son," the priest replied.

Leo shook his head. "Not in the people who did this, Father. Not one shred of good in them."

"I pray you're wrong."

"No, Father." Leo pointed to the head of the girl. "Pray for her."

"She was a runaway from a little town in Alabama," Lani said, walking in and laying a teletype on Leo's desk. "Seventeen years old. She must have come from a real loving home. Her parents said to bury her out here . . . providing the state will pay for it. They don't plan on coming out for the service."

Leo sighed, Ted looked very pained, Brenda shook her head at the callousness.

"I put out some jars around the office to try to collect enough for a small headstone."

"I have a better idea," Leo said. "I'll see to it that Dennis Potter hears of this. Any word on Dick Hale?"

"No. He's dropped out of sight."

"He'll surface," Brenda said. "And he'll start killing more homosexuals when he does. Our office did a psychological profile on him. Our in-house shrink says he blames gays for the death of his son. He said get ready for wholesale slaughter, if Dick stays on the loose."

"I'm afraid you're right and he's right." Leo picked up a sheet of paper and held it so all could see. "Small sporting goods store out on the edge of town was broken into last night. Several cases of canned food and bottled water were taken. Along with about two hundred 12-gauge shotgun shells, a .38 pistol, and several boxes of ammo for that. Also missing was a tent, sleeping bag, camp axe, knife, and other survival gear. If it was Dick—and I'll bet it was—looks like he's going to head for the timber and work at night."

"One thing's for certain, after all that shooting at the club the other night," Brenda said.

"What's that?" Leo asked.

"Dick seems to have overcome his aversion to blood."

Chapter 17

The subliminal messages continued to show up at the station, leading Ted and Brenda to believe that the Ripper was not an employee of the station. To continue would be foolish. Lani and Leo didn't buy that.

"The Ripper is an employee of KSIN," Leo insisted. "I feel it in my guts."

"But we've checked them all out," Brenda said. "Ten times over. We've put tails on every employee there. They're clean, Leo. Is there any word on Dick?"

"Nothing," Lani said. "Maybe the bastard did burn up in that fire. But I don't think so." She looked at Leo, who was staring off into space. "What's up, partner?"

"I'm going to be gone for two days, Lani. There is one thing we didn't check back in New York State." He stood up and slipped into his jacket. "See you." He walked out of the office.

"What the hell . . . ?" Brenda asked.

"We'll know in two days," Lani said, not a bit put out by her partner's actions. If his hunch fizzled, he would shoulder all the blame, and she would be left out of it. Besides, she had work to do here.

She just didn't have any idea how much work was about to be tossed her way.

* * *

Stacy Ryan arrived home from the station just about the time Leo's plane was taking off. She kicked off her shoes and headed for the bathroom for a long soak. A movement near the darkened hall slowed her. She turned. Dick Hale was standing there, a shotgun in his hands. He was grinning at her, his face unshaven, his eyes shining with madness.

"Now, Dick," Stacy said.

"Shut up, you dirty bitch cunt!" Dick said. "You made life miserable for me for too many years. Now it's payback time." He lifted the shotgun, and Stacy jumped for the bedroom door just as it boomed. Stacy locked the door and climbed out a window. She went running down the street, screaming just as loud as she could. Dick broke down the door and fired twice more at her, but by that time Stacy was out of range, running faster than she had ever run in her life.

A neighbor called the police, but by the time they arrived, Dick was long gone. Stacy Ryan, known to thousands as Tally-Ho, was unhurt, but badly frightened. She was placed under a twenty-four-hour police guard.

And the Ripper struck again. Just about the time a weary Leo Franks was checking into a motel in Albany, New York, two teenagers discovered the tortured and mutilated body of a young man lying on the shoulder of the road just inside the city limits of La Barca. The young man was alive, but just barely. He was rushed to a hospital and the cops gathered, hoping he would regain consciousness long enough to give them some information.

He did, gasping out a few sentences to a very shocked Lani Prejean seconds before dying. Since Leo had not checked in, she had no way of knowing where he was staying in Albany, or even if he had landed yet. But one thing for certain, she had some very important news to share with her partner.

Leo was waiting at the flower shop when Dan Jennings drove up. He did not seem at all surprised to see Leo. He smiled. "Where's the pretty one, Leo?"

Leo laughed. "In California. Dan, I need some answers."

"Come on in. I'll make coffee and we can talk. No luck with the Longwood twins, hey?"

"That's what I wanted to talk to you about."

Dan straightened up from unlocking the door and looked at him. "Sounds serious, Leo."

"It is."

Leo waited while Dan counted out the money for the cash register, turned on the air, and made coffee. He left the CLOSED sign on the door and waved Leo to the back. They sat at a small table with cups of freshly brewed coffee. "Now then, what's on your mind, Leo?"

Leo's question shook the priest right down to his shoes. He placed the cup on the table and thought about Leo's question for a moment. "The boys were born at home. Doctor, midwife, priest, and nun in attendance. I know that for a fact. The doctor and the priest are dead. Shortly after the birth, the Sister took a vow of silence, and has been in a convent up in Canada since that time. She wouldn't break it. The midwife, now . . . " He bit at his lower lip and stood up. "Wait here. I just might be able to help." He looked down at Leo. "You ask interesting questions, Leo. Very interesting."

He was on the phone in his small office for about fifteen minutes. Several times he raised his voice, almost shouting at whoever he was speaking with. He returned wiping his sweaty face. "I was her priest for a long time. I hated to intimidate her, but she finally broke down and told me. You were right, Leo. You were right."

Leo caught the afternoon flight out and was back in La Barca that night. He drove straight to Lani's house.

"Leo! Have I got news for you." She hustled him inside and insisted on making him some bacon and eggs and toast. With a large glass of milk. She talked as she worked. "There are three of them, Leo. A man and two women. The kid told me that just before he died." She looked into Leo's tired eyes. "What's wrong, Leo? What'd you find out?"

"Jack and Jim had a sister. The mother had triplets. Jack, Jim, and Janet."

"Triplets! Well . . . what happened to the girl?"

"No one knows. The midwife says the baby was given up for adoption days after being born. The doctor and priest are dead. The nun took a vow of silence shortly after the births. Dan Jennings finally got the midwife to confess about the girl. The Longwoods paid off everybody to keep silent about it."

"Why?"

"The mother rejected the baby at once. Wouldn't have anything to do with it."

Lani dished up the food and set the plate before Leo. "Eat, eat. So what happened to the girl?"

"Like I said, no one knows. And adoption records are permanently sealed. We'd have hell getting those records opened."

"There has to be a way."

Leo shrugged.

"You've got a theory, haven't you?"

He shrugged and ate his bacon and eggs.

"How could a mother just reject a newborn baby?"

"I've been thinking about that, too. The midwife says the baby was beautiful. Angelic, even. But Mrs. Longwood would not hold it, nurse it, nothing."

"That's . . . sick, Leo."

"Grotesque is a better word."

"So is killing five or six hundred people, Leo." She poured them both more coffee and sat down across the table. "Our resident shrink says they want to be caught." She said that with a smile, knowing what Leo's reaction would be.

"I think all that is pure bullshit! And I think it takes an absolute, babbling nitwit idiot to not know right from wrong. I am so goddamn sick of these liberal shrinks laying out yards of excuses for street slime and punks and thugs and—" He looked up at Lani's giggling and smiled. "Did it to me again, didn't you, kid?"

She touched his hand. "Go home and get some sleep, Leo. You've got bags under your eyes."

He finished his coffee and sat for a moment at the table. "The third kid ties in. I don't know how, but she does. She is the key to all this mess. I feel it. But how to find her? Where the hell is she? Who is she? Goddamnit, Lani, it's right in front of us. I know it is. I just can't get a grip on it.

"I'm whipped, for a fact. I called my wife from Albany and told her to stay up north with the kids, until we get this thing wrapped up . . . or until school starts. One or the other. If I can get the time off, I'll drive up and see her next weekend." He stood up and walked to the front door and opened it. "I'll see you in the morning, Lani. Thanks for the food."

Lani caught the glint of moonlight off of something metallic, and threw herself at Leo just as the shotgun roared. The slugs tore holes in the edge of the door. Lani scrambled for her pistol; Leo had left his in the car. Leo hit the light switch, plunging the room into darkness.

The shotgun roared two more times. One load shattered the front window, the second blast blowing holes in the center of the door, which had banged against the wall after the first charge and then slowly swung nearly closed.

Leo had crawled to the phone and called in. For all the good it would do. The shooter—and they both felt it was Dick—would be long gone by the time the units arrived.

"He's running away," Lani called. "Gone. It was a small man, Leo. Not Dick."

Leo wearily crawled to his knees. "Or a small woman."

"Yeah. Could be."

There were sirens in the distance.

Leo looked at the door. It was ruined. The front windows were blown out.

"You can't stay here tonight, Lani. Pack some things, and I'll drive you to a motel."

"I could stay with you, Leo."

Leo smiled. "My wife is understanding, Lani. But she ain't that understanding."

The next morning Carla Upton's maid called into the sheriff's office, in hysterics. Someone had shot Carla in the head at close range. With a shotgun.

Lani, Leo, Brenda, and Ted stepped over the CRIME SCENE, DO NOT CROSS tape, and walked into the bedroom. What was left of Carla was lying on her back on the bloody carpet at the foot of the bed.

The man from forensics said, "There is evidence of

shell case fragments embedded in the flesh. I'd say she was shot from a distance of no more than two or three feet. As you can see, it took most of her head off."

Blood, brains, hair, and bits of bone were splattered all over one wall.

Leo squatted down in front of the open door of a huge, walk-in closet.

"What is it, Leo?" Lani called.

"Dried mud. Whoever did this was waiting in the closet for her. Several pretty good impressions on the carpet. Small foot. Dick wears a size twelve wide. Get some shots of this, people. And some samples of the mud."

Lani had knelt down beside the body, being careful to stay out of the blood. She knelt there for about a minute, then stood up and turned to a plainclothes. "Print her," she said.

Leo cut his eyes. "Something wrong, Lani?"

"Yeah. This isn't Carla Upton."

One thing was for certain. The dead woman was not Carla Upton. The cops didn't know who she was, only that she wasn't Carla Upton.

"This is getting weirder and weirder," Sheriff Brownwood said, meeting with the quartet in his office. "Where the hell is Carla?"

"Maybe Dick grabbed her?" Brenda offered.

"To do what?" Brownie asked. "Dick hated dykes. Where was Stacy Ryan last night about midnight?"

"Says she was home in bed." Lani replied. "But she can't prove it."

"Lovers' quarrel maybe?" Ted asked.

"Tests on her hands and arms show up negative," Leo said. "She has not fired a gun."

"How about the will?" Brownie asked.

"Everything goes to relatives and various charities," Brenda said. "Stacy receives nothing."

"How old is the will?" the sheriff asked.

"Dated two years ago."

"We've now attracted the national press," Brownie said, a disgusted look on his face. "The city is filling up with reporters. This is making the Atlanta murders, the Hillside strangler, and the St. Valentine's massacre pale in comparison. And the press is eating it up. There was an emergency city council meeting just about an hour ago." He grimaced and shook his head, which was graying very rapidly now. "Unfortunately, I was in the building and decided to attend. It was awful. The mayor jumped all over the chief of police, called him an incompetent son of a bitch; the chief called him an ass-kissing motherfucker and then slugged him. Knocked his upper plate slap out of his mouth. Then the city council got into it, everybody fighting all over the place. Paul Ford gave Rebecca Staples a black eye, and she gave Paul Ford a busted lip. Knocked him right on his butt. That woman's got a right cross you wouldn't believe. The chief of police is threatening to quit, and the mayor is threatening to sue him. And the city council is threatening to sue each other. This is the goddamnest mess I have ever been involved in."

"Yeah? You just wait until the press learns about the mysterious third Longwood kid," Leo said. "And they will. Sooner or later."

"You're probably right." He stood up and walked to the door. "What can I say? Keep plugging. It's got to break."

The door hissed softly behind the sheriff. The four looked at each other.

"I wish I could be even that optimistic," Brenda said.

"The babies of rich people just don't disappear," Leo said, standing up. "Janet Longwood was either put up for adoption, given to someone else to raise, or kept in that great mansion until . . . "

"Until what, Leo?" Lani asked.

"Oh, shit, I don't know!" Leo picked up a metal ashtray and hurled it against the wall in frustration. It bounced off the wall and rattled to silence on the tile floor.

"I share your feelings," Ted said. "Believe me I do. We all do. Frustration is something good cops know well. Bad cops never get frustrated."

Leo slowly raised his head and looked at Ted. Brenda cut her almond eyes to stare at him. Lani took a deep breath as the same thought came to her.

"What?" Ted asked, looking at the others all looking intently at him.

"Who else would know where every unit is? Who would know the shifts? And who would know who is sick and who is kinky and who is having an affair with whom and who is dirty?" Leo tossed the questions out.

"I don't get it," Ted bitched. "What are you driving at, Leo?"

"One of the three Longwoods is a cop, or married to one, or a very good friend of a cop. I opt for them being a cop," Leo said.

"Yeah. In either the La Barca city PD, or in this department," Lani said.

"And yet another Longwood has to be free to move around and select the victims and grab them," Ted opined. "A woman with tremendous strength?" he questioned.

"I'll go along with that. But where does that put the third Longwood?" Brenda asked.

"I'll bet any of you or all of you that she's the new

general manager of KSIN," Leo said with a smile. "Stacy Ryan."

"But goddamnit, we ran her with the others!" Brenda objected.

"Sure we did. And she came out clean. Why shouldn't she? She is exactly who she says she is. Stacy Ryan was raised just outside of L.A. By a Harold and Betty Ryan, if I remember the printout right. Let's check out Harold and Betty Ryan. I mean, check them out with every agency we can."

"It doesn't wash, Leo," Lani objected. "Stacy Ryan checked out squeaky clean. She . . . " She frowned at Leo. "Why are you smiling at me like that."

"There is an outside chance she doesn't know she's a part of it," Leo said.

"Doesn't *know?*" Ted blurted. "How could that be?"

"Could be she's being manipulated by her brothers. Hypnosis maybe. The FCC sent inspectors in to every radio station in every community where murders such as we're experiencing occurred. They went in under false pretenses, but got the job done anyway. They checked old commercials. Not a trace of subliminal suggestions on any of them. And there have been no killings like these in any other market where Stacy worked. I think that Jim and Jack Longwood have been running wild all over the nation, killing at random. Somehow they found—using their enormous wealth—that their sister was in broadcasting, and here is where they planned to make their . . . well, final stand, so to speak. Go out in a burst of glory. They're playing a game. And it's called fool the cops."

"But one of those three is not a cop," Lani said.

"How so?" Leo looked at her.

"One of their *followers* is a cop. That would leave Jack and Jim free to roam and kill."

Leo thought about that for a moment and then slowly nodded his head. "Yeah. Yeah. I like that better. And it's a female cop, too."

"How do you figure that?" Brenda asked.

"In the latest assault, there was one man and two women, right?"

Brenda nodded her head and Leo smiled.

"Actually, this is Lani's brainchild. You both were there when she voiced it."

"I don't think I'm going to like this, not one little bit," Ted said. "I remember it."

"The sex-change bit," Brenda said.

Leo nodded his head, and Ted looked like he had a sudden attack of gas. "Sick, sick, sick," Ted muttered, then burped his opinion of people who have sex-change operations.

"Brenda, you check out Mr. and Mrs. Ryan down in L.A.," Leo said. "Lani, run a separate and comprehensive check on Stacy, from grade school through college. I'll start quietly pulling personnel records. I *do not want* internal affairs in on this." A lot of cops don't like the Internal Affairs Division. "Ted, what do you want to do?"

"I'd like to be excused."

Chapter 18

While the cops were trying to determine the identity of the dead woman in Carla Upton's bedroom, chase down Leo's new theory, find Dick Hale, and avoid the crush of press that had descended on the town, the Ripper went back to work. And the person or persons known as the Ripper was becoming more bizarre and hideously inventive in his or her methods of torture and mutilation. The next kidnapping and death was so brutal and savage, not even the sleaziest of publications would report all the details. After viewing the body of the latest victim, a young woman, and immediately losing his lunch, Sheriff Brownwood appealed personally to the FBI for help. But the Bureau was overwhelmed with work: terrorists were blowing up buildings all over the nation; a plot to assassinate the President had been uncovered; a plan by Muslim fanatics to kill members of Congress had been revealed. The Bureau just did not have the personnel to offer very much aid in the field.

The chief of police of La Barca stormed into the mayor's office, enraged over new remarks made by the mayor about the chief, and proceeded to beat the shit out of him. The citizens of La Barca found themselves with their chief of police in jail and their mayor in the hospital. A number of city cops, sympathetic to their chief—including detective Bill Bourne—quit. Brownie promptly hired Bill. The weary assistant chief of police handed the entire Ripper package over to the Hancock County Sheriff's Department.

"Thanks a lot," Brownie said sarcastically.

"You're very, very welcome," the assistant chief replied.

Brenda Yee returned from Los Angeles with her report on Harold and Betty Ryan. Not wanting to discuss anything about the case at the office—the walls were beginning to have ears—the four met at Leo's house.

"Jesus!" Lani said, looking around her. "I'll come over here and clean this mess up before Virginia returns home, Leo."

"She's used to my sloppy ways," Leo said defensively.

"No woman is used to this," Brenda said. "I'll help you, Lani."

"Can we get on with the report, please?" Leo pleaded, picking up a pair of dirty socks and looking around for someplace to dump them.

"Try the washing machine," Lani said, very drily. "I believe you'll find it in the utility room."

"Cute, Lani," Leo replied. "Very cute. I've been busy, that's all." He went into the utility room and returned, sockless.

Brenda cleared off a spot on the couch and sat down. "Harold and Betty Ryan are legit. Both of them very nice people. Ultrareligious. But they have had no contact with Stacy in over ten years. When they discovered her, ah, sexual preference, they told her to either shape up or ship out, so to speak. She shipped out and never went back.

"Stacy was adopted through a legitimate adoption

agency—church run. It's still in operation, very successful and very, very clean. The people there were nice and friendly and very firm. The man who runs the agency said there is no way on God's green earth he would ever open Stacy's records to me or to anyone else. He said he would destroy them first.

"Harold and Betty Ryan received a check for a thousand dollars every month for twenty-one years. A cashier's check. A total of two hundred and forty-two thousand dollars. Harold and Betty Ryan are native Californians. Never been in trouble with the law. Harold still works in the aerospace industry—same job he's had for twenty-nine years—and Betty teaches in a preschool facility. They both plan on retiring next year. End of report."

Lani opened a folder. "Stacy wanted for nothing while growing up. She graduated near the top of her class from UCLA. She went to work immediately after graduation and has been employed in broadcasting ever since. She has never been charged or arrested for anything. She has never received a traffic ticket. She pays her bills on time and has an excellent credit history. She drinks only socially and does not use drugs. She is very outgoing and makes friends easily. She's active in several charities. She knows she is adopted, and to the best of my knowledge has never tried to discover the identities of her real parents. And she is very distraught over the disappearance of Carla Upton."

Ted said, "Some of the financial affairs of the Longwood estate are handled by a New York law firm—Allen, Frank, Dennis, Williams, and Batson. They were totally uncooperative. Other affairs are handled by a law firm in the principality of Liechtenstein. The Longwood estate has quite a large amount of money in several banks there. To say the banks and lawyers

there were uncooperative would be the understate-
ment of the century. I queried people in our state
department. They told me that as long as United
States taxes are paid, and they are, accurate to the
penny, those banks don't have to tell me a damn
thing."

"I struck out in personnel," Leo admitted. "I
couldn't even come up with a possibility. I've known
most of the people for years. And you all know how
strict Brownie is about his people. We're rated as the
best department in the state. If a cop is involved, he or
she is on the La Barca PD, and I can't get into their
records."

Leo sniffed the air. "The coffee's ready." Then he
remembered he'd used every cup in the house and
forgotten to wash them. "Ah . . . "

"Never mind, Leo," Lani said. "There probably
isn't a clean cup in the house. Come on, Brenda."

"This is kind of embarrassing," Leo said, when the
ladies had left the room.

"They love to wait on a man," Ted said, jerking his
thumb toward the kitchen. "Women are born with
that sense of duty in them."

Leo smiled. "You, ah, ever been married, Ted?"

"No. No. The right one just hasn't come along for
me." He frowned. "I meet nice girls, but I just can't
seem to hold on to them."

"I wonder why?" Leo muttered under his breath.
Leo would never leave dirty socks on the floor or a
sink filled with dirty dishes if Virginia was within a
hundred miles of home.

Lani and Brenda returned, the coffee poured into
freshly washed cups. They had all sugared and
creamed and stirred and were relaxing when the phone
rang. Leo picked it up.

"Pig motherfucker," the voice said. The caller was

using one of those electronic voice disguisers, and Leo could not tell if it was male or female. Leo immediately flipped on the cassette-recorder attached to the phone. "Your wife and oldest daughter are next on the list. I'm going to butt-fuck your kid and tape-record her screams. I'll be sure to send you a copy. By the way, I know your wife is visiting her sister up north. I'll let you know if your wife has good pussy." The caller hung up.

Leo's face had not changed expression. But inside, he had turned ice-cold and hard as steel. His thoughts were murderous. He rewound the tape and played it for the others.

Ted stood up. "Give me the address, and I'll use my car phone to get San Francisco PD and have them provide around-the-clock protection."

"Thanks, Ted. It won't be for long. I know my wife. She'll want to come right back here."

"That's not smart, Leo," Brenda said.

Lani and Leo smiled, Lani saying, "Virginia and Leo met while Ginny was a cop here in La Barca. She's one of the best pistol and rifle shots I ever saw. She iced two punks during a liquor store holdup and shooting. The third perp got off a round that shattered her knee and retired her on disability. Leo arrived just then and shot the third punk in the head. There are a dozen or more retired cops in this area who owe Leo and Ginny their lives. They'll be so many guns around Ginny and the kids, a platoon of Marines couldn't get to her."

"Virginia Malone!" Brenda said and Leo nodded his head. "Sure. We studied her in the academy. That wasn't the only shooting she was involved in. She killed that kidnapper/child-molester."

"That's my girl," Leo said. "If the Ripper comes

around here, shortly thereafter the mortician is gonna be stuffin' cotton up his ass."

"He does have a way with words, doesn't he?" Lani said.

Sheriff Brownwood was angry through and through after listening to the short tape. "No goddamn street slime son-of-a-bitch-punk-bastard asshole threatens the family of any of *my* people and gets away with it!"

"Calm down, Brownie," Leo said.

"Calm down's ass!"

"I've got her covered, Brownie."

"She'll be safer here than in 'Frisco."

"She'll be here late this evening. Two buddies of mine are escorting her and the kids home."

"That's not enough personnel. I'll call the highway patrol." He reached for the phone.

Leo laughed and caught his arm. "Wait, Brownie. Wait. Sit down. Please. That's better. It's Dick Klimer and Stu Powell with her. Two cars, front and back of hers."

The sheriff relaxed. "Oh, well. That's better. Nothing could get by those two apes."

"And the highway patrol has already been informed of the move down."

"Better yet. Sorry, Leo. You know how I feel about people who threaten a cop's family."

His secretary buzzed him. "Dennis Potter on the line, Sheriff."

Brownie picked up. "That's right, Dennis. How do you find out these things? What? No, no. We'll have her covered. Yes, we will. I . . . Dennis. I . . . Dennis, if it will make you feel better, I'm sure Leo would be more than happy to have you handling security. I'll ask him and get right back to you. Thank you, Dennis."

Brownie looked at Leo. "How the hell does he find out about things like this?" He held up a hand. "If you know, don't tell me. I don't want to know about it. He says he'll have the best security people in the world here by midnight, if you want them, for as long as you want them."

"Sure," Leo said. "I know that quite a few of the retired operations people from CIA go to work for Dennis, and he employs his own private army of ex-military types. SEALs, Special Forces, Rangers, Air Force Commandos. I'll be happy for them to guard Ginny and the kids."

Brownie called Dennis and it was set.

Leo rejoined his team and went back to work trying to catch the Ripper. By eight o'clock that night, four men appeared on Leo's porch. They were all in their mid to late forties. Two were of medium height, one was tall, the other was short. They all had the same expression in their eyes and on their faces. Nothing. Cold, with no other emotion showing. Pete, Sam, Ralph, Martin.

Leo was surprised when the fifth member stepped up and it was a woman, and a very attractive woman at that. She looked to be about thirty-five.

"That's Leslie," Pete said. "She goes with your wife and daughters where we can't go. If you get what I mean."

"I got it. Come on in and meet the family."

Inside, with Leo's family, the demeanor of the security team changed, becoming open and friendly, but still retaining that edge of alertness. When the team's suitcases and trunks were opened, Leo stared in envy. Everything from night-vision equipment, to the very latest in weapons, to stuff that not even the experienced Leo could recognize.

Leo relaxed. His family was safe.

"We can't just go to Stacy and lay it all out on the line to her," Brenda said, during the morning meeting of the Ripper team. "That would be a terrible shock to her."

"No," Leo agreed. "But what we can do is explain to her about the hidden messages behind the tapes at the station, and ask her if she would consent to work with us. Then we could gradually work up to the real objective."

"It's still going to be one hell of a shock to her," Lani said.

"Do we have a choice in the matter?" Ted asked.

They all agreed: no.

"Incredible," Stacy said. "I've heard of subliminal suggestion, of course. We studied it during many of my broadcast courses. But a lot of people claim it doesn't work."

"It works," Lani told her. The team had agreed that Lani and Brenda would be the first to approach Stacy with the idea. The men would come in afterward. "And we'd like you to help us find the Ripper."

"Certainly," Stacy agreed without hesitation. She sighed. "Any word on Carla?"

"Nothing," Brenda answered. "And we don't know who the dead woman is either."

"This whole matter is just . . . bizarre. I mean everything. The Ripper, Dick Hale, Carla. Everything. Is it all connected?"

"Yes," Lani took it. "And your help is going to be invaluable to us. Believe that."

"I don't see how."

"You will."

Two weeks passed uneventfully. No more bodies were found. Dick Hale did not surface. No attempts were made on the lives of Virginia Franks or the children. No trace of Carla Upton was found. Stacy Ryan was named permanent general manager of KSIN broadcasting. June Hale was placed in a mental institution; a very exclusive, very private, and very expensive one.

Since nothing exciting was happening, most of the press left town to work other, more newsworthy stories around the nation. War, pestilence, famine, and gut-wrenching personal tragedy were the stuff that ratings were made of. It was just plain boring around La Barca and Hancock County.

But the cops and the security team guarding Virginia Franks and the kids knew this was nothing more than a lull before another violent, bloody storm of torture, perversion, and death. The pause was deliberate on the Ripper's part.

Stacy could not identify the voice behind the suggestions on the tapes. Cal Denning isolated the voice and cleaned it up, but to no avail. Neither he nor Stacy had ever heard it before.

Unknown to Stacy, she was given a series of PSE tests, the most skilled operator in the state located in another room. She passed every test without a hitch. Stacy Ryan knew nothing about the Ripper.

As the dog days of summer struck in full force, so did the Ripper and Dick Hale. And this time, for the cops, it was very close to home.

Chapter 19

Tony Moreno was two years away from retiring from the Sheriff's Department. He had decided to pull the pin after twenty-five years behind a badge. He and his wife, who worked as a bookkeeper in a local factory, had just put their last chick through college. Tony was going to work part-time as security for a local firm for a few years, and then he and his wife would really retire and do some traveling.

His radio crackled. "HC 135."

"HC 135," Tony responded.

"See the woman, 11074 River Oak Drive. Signal 34."

"Ten-four." Prowler, Tony thought. Not good, but a damn sight better than a domestic disturbance. Cops hate domestic disturbances. You separate the man from hammering on his wife, and the wife many times will turn on you. Tony still carried the scar on the back of his head where, after he'd pulled the man off his wife, who was doing his best to rearrange her face with his fist, and doing a pretty good job of it, the woman had picked up a Big Ben alarm clock and smashed it against the back of Tony's head. Then after all that was straightened out, the woman dropped the charges against her husband.

River Oak Drive was way to hell and gone out in the country. The house was dark when Tony pulled into the drive.

"HC 135 dispatch."

"Go ahead."

"I'm 10-97." Arrived at the scene.

"That's 10-4, HC 135. Zero three three five hours."

"Where was the woman supposed to be?"

"Inside. Said she was afraid to come out."

"Ten-four."

That was the last voice communication anyone ever received from Hancock County unit HC 135.

When repeated attempts from the dispatcher failed to get a response from Tony Moreno, every deputy in the county was alerted, as well as the La Barca PD.

Deputies found the unit at ten o'clock the next morning, parked in a ravine about ten miles from La Barca. At four o'clock that afternoon, Sheriff Brownwood got a phone call.

"Listen, Sheriff," the electronically altered voice said. "Listen to your deputy scream his life away."

Brownie became physically ill listening to the tortured screaming of Tony, as the call was being traced. He finally had to leave the room.

"Pay phone out on 168," he was told.

"Roll!"

But there was nobody there. Only the phone taped to a tape recorder with the tape on a continuous loop, and an envelope containing a very profane and mocking note printed in large block letters using a ruler, which eliminates a handwriting expert's testimony. The deputies, including Leo and Lani, Brenda and Ted, followed the directions and found the remains of Tony Moreno about an hour later. He had been completely skinned, from the soles of his feet to the top of his head.

"I'll go tell his wife," Brownie said, his voice choked with emotion, both sadness and anger.

For the first time since the Ripper began the barbarity in California, a civilian was allowed to see just how savage the attacks were. Stacy Ryan was brought to the scene and allowed to view the remains of Tony Moreno. She passed out.

The newly appointed chief of police of La Barca opened his personnel records to Leo. On that same day, three officers abruptly quit the force and dropped out of sight. Sam Bolling, Mark Jeffreys, and Anita Rush.

"Run them all the way back to the moment of conception," Leo said. "And put out an APB." Some departments use what is called BOLO. Be On the Lookout.

The three former La Barca police officers vanished without a trace. Leo and Lani tossed their apartments and found damning evidence of their involvement with the Ripper, and the theory that it was a killing club proved out. Books and magazines of the most perverted type were found: S & M, child pornography, torture, and depravities so horrible they were unspeakable in nature. They found address books and immediately started alerting other departments nationwide. But of the several hundred names, only a few were picked up for questioning. The others had been tipped off and had split for parts unknown.

Leo and Lani flew to Indianapolis, a city that had recently reported several copycat murders, and where one of the names found in Sam Bolling's address book had been picked up. A team of Indianapolis cops had sweated the suspect, and he finally broke.

"You're not gonna believe this guy," a detective

lieutenant told Leo and Lani, after picking them up at Indianapolis International/Weir Cook Airport. "This is something right out of a horror story. We've got people digging right now, and so far we've uncovered the remains of a dozen people. And he's a DJ, too," he added softly. "Local hard rock station."

"Have you made that public yet?" Lani asked.

"No. I figured you guys would want a lid on that."

"Right. Thanks."

"The Bureau been notified?"

"Yes. But we can't expect much help there. I guess you haven't heard the news. It just broke. Big plot was just uncovered to kill the President and half a dozen senators and representatives and members of the Supreme Court. Every federal agency you can think of is busy working on that. This perverted mess we've got is pretty much going to be in the hands of locals."

"You notified the FCC?" Leo asked.

"Right. Inspectors have already begun working to pull the tapes with subliminal suggestions on them."

"It's nationwide then," Lani said, as much to herself as to the others.

"We think so. Already a dozen departments have responded to our private calls, and discovered cells, or would-be cells, in their cities."

The DJ, who looked as freaky as the music he played sounded, was defiant and sullen. "Motherfuckin' pigs from California," he snarled at them. "And a cunt, too. How'd you get here? Ride your surfboards?"

It took every fiber in Leo's being to keep him from backhanding the punk out of the chair. Tony Moreno had introduced Leo to Virginia.

"Death is the ultimate high, man," the freak said. "I dig death. Can't wait for it."

"Hopefully you won't have a long wait," Leo said,

knowing full well that even if convicted of his heinous
crimes, and even if Indiana had the death penalty, the
freak might be on death row for years before he was
gassed or juiced or given a lethal injection, the latter
being one of the most ridiculous things Leo had ever
heard of. People like this freak showed no compassion
to their victims, so why in hell should society show
mercy or compassion to them?

Most cops Leo knew shared that opinion.

The freak had admitted the existence of a killing
club in the city; he'd admitted his part in altering the
tapes at the station; and he had freely and openly
admitted his part in several killings. But he would give
no names.

"I hope you do torture me," he said with a grin. "I
groove on pain, man. We all do. If it feels good, do it."
He looked at Leo. "You ever been fucked up the ass,
man?"

Leo grimaced at just the thought.

"It's neat, man. There ain't nothin' like a dick up
your ass. I told the pigs here to put me in with the
meanest, big-dicked nigger they got locked up. I—"

Leo tuned him out and left the interrogation room
to go wash his face with cold water. When he stepped
out of the men's room, Lani was leaning up against a
wall in the corridor, her face shiny with sweat. Her
breathing was ragged. Leo put a hand on her shoulder.
"Steady now, Lani. Stand tough."

She nodded her head and said, "Leo, there might be
hundreds of these perverted sacks of freaky shit out
there."

"I know it."

"Did you see all the S & M paraphernalia they got
from that . . . thing's house?"

"Yeah, I did, Lani."

"Leo, I wanted to kill that bastard. I wanted to pull iron and shoot that son of a bitch."

"I know, Lani. So did I."

"So did all of us on this case," the lieutenant said, walking up and hearing the last. "Wanna hear something rich? This punk says if we put him in isolation, he's going to sue the department. Anyway, I wanted to tell you that we just picked up two of his equally freaky friends. Now we have two more places to dig. You want to come along?"

"That's why we're here," Leo said.

The stench was so foul, all in attendance had to wear protective masks. No one could work in the cellar of the long-abandoned farm home for very long. It was just too much to ask of a normal human being. Several street-hardened cops had fainted at the uncovered sight. All present had puked their stomachs empty. The smell of rotted tortured death permeated the clothing of the living. Holes were knocked in the walls, and generators set up to pump in fresh, clean, outside air. It helped, but not much.

The freak had been brought out from jail. He was excited at the sight. "Yeah, yeah!" he hollered, pointing as much as his belly-cuff chains would allow. "See that little cunt kid there? I done that. I cummed all over myself just before she died. I never cummed like that before in my life! It was wonderful!"

One cop had to be physically restrained by other cops. He was mad as hell, climbing out of the hole with a shovel in his hand, fully intending to hammer the freak's brains out. He had been the man who uncovered the badly mutilated body of the ten-year-old girl, so eloquently eulogized by the freak.

Lani and Leo drove to another dig site. This one,

like the one they'd just left, was far out in the Indiana countryside. This one had been pointed out by another just-arrested geek friend of the first freak, who was riding in the lead car.

"I got a bad feeling in my gut," the Indiana cop said. "I got a hunch that before this is all over, this is going to be the worst rash of killings this nation has ever seen."

"So do we," Lani spoke for both of them.

"Thirteen bodies so far," a very tired-looking cop said, taking a break from the digging. "This is an old one. The bodies are badly decomposed. It's grim in there, Al. I mean, real grim."

"Lemmie see, lemmie see!" the second freak hollered. "Man, I love the smell of death. Can't you dig it? Oohhh—I think I just cummed in my shorts."

The weary and dirt-stained cop's hands tightened on the handle of his shovel.

Al gave the punk a shove away from the hard-eyed cop. "Move, asshole. You want to see this place, let's go see it."

Lani paused for a moment to look at the cop with the shovel. She jerked a thumb toward the manacled geek. "How do they get that way?"

The cop shrugged tired shoulders. "God, I don't know. Luckily my kids hate heavy metal and rap and shit music. Believe it or not, they both like jazz and big band. Hell, I don't even like jazz. Sounds like half a dozen musicians each trying to out-blow the other!"

Lani chuckled and patted the cop on a sweaty shoulder. She walked toward the dig site.

"Brace yourself," the cop called.

"I got nothing left to puke up," Lani said.

"Me, neither," the cop replied.

Leo blocked her way into the old barn. His face was pale. "Forget it, Lani. There is no point in you going in there. We'll soon have our share of digs back home, I'm thinking."

She ducked under his arm and stepped inside. She was back in under a minute, a tad green around the mouth. "Gimmie a cigarette, Leo."

"We both quit, Lani. Remember?"

"So I started again. I gotta find a cigarette."

"You don't need a cigarette, Lani"

"Goddamnit, Leo!" she flared. "I'm a grown woman. If I want a goddamn cigarette, it's my goddamn business. Goddamnit!" she added.

A nearby cop held out a pack. He and Leo exchanged glances, both of them sensing that Lani was near the breaking point for that day. And both of them knowing they were very near that same breaking point. The breaking point knows no gender. When enough is enough, the mind closes down.

Lani took the cigarette and the light. The cop held out the pack to Leo. Leo sighed and took one. "Why the hell not?" He lit up and looked at the uniform. "You been smoking long?"

"I quit five years ago. I just started up again this morning. Out here."

Leo nodded. "I sure don't blame you one little bit. I think I'll get drunk tonight."

"I *know* I'm gonna get drunk tonight," the uniform said. "But before I do, I'm gonna make love to my wife and hug all three of my kids. In that order." He gave Leo the nearly full pack. "Take them. I went into town and bought a carton." He toed out his smoke, picked up a shovel, and with a sigh, reentered the old barn turned death house.

"Do we want to go to the third site?" Lani asked, puffing furiously.

"I don't."

"What do you want to do?"

"I want to go home, Leo. There is no more we can do here. Al says he'll fax us the freak's statements ASAP."

"There's a flight out at 6:55 in the morning. We can be on that one."

"Anything this evening?"

Leo took a timetable pamphlet from his jacket pocket and checked the flight times. "No. We missed the last one."

Lani puffed. Coughed.

Leo glanced at her. At least the smoke was helping to kill the terrible stench of rotting bodies. "I have a hunch we'll just be jumping from one bad situation to another equally bad situation."

"We're gonna have to set up a task force, nationwide. And we're gonna have to do it quick."

"Agreed."

"The FCC is gonna have to work with us on this. They're gonna have to assign as many inspectors as possible. We've got to convince them of that."

"I don't think that will be a problem."

Al had left the murky confines of the old barn and joined them on the outside.

"We're on a statewide net right now," the Indianapolis cop told them. "By this time tomorrow, we'll be nationwide. The FCC is handing us everybody they can spare. I figure in seventy-two hours, we'll be rolling nationwide to get the subliminal suggestions off the air."

"And maybe have some sort of a handle on the cults, the clubs, whatever the hell they're called," Leo said.

"We code-named this the Killing Clubs."

"The press will love that."

"Fuck the press," Al said bluntly.

Lani smiled. "Another thing we share in common."

A uniform walked up. "Dispatch says homicide pulled in two more suspects. They're talkin' about a fourth site."

"Jesus Christ!" Al said, wiping his face with a handkerchief. "And this is just one small city. What's it going to be like nationwide?"

"Chaos," Lani said softly.

Chapter 20

Lani could not have chosen a better word to describe the mood of the country after the news spread. FCC investigators began finding taped subliminal suggestions in every major market and many smaller ones. Police began finding death pits all over the nation, border to border, coast to coast. The vice president's wife—who had been complaining about certain song lyrics for years—was quickly appointed chairperson of a commission to study song contents, programming, musical groups, whether a minimum age limit should be set to attend heavy metal and rap concerts, and so forth. Musicians and singers began screaming about the constitutional right of free speech.

"We're getting off the track here," Leo said, sitting at his desk. He tossed the morning paper into the wastebasket. "It's subliminal suggestions we're looking for, not song lyrics."

"There are those who think the lyrics of certain songs drive some listeners to commit crimes," Ted said.

"It certainly does me," Sheriff Brownwood said, pausing at the open door. "Makes me want to kill the son of a bitch singing it." He walked on.

Since the death of deputy sheriff Tony Moreno, the

Ripper had ceased killing in Hancock County . . . that is, as far as the cops knew. Dick Hale was still on the loose, but laying low. Carla Upton had not been found. The number of bodies found nationwide had far exceeded Lani and Leo's original estimate. Over two thousand tortured and mutilated bodies had been dug up, and the body count was climbing every day. Citizens were arming themselves in record numbers, some gun stores selling out their entire stock in one day. Over fifty radio stations and four TV stations had been shut down by FCC inspectors. Going dark, in broadcasting language. Arrest warrants had been issued for more than three hundred people nationwide; but the suspects appeared to be as slippery as quicksilver. Only a handful had been arrested and charged. They freely talked, boasting about their part in torturing and killing, leading the police to new and larger death pits.

Leo was studying Lani, who sat deep in thought at her desk. "What's on your mind, Blondie?" he asked.

"We were the ones who uncovered this snake pit," she said. "So we'll be the ones right on the top of the killing list of these geeks and freaks and weirdos. You and me, Leo. And probably Ted and Brenda, too."

"Yeah. You're right. So?"

Sheriff Brownwood had stepped into the office and was listening.

"Over three hundred arrest warrants have been issued nationwide, but only a few suspects have been picked up. Those on the loose have apparently gone hard underground. We've all agreed that a contingency plan had been worked out in advance, knowing a day of discovery would come."

"Yeah. So?"

"So we're all convinced that the Longwood boys are in charge, so to speak, of this killing club, right?"

"Right," Brenda said. "Where are you going with this, Lani?"

"It's not where I'm going," she said. "It's where those still on the loose are going."

Brownie had poured a cup of coffee. He dropped the cup on the floor and whirled around, facing Lani. "You think they're coming *here?*"

"That seems the logical conclusion to me, yes."

"Why?" Ted asked.

"For their grand finale. One final day, or night, or week, or month of killing frenzy. Look, cops nationwide have connected every suspect; albeit loosely, but they are all connected. These goddamn freaks even had a newsletter. You've all seen it. Or copies of it. Jim and Jack Longwood have spent years setting all this up. Everywhere they traveled, they set up a cell. Those cells grew from the cities and spread out into the countryside. We've now proven that that broadcasting school the government just last week put out of business was the brainchild of the Longwoods. They financed it and taught selected people the craft of subliminal suggestion. Those people went out all over the country, and put that to work. Those freaks in Indiana confirmed it. Jim and Jack Longwood are here. Right here in Hancock County, laughing at us. All those on the suspect list are disciples of Jim and Jack Longwood. They worship those two weirdos. Where else would they go?"

"Yeah," Brenda said softly. "It began on the East Coast, and it will end on the West Coast. It fits. I buy it."

"Lani," Brownie said. "Two six or seven-year-old boys couldn't have set this up—it's too elaborate!"

"No. They didn't. Not then. This plan came later on. Probably right before they killed their parents. Everything they've done has been a plan to throw off the cops. The classic movies, the classic music. That was laid down as a false trail, and we bought it. KSIN is the only classic radio station in the nation that has been directly tied in. All the rest were hard rock and heavy metal and rap. All youth-oriented. A few hidden messages were found in other stations, but damn few. We've been had, people. We got screwed, and didn't even get kissed in the process."

"And you think these two hundred and seventy-five or so freaks are coming here to go into a blood-lust frenzy?" Ted asked.

"I think that's what Jack and Jim Longwood *want* us to think."

"Why?" Brownie asked.

"I haven't figured that one out yet," Lani admitted.

"Mary had a little lamb?" Leo asked.

Lani shook her head. "Another false trail. Means nothing."

"The half brother and sister?"

"I don't think they exist. I think that story is bogus. It was planted around town, school, and in Karl and Anna's minds by the boys. They spread it around. They told Father Daniel. You know how people like to talk to those who work for the very rich. Human nature."

"Those two who attacked us back at that old school?" Leo asked.

"We start doing some digging—when we have the time—and I think we'll find those two were in some mental institution with Jack and Jim. Recruits, that's all."

"This is a lot of fishing and guessing, Lani," Brownie said. "But I tend to lean in your direction. This whole case has been goofy from the start. Leo?"

"Yeah. I'm with you. This case, right from the beginning, has had all of us acting like a one-armed paperhanger. At least Lani's theory makes some sense. Nothing else about this screwy mess does."

All four of the investigators were losing patience. Brenda Yee threw a stack of file folders on the table. "Goddamnit!" she yelled, causing Brownie to almost spill his newly poured coffee down the front of his shirt. He gave the state investigator a very pained look. "What does Carla Upton have to do with this case?" Brenda asked, looking around. "Did she stage her own death? If so, why? She was, is, whatever, a rich woman, and from all we can find, a very happy one. If she was kidnapped, why the elaborate setup? Who was the dead woman? Was her death unrelated to this case? If not, how does it tie in with the freaks?"

"It all ties in," Lani said softly. "We just haven't found the right sequence of ribbons and bows, that's all. The Ripper is playing with us, taunting us, mocking us." She cleared her throat. "Okay. Let's lay it out on the table. One: we stopped the Ripper's game of subliminal suggestion. Two: every DJ, copywriter, engineer, secretary, salesperson over at the broadcasting complex checks out nine ways to sundown. They're clear. Three: we know how the Ripper used to lure his victims to their death. We stopped that. Four: is the Ripper now picking the victims at random? Or has the Ripper come up with a new scheme in choosing victims? Five: where the hell is Dick Hale? The man is not any sort of outdoorsman. Dick's idea of roughing it was a weekend at the Sheraton."

"Forget Dick Hale," Brownie said. "Let Homicide handle that one."

Lani shook her head. "He's part of it, Brownie. In a strange and tragic way."

"Well, pardon me. I thought we cleared Dick of any involvement with the Ripper?"

"Yeah," Leo said. "Me, too."

"We did. But not his daughter."

"What are you talking about?" Ted asked.

"I've got Cal going over that tape that Dick played for us that day at his house. You know, the one where the woman called about information that would clear Dick?"

"Yeah. So? You think that was Sue Hale on that tape?"

"Cal's doing voice comparison analysis right now. He had old tapes over at the station of Sue, fooling around in the commercial room. He should be through at any moment."

"Jesus God!" Brownie said. "Dick's own daughter set him up. What a charming family that was." He looked at Lani. "I see what you mean about it being strange and tragic."

"What got you leaning in Sue's direction, Lani?" Brenda asked.

"That's a cold little bitch, people. I've been doing some snooping around; asking some people about her. And if Cal finds out that's really Sue's voice on the tape, this case is going to go right through the ceiling." Lani rose and refilled her coffee cup with fresh coffee.

"Well, don't stop now!" Leo said. "Come on, give."

"For the past year, it seems that Sue has been offering sex, including oral and anal, to certain high school boys, and girls, if they would agree to join a secret club—"

"Oh, *fuck!*" Brownie said. "Now we have juveniles involved in this mess."

"Yeah." Lani stared down into her coffee cup for a moment. She looked up. "I got to thinking about how cold Sue was when her father was arrested. I checked the visitor book. She never came to see him. And they were supposed to be such a happy, close-knit family. Boy, was that a facade!"

"How many boys and girls?" Brownie said in a very tired voice.

"Fifty or so."

"God!" the sheriff whispered.

"Her brother was part of that club," Lani added.

"You mean . . . " Ted cleared his throat. "Sue and her brother were . . . ?"

"Apparently so. The one kid I spoke with—who is clear, by the way—who even came close to leveling with me, said that Sue felt she could cure her brother's homosexuality by having sex with him."

"Next you're going to be telling me that the mother also had sex with her son," Brownie said, the words sounding like he had a very bad taste in his mouth.

"Yeah, that's right," Lani told him. "And with her daughter, too."

"I think I'll retire after this term," Brownie said, very wistfully. "Me and the wife move up into the mountains. Talk to squirrels and birds and deer and other critters. To hell with humans."

The phone rang and Lani picked up. Cal Denning calling from KSIN. "I called in a friend from L.A. to verify my findings. It's a match, Lani. No doubt about it."

Brownie put his face in his hands. "Wonderful. Just fucking wonderful!"

Moments after the first teenager was picked up, Sue and the other kids involved in the killing club took off for parts unknown. When the cops came knocking on the front door, the parents were angry, disbelieving, and dismayed.

"Not my Paul. Not my Pat. Not my Lisa. Not my Johnny. Not my Frank," was the usual response.

Parents should be required to ride with cops at least

one night a week. That experience just might open their eyes to some truths they would ordinarily deny to the grave.

But that won't happen, and many incredibly naive parents will continue to be shocked and saddened and angry when the local cops show up at their door with some distressing news concerning their perfect children.

La Barca was no different from any other small to medium-sized city. It had its normal share of runaways, drifters, social dropouts, dopers, hookers, gangs, and unexplained disappearances. Nationally, thousands of people disappear every year, never to be heard from again. There are all sorts of theories as to what happens to them, ranging from alien kidnapping to white slavery in some Moroccan bordello. The sad truth is, in reality, no one really knows.

Lani and Leo, Ted and Brenda started looking through the La Barca PD and Hancock County Sheriff Department's missing persons files.

"It's been running unusually high the last couple of years," the clerk in missing persons noted.

"I wonder why?" Lani said, only slightly sarcastically.

The clerk did not pick up on that, but the rest of the team sure did. Leo especially, for he, too, was thinking about those pits back in Indiana, filled with tortured, mutilated, and rotting bodies. They knew it was just a matter of time before something very similar was discovered in Hancock County.

Outside the building, leaning against their cars, Leo said, "Fifty kids just don't vanish in a town the size of La Barca. L.A., Chicago, New York City, yeah. But not in La Barca."

"So what are we doing wrong?" Brenda asked.

"We're not thinking like a kid," Ted said, and that got everybody's attention.

"Go on," Leo said.

"The kids have got to eat. But they're not going to be fixing lamb chops and brussels sprouts and so forth. They won't be going to the supermarkets."

"Junk food," Lani said. "Cokes and Pepsis and chips and candy bars and peanut butter."

"Right."

"Small convenience stores on the edges of town," Leo said. "And alert all units to look out for kids who were not on our list, buying sacks of junk food and heading out of town with it."

"Maybe not just out of town." Brenda snapped her fingers. "All those warehouses down by the docks. Especially the ones no longer in use."

"Yeah," Lani said. "There's about a mile of them. Some of them scheduled to be torn down. We've been concentrating looking *outside* of town."

"The old amusement park is down there, too," Leo said. "It's been condemned for years. And that place is honeycombed with basements. Dandy places to hide. Or dispose of a lot of bodies," he added, then glanced at Lani. "We'll stay off the air with this. You can be sure these kids have access to a scanner, and have all our frequencies programmed in. They're listening. And don't discount the very real possibility of some of their parents helping their kids to hide from us, and bringing them food and bedding and clothing and so forth."

"We need more people," Brenda spoke the obvious.

"Well, we don't have them," Leo said. "Listen, we've got to assume that many of these kids are armed. That kid we picked up and sweated was carrying, so some of the others are, too. The goddamn parents wouldn't tell us if any firearms were missing, and that's a dead giveaway that some guns were taken. Everybody carry extra speedloaders or clips, and everybody fill a pocket with extra shotgun shells. I want us all in body armor. Put fresh batteries in your flashlights. We'll pull some uniforms off traffic to assist us. If we can grab half a dozen of these kids, we can break them, and to hell with what Juvenile thinks about it. They won't know anything about it until we sweat the truth out of the kids. This may be the break we've been looking for. Let's go."

Chapter 21

"You really think some of the parents are helping their kids, Leo?" Lani asked, as they drove toward the docks.

"I'd bet a month's pay on it. Many parents can't control their kids nowadays, for a variety of reasons. But instead of mommy and daddy looking inward to find the solutions, they lash out at law and order and discipline and the cops. I'm not telling you anything you don't know, Lani."

"But you've got a whole house filled with kids, Leo. And they've never been in trouble . . . that I know of."

"Lani, when I'm not working, I'm with my kids. You know that. Ginny and me started out that way with the first one, and it'll be that way until the last chick leaves the nest. One night a week is family night. We play games, talk, discuss anything that might be troubling them—and we do it together."

"There's got to be more to it than that, Leo."

"Oh, there is. Sure. None of my kids were born with the bad seed in them."

"You really truly believe in that, don't you, Leo?"

"Damn right, I do. And I think you do, too."

"For the most part, yes. How come your kids don't care much for sports, Leo?"

"Because their father and mother don't like sports. I don't believe in this sports hero crap. They're not heroes. They're fine athletes. Not heroes. They're not role models, and there is no reason they should be. They're human beings just like the rest of us, with all the flaws and frailties. Ginny and I read, we both have a deep love of fine music, and we put books in our kids' hands at a very early age. We didn't sit for hours in front of a TV acting like idiots, because somebody could dribble a basketball or hit a baseball better or catch a football better than the other fellow. You better get me off this subject, Lani," he said with a smile.

She laughed and cut her eyes toward him. Leo was as near to being the perfect father as any man she had ever known. He and Ginny had raised four good kids: polite, hardworking, respectful. She knew for a fact that Leo never had to criticize his kids's choice of music, for while they liked rock and roll, they did not listen to heavy metal or rap or hard rock. She smiled a secret smile. However, Leo's kids knew just how to manipulate him, and just how far he could be pushed.

Four county units had joined the team, staying well behind Ted and Brenda's car, at staggered intervals. Leo knew the press was watching the cops closely. If there was to be a shoot-out, he didn't want a bunch of civilians around. That was one reason. The main reason was he didn't want the press to see him sweat any kid they might find, for he was going to get the truth, one way or the other.

"I know that look in your eyes, Leo," his longtime partner said. "It scares me. These are kids we're dealing with . . . providing there *are* any kids in these old warehouses." She knew what his reply would be, and she wasn't disappointed.

"Kids stop being kids when they get a driver's license. Then they become adults. Like it or not."

"You're impossible, Leo."

"Nope. I'm a realist, Lani."

"Stubborn, too."

"Not necessarily. It's just that I'm usually right."

She groaned. "I don't see how Virginia lives with you."

"True love smooths out the bumps in the road."

"You're also full of shit, Leo."

They were both laughing as Leo parked the car beside the heavy duty chain-link fence the county had put up around the old, long-abandoned warehouses and got out.

"You people in body armor?" Leo asked the six uniforms. Four men, two women. They were. "Extra rounds for sidearm and shotgun?" They all patted their pockets and nodded their heads.

Four more units pulled up, and Leo assigned the additional eight uniforms to patrolling outside the fence. "If the kids are in those warehouses, there is no way we'll round them all up. Some will cut and run. Grab as many as you can. But be careful. These aren't choir boys and nuns-to-be we're dealing with. Let's go."

So far, the operation had not drawn the attentions of the press. Leo hoped it would stay that way. Leo used the key he'd gotten from county maintenance to unlock the gate, and they drove in. He did not secure the gate. That wouldn't have done any good. The kids, if they were inside the huge compound, had found another way in and out.

Leo sent the uniforms to the far end, about a mile away. "We'll start working toward the middle." He shucked a round into the slot of his 12-gauge sawed-off. Double ought buckshot. "Ted, you and Brenda take the second warehouse. Lani and me will work the first one."

The warehouses were huge, dirty, dusty, cobwebbed, and poorly illuminated; the windows darkened from years of dirt. The teams worked for over an hour and found nothing. Leo had anticipated that, figuring that if the kids were here, they would be close to the center of the long row of buildings.

The instant Leo pushed open the door, he knew he'd found at least some of the kids. The entrance was free of cobwebs, the dust marked with the soles of tennis shoes. Using hand signals, he told Lani he would go in first, rolling toward the right. She nodded her head, indicating she would follow, but rolling to the left.

Leo winked at her, and then was inside the cavernous warehouse. Lani was a second or so behind him. The building was a jumble of crates and junk. The smell of fried chicken was strong. Somebody had recently visited the Colonel and brought back a couple of buckets. Using his walkie-talkie, Leo signaled the others that he felt he'd struck paydirt. He ordered all the uniforms to cover the sides and back of the warehouse. Lani and Leo waited until the signal came that everybody was in place.

"All right, kids!" Leo called, his voice echoing in the huge old building. "Sheriff's department. Give it up."

His words brought a hail of automatic-weapons fire from amid the boxes and crates and other junk in the center of the warehouse. The bullets whined and howled and tore holes in the old wood.

"Uzis!" Lani said, flattened out on the floor. "Where the hell did these kids get Uzis?"

"Jim and Jack Longwood," Leo replied, during a lull in the wild shooting. "The bastards thought of everything. Crawl to the door and roll out. We're outgunned here. I'm right behind you." Leo called for all the cops outside the fence to stay head's up, and then he rolled for the door. Outside, he radioed dispatch and called for backup and tear gas.

Within minutes, the warehouse was surrounded by uniforms from the La Barca PD and the Hancock County Sheriff's Department.

"Fill that warehouse with tear gas and drive them out," Leo ordered.

Tear-gas grenades were fired through the windows and seconds later kids began staggering outside, half-blind with tears running out of burning eyes. But they weren't going down easy. Many came out firing automatic weapons, spraying the area with bullets. The cops were in no mood for fun and games. Those kids who came out shooting, got lead in return. That stopped it. The kids still standing dropped their weapons and put their hands up.

By now the press was all over the place, having electronically snooped with scanners, and they witnessed the shootings.

"Now we're in for it," Brownie remarked, his own eyes stinging from the drift of the gas. "I can just see the headlines and hear the TV anchors weeping and blubbering about this. Sometimes I wonder who's side they're really on."

"Not ours," Leo said tersely. "You can bet on that."

"Police brutality!" Agnes Peters squalled from behind the CRIME SCENE tape. "Baby killers!"

Brenda Yee "accidentally" dropped a tear-gas canister in the middle of the knot of reporters, local, state, and national, and that broke it up long enough for the cops to hustle the kids into the backseat cages of units and into police vans and transport them to booking and interrogation.

"Somebody remind me to recommend a medal for her," Brownie said, smiling at the coughing, crying, choking line of reporters.

"Goddamn you, Sheriff Brownwood!" Agnes Peters yelled. "That fascist bitch did that deliberately."

Lani grabbed Brenda before she could jack Agnes's jaw and pulled her away.

"The public has a right to know!" another reporter gasped out the words, tears streaming down his face.

"Come on," Leo said to his team. "We've got work to do."

"Fuck you, pig!" the sixteen-year-old girl told Brenda in one interrogation room.

"Go suck a pig's dick!" a seventeen-year-old boy told Ted in another interrogation room.

Yet another seventeen-year-old punk lay on the floor of the interrogation room, his mouth bloody and his eyes shocked at what had been done to him. Leo jerked him to his feet and popped him again.

"Hey, man!" the punk said. "You can't do this to me. I'll sue you."

That remark caused him to kiss the floor again.

"We can do this easy or hard," Leo told him. "It's all up to you."

Lani suddenly rushed into the small room, shoved Leo hard, then started yelling at him. It was quite a performance; classic good cop/bad cop. She shoved Leo out of the room, into the hall, and said, "Goddamn you. This isn't the way we do things around here." She grinned at him, Leo winked at her and wandered off to find a cup of coffee.

Lani helped the weeping young man to his feet and brushed him off and patted his tears dry with a handkerchief. She resisted a very strong impulse to drive one knee into his nuts and use a nightstick on his head. Instead, she started mothering and comforting the craphead. It didn't take long before he was spilling out his tale of woe to the very pretty and oh-so sympathetic lady.

It doesn't work all the time. But this time it did.

"Did you cut the prick a deal?" Leo asked.

"Had to," Lani said. "DA went along with it. He'll do some easy time in return for testimony. We have a death pit, Leo."

"I figured we would. But I'll bet you there is more than one out there."

"No bet. You better stay out of sight of the prick, Leo. I've got him convinced that it would work to his advantage not to sue us for brutality."

"All right. How about the other young people?"

"A few are talking. Most are arrogant and sullen and silent."

"You ready to go view the death pit?"

"No. But we have to do it. I've sent uniforms out to cordon off the place. There'll be press everywhere."

"Tell Brenda to bring along another tear-gas canister."

Doesn't take long for a cop to get hard to terrible sights, from man's inhumanity to man, to needless violence, accidents, dead babies, blood and gore. But even the oldest and most hardened cop can lose it every now and then.

Leo stopped by the side of the man who had been his field-training officer; one of the toughest men Leo had ever known. The man was sitting on the ground, crying. He was about five hundred feet from the cordoned-off area.

"Paul?" Leo asked gently.

The street-hardened deputy looked up. "I've got

thirty years in, Leo," he said, wiping his wet cheeks. "I have never seen anything like what we found in that basement over there."

Leo and Lani squatted down beside the man.

"What's over there, Paul?"

"You told me about the pits back in Indiana. This is worse. Whole families over there, Leo! Mother, father, kids, babies, dogs, cats. Some of them skinned whole. I figure the Ripper got families on vacation and somehow lured them to . . . wherever he did his rotten work. The whole basement is a big dug-out pit. Lime scattered over the bodies. I counted twenty-seven before I lost it and had to leave. I went down three layers of bodies, Leo. Those on the bottom are badly decomposed. Maybe a year old. I figure that's how long he's been working out here." He shook his head. "Hell, maybe longer than that. This is just the first one we've found. There's sure to be more."

Leo patted the older man on the shoulder and stood up. Looked at Lani. As one they started up the slight incline to the country house. The smell hit them hard. With the bodies now disturbed and the basement windows opened, the smell was really bad. Lani and Leo walked around the rear of the house, squatted down, and looked in through the outside cellar door. Back in Indiana there had been no babies, no smaller children, no family pets. All that had now changed.

Brenda and Ted climbed up, knelt down, and took a look. Both of them paled. Brenda pointed. Lani noticed her hand was shaking. "Those are . . . little *babies!*"

"Yeah," Leo whispered. "Killing adults is one thing. Killing and skinning babies is quite another."

"The press is about five minutes behind us," Ted said, holding a handkerchief to his nose.

"CHP is going to hold them at the foot of the hill," Lani said.

Brownie stepped out of the basement, his face pale and sweaty. "I want a total lid on this, people. Not one word to leak out about the babies and the family pets." Brownie was an animal lover, and was strong for the humane treatment of animals. He also knew the power of several animal activist groups. The last thing he needed right now was for some of them to get involved. He looked at Leo. "How's Paul?"

"Pretty shook up."

"Even the toughest men have a breaking point," Brownie said. He glanced down the hill and up the road. "Oh, shit! Here comes the press. Looks like about a thousand of them."

"But it's good for the economy," Lani said with a straight face. "They drink a lot."

Brownie cut his eyes. "You've been around Leo too long, Lani. He's corrupted you." He looked at Brenda. "You stay away from down there. That bunch has got it in for you."

"It was an accident, Sheriff," she said innocently. "I swear it was. I would never, ever, do anything to cause harm to come to the good friends of law enforcement."

Brownie fixed her with a very jaundiced look. "Did anybody ever tell you that you were full of hockey-poo."

Brenda smiled. "Hockey-poo? No. But I've been told a lot of times that I was full of shit!"

Chapter 22

Dealing with juveniles is a pain in the ass. Cops have to put up with irate parents, many of whom are simply too naive to believe that their wonderful, precious, darling kid could ever do anything wrong. There just has to be a mistake. Then one has the social workers to contend with. Then the liberal press feels compelled to stick their noses into it. And one must never, ever forget the lawyers (although many cops would certainly like to). And if there is shooting involved, it just gets worse and worse. All in all, it can turn into a great big mess. Most good cops will admit, albeit reluctantly, that the safeguards (at least most of them) are necessary to protect the innocent. But they sure as hell don't have to like them.

Brenda tossed the file folders on the long table and sat down, a disgusted look on her face.

"Two of the wounded kids had nothing to do with the killing club. They just wanted to be with their friends. Four others, thank God unharmed, also had nothing to do with the Ripper. But their parents and their lawyers say the kids suffered terrible traumas due to the shooting and the sight of their friends being gunned down by the police. About fifty million dollars apiece, and their traumas will be eased enough for them to resume normal lives."

"I'm just overwhelmed with sympathy for them," Leo said. "I suppose, since we were the ones who initiated the assault, that the four or us are prominently named in the suits?"

"Of course. The sad thing is they'll probably get some money out of the suit."

"Show the jury pictures of the death pit," Lani said.

"That probably won't be admissible as evidence, since the pit was uncovered after the shoot-out," Ted said. "That's just a guess on my part."

Leo had been studying the reports. He shook his head. "Not one of these kids come from what could be called poor families. Most of them are upper middle class. Only a few from broken homes. Many of them have their own cars and a nice allowance, and only a few of them actually do any work. I don't understand it."

"They don't want for anything," Brenda said. "If everything is handed to you, where is the desire to strive? Both parents work; can't spend much time with the kids, so they over compensate by handing the kids expensive things. The kids have too much free time without adult supervision." She smiled. "That's what the shrinks will tell you."

"Do you buy that?" Lani asked her.

"Hell, no! Both my parents worked long hours. We were certainly upper middle class. I was a latchkey kid before the word came into vogue. But I couldn't turn on the TV and see near-naked people doing weird things on music videos. Teachers could still discipline and teachers still taught . . . without being in fear of their lives. I went into my teens in the early seventies. Of course, those were the days before drive-by shootings and gunning down cops became the norm. My group didn't throw concrete blocks off of overpasses onto oncoming traffic for kicks. Political correctness had yet to come. But then, I always knew what I wanted to be. Ever since I was a little girl. I wanted to tote a gun and *walk tall!*" She laughed and stood up, doing a slow pirouette. Brenda Yee was about five feet, two inches tall, at best. That got a laugh from everybody.

Brownie shuck his head in the room. "A new will signed by Carla Upton has just been found in a hidden wall safe in her home." He smiled, letting the suspense build a bit. "Everything goes to Stacy Ryan."

"I knew nothing about any new will," Stacy said to Brenda. "Please believe me. I knew nothing about it."

In the other room, a technician was secretly monitoring her voice with the latest model of what is called a Psychological Stress Evaluator . . . the newer model was a machine that the general public did not know about and would not know about, if the authorities, both civilian and government, had anything to say about it. The findings were not admissible in court, but it gave the police a starting point. "She's lying," the technician said.

"You're sure?" Lani asked.

"The machine is."

"Do you know anything about any family called Longwood?" Brenda asked.

"No. Nothing. I mean, I've heard the name used. Probably in movies or books. But I don't know anyone named Longwood."

"She's lying," the technician said. "Her throat tightened up so close, I'm amazed she was able to speak."

"You are sure of that?" Brenda pressed.

"Oh, I'm positive," Stacy said.

"Lying," the technician said. "And yes, I am sure."

"Like the fellow wrote," Leo muttered. "Curiouser and curiouser."

Long after Stacy had left the building, the four cops sat behind closed doors and talked about this new development.

"Why fake the death?" Lani asked.

"So she can collect the money and estate, and still keep her sweetie around for fun and games," Brenda replied.

Ted looked very pained at that.

"And then to torture her and skin her alive," Leo added.

"Jesus!" Ted said.

"And keep the face in preservative forever and ever," Lani said.

"I'm going to the bathroom," Ted said, standing up and walking out of the room.

When the door had closed, Brenda said, "He's as cool as any person I have ever seen in a shoot-out or hostage situation. He handles stress well, but not the gay community. He is absolutely opposed to that life-style."

"And you?" Leo paused in the poured of a cup of coffee.

Brenda shrugged. "I like men, period. I got me a regular feller back home. I tolerate gays. How about you guys?"

Lani said, "Like you, I tolerate them."

Leo sat down at the table. "I don't condone their lifestyle. But as long as they keep it to themselves, I can live with it. Just don't flaunt it in my face, or teach my kids that it's all right."

Brenda smiled. "We live and work in a hell of a state to feel the way we do, don't we?"

Ted threw open the door, startling everybody. "Another body, gang. Let's roll!"

This one had been placed in a seat in the center of the auditorium of a local theater. The theater manager had discovered the body just before opening up for a Saturday matinee. The opening was going to be delayed for a while.

The Ripper was developing a very macabre sense of humor. The feature movie for that weekend was the updated version of *Jack the Ripper;* a soft drink container had been fitted into one stiff hand, a box of popcorn in the other. The victim had been skinned. It was Carla Upton.

"Very funny," Leo said. "Real neat touch on the Ripper's part."

"Get that horrible-looking body out of my theater!" the manager yelled, hopping from one foot to the other in the aisle. "I've already thrown up twice, for god's sake."

"Shut up," Leo told him. "I hear something." Then they all heard it. A very faint sound of bells. Tiny bells. "It's coming from the stage." He pointed a finger at the manager. "You stay here. Go count your money, or something"

"I demand to be allowed into this theater!" the shrill voice of Agnes Peters could be heard from the lobby. "You goddamn bullyboy! You fascist pig. Oppressor of the minorities."

"Lady," the cop's voice came to them. "Take a look at my face. If I got any blacker, I could star in Tarzan movies. Don't accuse me of oppressing the minorities."

"Big ugly ape!" Agnes yelled.

"My mammy thinks I'm cute."

"Gene Clark," Lani said to the group. "Agnes will never get past him."

"He's got a wild sense of humor," Ted said.

"Yeah," Lani said. "He got exasperated at his wife a couple of years ago. She couldn't decide what he should wear to a costume ball the sheriff's department was putting on for charity. He told her if she came home with one more costume from the rental shop, he was going to stick a broomhandle up his ass and go as a Fudgesicle."

Brenda could not contain her laughter, and even Ted chuckled. It was defensive laughter. Gallows humor. Something to ease the strain of a terrible job.

The humor faded as the cops stepped between the curtain and the screen. A young woman was hanging there—or what was left of her. The naked and mutilated body was hanging upside down. It was swaying gently in the rush of air from a big air-conditioning vent. Tiny little bells had been tied on each finger. As the body swayed, the bells tinkled. She had been skinned. But she was still recognizable. Sue Hale.

"Oh, hell!" the anguished voice of Gene Clark ripped the silence. "The bitch kneed me in the nuts. She's got a camera. Stop her."

The theater manager stepped in front of Agnes on the gently sloping aisle and Agnes ran slap over him, knocking him sprawling, rolling ass over elbows down the aisle. A uniform grabbed at her, and she socked him with her purse.

She came to a halt at the floodlighted scene of what was left of Carla Upton. "Whoops!" Agnes said, then lost her lunch, the vomit spraying another uniform who had the misfortune to approach her.

"Jesus Christ, Lady!" he hollered, frantically backing up and digging in his pocket for a handkerchief.

"Fuck you, pig," Agnes said, whipping out her camera and taking a few shots of Carla.

The projectionist had come in through the back door and didn't have the foggiest notion what the hell was going on down on the floor. "Hey, Albert! Where are you?" he yelled to the manager, who was just then getting groggily to his feet, down near the stage. There was a big bump on his head where he'd impacted with several seat frames on his way down. "Let's see if that jerk fixed the curtains."

He hit the switch and the curtains parted.

What was left of Sue Hale swayed to the sound of tiny bells.

Agnes let out a squall that would have put Cochise to shame. Then she did a little dance in the aisle and passed out.

"Go get her camera," Leo said. "And break the goddamn thing." He walked to the edge of the stage and called for the manager. "You'd better post a notice at the box office. You're not going to be open this afternoon." There was no answer. Leo's eyes searched the cavernous interior. He finally found the manager, passed out cold on the floor.

The bells on Sue's fingers tinkled softly as she swayed.

"Sarge, you really want me to break this camera?" a uniform called from the floor.

"No. Just expose the film. She's gonna write about this, but at least she won't have pictures."

"She'll probably sue us," Lani said.

Leo looked at his partner and smiled. "She'll have to get in line, won't she?"

Dick Hale was quite mad. But like so many insane people, he possessed an uncanny ability for rationalization . . . in certain areas. He could function normally. He could survive and clean himself and prepare food. In other areas, he became more animal-like. Perhaps it is a throwback to a million years ago; perhaps we all retain some dark memory of that time, buried deep in some far reaches of our brain.

Dick had grown a beard and allowed his hair to become long. He had lost a great deal of weight. He looked and acted like a bum. Only someone who had known Dick Hale extremely well would have been able to recognize him in his current state. Dick Hale now lived in the shadow world of the homeless, and acted the part.

He had cached his weapons and ammunition in a safe place and carried only a small pistol with him when he ventured out of his resting place, to search for food near an abandoned city dump on the outskirts of La Barca. During the day he rested, at night he prowled.

Using a small portable radio he had stolen, Dick heard the news about his daughter. He did not care. He had heard on the same newscast about Carla Upton. He was delighted with that news. Reading a tossed-away newspaper, Dick learned that the Hancock County Sheriff's Department was being sued by dozens of parents and several reporters. The parents' children had suffered terrible traumas during the shoot-out at the old warehouses . . .

"Horseshit!" Dick said.

. . . and the reporters charged that they had been deliberately tear-gassed while doing their jobs.

"Horseshit!" Dick repeated.

Agnes Peters was going to sue the sheriff's department, charging police brutality and damage to her camera.

"Horseshit!" Dick said again. Then he smiled. Mad-

ness shone brightly in his eyes. A little bit of slobber
appeared at the corners of his mouth. He began grunting incomprehensively.

Even though the coppers (Dick was a great fan of
Bogart and Robinson gangster movies) were looking
for him, Dick held no special rancor for the bulls. But
he hated Agnes Peters, in the past often referring to
her as a dyke (she wasn't) bitch (she was).

Now Dick had a plan. He'd help the flatfeet. Yeah,
he could do that. He'd be one of the good guys.

Now if he could just remember where he hid his
shotgun.

Chapter 23

Those kids taken into custody knew very little about the leadership of the killing club. Sue Hale had been their go-between, and Sue had been forever silenced. And like the DJ back in Indiana, many of the kids were masochistic, enjoying both the giving and the receiving of pain. But these weren't tough street kids who operated under some code of silence; once one started blabbing, implicating others, those who had the finger pointed at them started pointing back. Two more pits were uncovered and that seemed to be all. But the death toll in and around La Barca had climbed to over two hundred men, women, and children.

"It's going to be years before this is over," Ted said. "The attorneys for each kid has asked for separate trials. Since some of the kids are fourteen and fifteen years old, there probably won't even be a trial for them."

"The latest will of Carla Upton is legal and will be upheld," Brenda said. "Those who witnessed it said she was not under any duress, and was perfectly lucid and rational at the time. Stacy Ryan is a very rich young woman."

"She is also a liar and probably a murderer and God

only knows what else," Leo said sourly. "The only problem is, we can't prove it."

"We've backtracked her previous statements, Leo," Lani said. "We don't have anything on her. She's clean."

"She's got to have slipped up somewhere," Leo muttered. "But she won't slip now. She's sure to know, or at least suspect, that we've got people on her like white on rice twenty-four hours a day. I just don't understand her. I first I thought she might be unknowingly manipulated by her brothers. But she lied when questioned about the Longwood name. The operator said it scared the crap out of her. She lied about having no knowledge of the new will. What the hell is her game?"

"Blood is thicker than water," Lani said softly.

"What do you mean?" Leo asked.

"What we talked about back in New York . . . seems like years ago, now."

"The supernatural, Lani? Aw, come on. I can't believe you're still hanging on to that ragged thread."

"No, I mean it, Leo. What's been happening is just too weird to explain away using normal terms. Look, we've about exhausted all other avenues, right? So why not take a walk down another path for a while?"

"I don't believe in any of that crap!" Ted's words came quickly.

"I do," Brenda spoke very softly.

Ted looked at her. "You can't be serious!"

"Why not? Look, it would take a closed mind not to admit that there is a lot of weird shit going on in this world that nobody can explain away. I used to date an airline pilot. He told me that he's seen stuff up in the sky that he didn't know what the hell it was or where it came from. A lot of pilots have seen weird stuff. The airlines made them all shut up about it. They don't even enter it in the logs anymore. And I know that for a cold fact. Back here on the ground, I've personally witnessed psychics work, leading us to dead bodies. It caused goose bumps to rise up on my flesh. Things that go bump in the night are real, Ted. They've been documented, photographed, and filmed in action too many times to shrug off."

"Nonsense!" Ted huffed.

"Screw you!" Brenda muttered.

"I looked up two words last night," Lani said. "Pure, and evil. Pure: absolute. Evil: the force in *nature* that governs and gives rise to wickedness and sin. And do any of you know what the very last definition of evil is?" She looked around as they all shook their heads. "Satan."

Leo did his best, but he could not suppress a shudder. Brenda rubbed at a sudden coldness on the back of her neck; her palms were clammy. Ted looked down at his bare forearms. They were covered with chill bumps.

"You remember the name of that psychic, Brenda?" Lani asked.

"I won't ever forget it. Anna Kokalis."

"What are we looking for?" Leo asked.

"I don't know," Lani admitted. "Let's talk to her and see if she will help us. What have we got to lose?"

"Credibility, for one thing," Ted said, but he knew he was outvoted in this matter.

Agnes Peters parked her BMW in her garage and walked back to close the garage door. Just as her foot slipped on a small spot of oil, throwing her off balance, a shotgun roared from the darkness beside the house. Had she not slipped, the buckshot that tore a hole in the garage wall would have blown her head off. Agnes screamed and made a dash for the door. The shotgun roared again, the buckshot blowing out the back window of her car. Agnes fumbled for the key to unlock the side door. The shotgun boomed again. The buckshot missed her, but it did tear the side mirror off of her car and send tiny bits of glass and metal in her direction. Several pieces of glass and metal came to a stop, when they impacted and penetrated about an inch into Agnes's butt.

"Yowee!" Agnes shrieked, just as she unlocked the door and fell tumbling into the kitchen.

The shotgun boomed again, and blew the glass panels out of the side door. The glass and bits of wood sprayed Agnes just as she was crawling to her feet, putting several small cuts on one cheek. Agnes thought she was mortally wounded, she let out a squall that sounded very much like an angry grizzly and took off at a run for her bedroom.

Naturally, since Agnes believed in the confiscation of all privately owned firearms—except those in the hands of certain selected, highly intelligent, morally responsible, and very elitist people, such as herself—she owned a pistol. A big pistol. A Dirty Harry special. Which she had never fired. She ran to her bedroom, snatched up the .44 mag from her nightstand, assumed a two-handed shooting position, just like in the movies, pointed the muzzle in the general direction of the garage, and pulled the trigger.

The recoil numbed Agnes's arms from hands to elbows and knocked her flat on her butt on the carpet. The slug, traveling at about the same speed as an F–16 with afterburners roaring, rocketed down the hall, through the open side door, through a garage window, right through the house next door, and came to rest in the tiled shower stall of the home at the end of the block. Agnes got to her feet and fired four more times.

She ruined a mixer in her kitchen, a microwave in the house next door, an outboard motor in another garage across the street, and blew out the side window, tore off the rear-view mirror, and punched a hole in the windshield of the car that was passing by, which happened to belong to a local Baptist minister.

"Jesus fucking Mary!" the minister hollered, momentarily reverting to his teenage years in St. Louis. He floored the pedal and ran up into the lawn of another homeowner, who had stepped out onto his porch to see what all the shooting was about. The homeowner had just enough time to leap for his life as the now out of control Toyota climbed the porch and entered his living room, coming to rest in his dining room.

"Son of a bitch!" the minister said.

Agnes, knocked against the wall of her bedroom by the recoil of the powerful handgun, was deaf as a post for several minutes, and her arms were numb clear up to her neck.

"Call the goddamn cops!" she squalled, putting such volume behind the words that the homeowner across the street, who was crawling out of the bushes by the side of the house, could plainly hear the plea.

But a patrolling unit from the La Barca PD had heard the shots and was pulling up just about the time Agnes, still clutching the .44 mag, staggered out onto her front porch.

"Drop the gun!" the officer yelled at her.

Agnes dropped the .44 mag. On her foot. Breaking two toes. "Don't shoot me, you pig son of a bitch!" she screamed at the confused officer. "I'm the one being shot at!" Agnes sat down on the steps, both hands holding her injured foot. "You goddamn ignorant ape!" she yelled at the cop, just as two more city units came screaming up.

Sgt. Gene Clark, who was working the second shift that week, jumped out and took a look at Agnes. "Oh, shit!" he muttered. He pointed to an officer. "You see what's wrong with her," he ordered.

"Thanks a lot," the cop said.

Agnes shifted position on the porch, putting weight on the shot-up cheek. She hollered and jumped to her feet. "I'm wounded, goddamn it! Call an ambulance!"

"Where?" Gene yelled.

"In my ass, you pig bastard!"

"Shot her right in the brains," Gene muttered.

"I heard that, you Gestapo son of a bitch!" Agnes shrieked. "I'll sue you!"

"Will somebody get this goddamn car out of my house!" the homeowner yelled.

By the time the police got everything sorted out, Dick Hale was long gone.

"I wish I could have seen it," Lani said to Leo the next morning. "I'd have given a hundred dollars to see Agnes Peters get shot in the ass."

"That's not the half of it," Brenda said, sitting down. "Sergeant Clark arrested her for possession of an unregistered handgun. Seems she didn't have a permit for it. Now she's screaming about living in a police state."

"She just can't seem to get her priorities in order," Leo said, unable to hide his glee at Agnes Peters getting shot in the ass.

"You think it was Dick Hale?" Ted asked the group.

"Oh, sure," Lani said. "He's hated Agnes for years. They've despised each other since high school."

"Too bad Dick can't stumble up on the Longwood boys with his trusty shotgun," Leo said wistfully.

"Don't let the press hear you say that," Brenda warned.

"Heaven forbid!" Leo looked upward. "Not those purveyors of truth and justice. As they see it," he added very drily.

"Don't let them hear you say that, either," Ted said.

The phone rang and Lani picked up. A second later she muttered, "Jesus!" and hit the record button on the cassette recorder attached to the phone. She listened without saying a word. She slowly replaced the phone in the cradle and rewound the tape. "Listen to this," she said.

The voice was electronically altered, and they could not tell if it was male or female. But the message pushing through the tiny speaker was very clear.

"The time has come to end this game.
To reach the summit of my fame.
The blood must flow and the screams be heard.
Now try to stop me, you pig-snout turds!"

A second voice was added. It said in a singsong voice: You'll hear from me again!"

They could all clearly hear the piano music playing in the background. It was "Mary Had A Little Lamb."

"So what do you propose we do?" Brownie asked, leaning back in his chair. "Declare martial law, call out the national guard, and order a dusk-to-dawn curfew?"

"That'd be the last thing I'd want," Lani said. "Even if it were possible. The Ripper would just pull back and wait us out."

"Stacy Ryan?" the sheriff asked.

"Calm and cool and making no bobbles. She gets

up, goes to work, has lunch at her desk, and goes home and stays," Brenda said. "Her phones are tapped at home and work. We've got people on her twenty-four hours a day. We know everything she does and much of what she says. She has made no calls from any pay phones. She has had no visitors at her home since surveillance began."

"The judge was very unhappy signing that phone-tap order," Brownie reminded the four cops. "We don't have one shred of court-admissible evidence against Stacy Ryan. If we don't have something concrete in a few days, he'll rescind that order." He held up his hand in advance of the vocal objections he knew were coming. "I'm just telling you all the way it is. I think Stacy Ryan is guilty as hell. I think she's involved in this mess up to her neck. Now go out and prove it."

Walking down the hall after leaving Brownie's office, Lani muttered, "Go out and prove it. What the hell's he think we've been trying to do all summer?"

"He's taking all the heat on this," Leo said. "The press is on his ass, the public is on his ass, the DA is on his ass, the governor is on his ass. I'm surprised Brownie hasn't lost his cool and punched someone."

"The attorney general is on our asses, too," Brenda said glumly.

"Hard!" Ted added. "After the chewing I got this morning from Sacramento, I'm just very thankful I still have the seat in my pants."

Brenda looked to see and Ted sighed.

"We can't sweat those kids any harder," Lani said. "Juvenile is pissed off now. Mommy and daddy's little darlings have been complaining about the interrogations. Their attorneys said we've got all we're going to get from them."

"Yeah," Leo said. "Because of their tender age, the

DA is cutting deals left and right. Some of those little monsters will be back on the street in two to three years. What am I saying? Hell, *some* of them are back on the streets *now!*"

But if Dick Hale had his way, they wouldn't be for long.

Chapter 24

"Monstrous!" Dick said, reading the day-old newspaper he'd found in the street. He wadded it up and tossed it aside. "There is no justice in this world." He slobbered for a moment, then picked his nose, and farted.

Dick picked up the ragged, old, discarded topcoat he'd found, and took out his knife, cutting away a few threads that lingered after his tailoring job. The back of the coat would be perfect for what he had in mind. Part of one sleeve would do nicely, too. He'd already fashioned that. He'd found a pair of long-handled underwear amid the trash at a newer landfill, and carefully washed and dried them. He'd found a pair of boots and repaired them with some strips of leather shoelaces. Dick was going to bring justice back into society. He'd by God show everybody what he was made of! He'd become a legend that people would be talking about for years to come.

Yeah, but not quite like Dick imagined in his sick mind.

"We know you didn't have anything to do with those terrible crimes," the mother said to her son at the dinner table.

"Of course, I didn't," the lying, little, beady-eyed zit-head replied smoothly. "I just wanted to be with my friends."

"That's only natural," the father said.

"The cops beat me every day I was in jail," the prick said. "And they tried to make me have oral sex with them, too. They're really terrible people."

"We know," mommy cooed. "And we're going to sue them for that. Our attorney says you'll be rich." Translation: *we'll* be rich, and the attorney will be richer.

Tommy Williams had taken an active part in a dozen of the torture/murders/rapes. He'd been a leader of one of the youth cells. He had planned and taken part in the kidnapping of many of the victims. Tommy Williams had begun his career of perversion and evil as a very young child, torturing dogs and cats and birds. That had been called to the attention of his parents, but, of course, they didn't believe a word of it. Naturally. Mommy and daddy's precious, little, perfect darling would never, ever, do anything like that.

How could they be so sure? Why, they asked him.

Mr. and Mrs. Williams did not see the dark shape slipping silently into their backyard. A rather peculiarly dressed shape, wearing an eye mask and a cape over long-handled underwear and flat-heeled boots.

Mommy and daddy left to go to the club for drinks and dancing, and Tommy was alone in the house. He was under court order not to leave the premises, and he had enough sense to obey that order. He wandered aimlessly from room to room. He put heavy metal on his stereo and turned the volume up to an ear-splitting level. "Stupid goddamn cops," Dick Hale heard him mutter, just before the sounds of shrieking and howling and banging and thumping filled the night air and caused neighbors to wince in annoyance and dogs to howl.

"Turn down that damn racket!" a neighbor hollered over the fence.

"Fuck you!" Tommy shouted. Such a polite, young man. Very respectful to his elders and so considerate of the rights of others.

"I'll call the cops!" the neighbor shouted.

"You do and I'll poison your dogs!" Tommy yelled.

The neighbor knew the punk would do just that. He'd poisoned other dogs in the neighborhood, when people had complained about the music. The man closed up his house, flipped on the air-conditioning, and turned up the volume on the TV. For the thousandth time, he wished Tommy Williams would fall off the edge of the world and burn forever in the pits of hell. He would get at least part of his wish that evening.

Tommy Williams walked back to his bedroom and opened all the windows and turned up the volume just as loud as his speakers could take. He smiled an evil upturning of the lips, as he walked back to the den. Tommy opened the sliding glass doors and looked out. He blinked and stared.

"What the fuck?" he said, and stepped out into the lawn. "Hey, you!" he shouted. "You with the cape! What the hell do you want?"

"Justice," the caped figure said.

"Justice?"

"That's what I said. Are you deaf from listening to that crap you call music?"

"Hey man, go screw yourself, you goofy-lookin' bastard. And get off this property."

"No."

"I ain't believin' this shit," Tommy muttered. "How come all the nuts move into this neighborhood."

The area would soon be minus one.

"You're a murdering piece of trash," the caped and masked figure said.

"Yeah? Well, the cops couldn't prove it, and neither can you. So haul your ass on out of here."

That was the last thing Tommy Williams ever said on the face of this earth. Tommy would murder and torture no more humans, no more animals, and he would never again annoy his neighbors with loud music. The caped figure lifted a shotgun and blew Tommy's head all over the sliding-glass doors. The music was so loud, the shotgun blasts could not be heard over the grunting and groaning of the singers and crashing of cymbals and the roar of guitars.

The caped man stepped into the house and walked toward the source of the music. He stood in the doorway and blew the offending stereo into a jumble of pieces.

"Thank you, thank you, thank you!" a neighbor hollered.

"You're welcome," the caped and masked man muttered, then walked out the back door, stepping over the headless body of Tommy Williams. He paused for a moment, looking down at the body, unaware that several neighbors were staring out their windows, wondering what had happened to bless them with such quiet. "Punk," the man said, then walked on.

"The woman over there said it was Batman," Gene Clark told Leo, pointing.

"The neighbor across the street said it looked like Zorro to her," another uniform said.

"The kid on the other side of the house swears it was Flash Gordon," a deputy said.

"Oh, hell, it was Dick Hale," Leo said. "The fool has gone completely around the bend."

Lani looked down at the blanket-covered body of the headless Tommy Williams. "There is justice in the world after all," she whispered, careful that the sobbing mother and father holding on to each other in the den would not hear her words.

"Yeah," Gene Clark said. "This was one sorry punk."

"Easy," Brenda said. "Agnes Peters just drove up."

"Somebody be sure to ask her if her ass is healing nicely," Leo said with a smile.

None of the cops present could work up even a modicum of sorrow for the kid sprawled in death at their feet. Tommy Williams had been giving the La Barca PD and the Hancock County Sheriff's Department headaches for years. But being a semiprecious juvenile, he had to be handled with kid gloves. Up until now.

"Oh, my baby!" Mrs. Williams squalled. "Why? He was such a good boy."

"Excuse me while I look for a place to puke," Sergeant Clark said, upon hearing those words.

Mr. Williams stepped to the glass doors and pointed a trembling finger at the knot of cops on the patio. "You goddamn cops better find out who did this," he threatened.

A neighbor, who was standing on his own property, peering over the five-foot-high security fence, said, "Goddamn punk finally got what was coming to him."

"What a terrible thing to say at a time like this!" Agnes Peters hollered from the side of the house, standing behind the yellow and black CRIME SCENE—DO NOT CROSS tape.

"Why?" the neighbor questioned. "It's the truth.

You should try the truth sometime, *Ms.* Peters. It would be a refreshing change."

"I'll whip your ass, Beeson!" Mr. Williams shouted.

"Come on," the neighbor said.

"How dare you say that to me!" Agnes hollered.

"How's your ass, Agnes?" Lani asked.

"You can't say those things about my boy, Beeson!" Mr. Williams screamed.

"I just did, Williams," the neighbor said quietly. "And I don't apologize for it."

"Shut up," Leo warned, pointing at the man. "No matter what you thought of the kid, can the nasty remarks for now."

"Your ass is mine, Beeson!" Mr. Williams shouted.

"I doubt it," Beeson said, and stepped back into his own house.

"I'll kill that no-good rotten son of a bitch!" Mr. Williams said.

"Just remember that a half-dozen cops heard you say that," Lani reminded him.

Someone else heard him say it, too.

Every cop working the case felt that Stacy Ryan was guilty as hell. But no one could prove it, and Stacy Ryan was staying squeaky clean. No one challenged Carla Upton's will, and Stacy was now legally a rich, young woman.

Sensing that public opinion was running high against the young people involved in the hideous torture/murders, and the majority of the public would not tolerate them making a martyr of the dickhead, the press played down the killing of Tommy Williams . . . instead of their usual weeping and sobbing and hanky-stomping. Even Agnes Peters decided not to write about the killing.

But all that was about to change.

The teenagers (all minors) who had been freed from jail, met secretly the morning after Tommy Williams was killed and came to the conclusion that someone was stalking them and that their lives were in danger. They called their attorneys, and the lawyers asked for a meeting with the chief of police of La Barca and with Sheriff Brownwood.

Brownie was the first to speak after hearing the astonishing request. "Get out of my goddamn office!" he angrily told the group of attorneys.

The chief of police grabbed a fistful of one attorney's shirt and tie and drew back his right fist, about two seconds away from popping him, when a deputy wisely grabbed his arm and pulled him away.

"It's a legitimate request, Sheriff," a lawyer said. "The young people are in danger. They're being stalked."

Brownie almost said that he hoped the stalker got every one of them, but he bit that off short of speech. "There is no goddamn way this office is going to provide security for that pack of savages!"

"Ditto for my office!" the chief of police said.

"Then you leave us no alternative, but to seek a court order forcing you to do so," another attorney told the top lawmen of city and county.

That did it for the chief. He lost his cool and wrapped both big hands around the neck of the attorney and starting choking him and shaking him like a doll. Brownie, the deputy, and the assistant chief of police finally separated the two men, and when the lawyer caught his breath, he predictably yelled, "I'll sue you!"

The chief of police balled one hand into a huge fist and knocked the attorney right through Brownie's office door.

While that was going on, Williams's neighbor, Mr. Beeson, an insurance agent, was driving out into the country to see a prospective new client. He was found around four o'clock that afternoon, shot four times in the back of the head with a .357 mag.

Mr. Williams was immediately picked up for questioning.

"I was alone, driving around, trying to clear my head," Williams said. "My son was *killed* last night, you bastards! This is a very trying time for me and my wife."

La Barca homicide detectives tossed the Williams home and found a stainless steel .357 mag.

"That isn't mine!" Williams said. "I don't own a gun."

"Test his hands," the chief said, after meeting with Leo and Lani. "This thing stinks like a setup."

Tests proved that Mr. Williams had not fired any type of gun that day.

"Try to recall who was in the crowd last night," Lani asked all the cops who had been present at the Williams home. "Somebody heard Williams threaten Beeson."

"There must have been several hundred people who eventually gathered around there," Ted said. "We had to block off the street to traffic, remember? And Williams was shouting when he threatened Beeson."

"Okay," Leo said wearily. "We reconstruct the scene. Try to remember everybody you saw at the Williams home. Don't leave out anyone just because they're a cop, an EMT, a doctor, a minister, a respected member of the community, or a friend. Let's meet back here in the morning."

* * *

"Ten possibilities," Brenda said. "Two of the kids there used to buddy with some of those kids we arrested. Seven people who have kids arrested were present, and one Patricia Sessions."

"That name is familiar," Ted said.

"She's a salesperson out at KSIN TV."

"She live close by?"

"She lives clear across town."

Det. Bill Bourne, who had left the La Barca PD to work for the sheriff's department, slowly raised his head. "Wait a minute. Hold it. Why does that name ring a bell with me? Give me a second, folks." He got up and walked around the room for several minutes. Then he snapped his fingers. "Got it! My wife saw them at the airport in L.A. Last year. Alice had taken a commuter flight down to visit her sister. They were boarding a plane to Mexico. All three of them, together."

"All three?" Brenda said. "Who?"

"Carla Upton, Patricia Sessions, and Stacy Ryan."

"Now let's go visit the arches and get some food to

Chapter 25

Before they could react, the phone rang. The psychic, Anna Kokalis, had arrived.

"Show her in," Lani said.

Brenda had deliberately not told Ted much about Anna, and she was amused at the expression on his face when the woman walked in. Anna was in her early thirties, very petite, very shapely, and very pretty. Her hair was as black as a raven's wing, and her skin was smooth and flawless. Her eyes were gray, and slightly Slavic-appearing. She was introduced all around.

"Nice to see you again, Lani," Anna said. She had a very soft voice.

Leo took one look at the expression on Ted's face and winked at Lani. Ted was smitten—hard.

"We've got a bit of a problem here, Anna," Brenda said.

Anna's smile was sad. "You have more than that, and you know it. You would not have contacted me, if you felt any other way."

"I'm the one who convinced the others to bring you in," Lani said.

"I know," the woman replied.

Lani wisely decided not to pursue that. She really wasn't sure she wanted to know how Anna knew. "I alone am firmly convinced that something . . . well, beyond the normal is at work here."

"The supernatural?" Anna asked.

"That or something very close to it. Let us walk you through this thing, starting with what Leo and I found out in New York State."

Anna sat for twenty minutes, listening to the detectives retrace their steps. She asked no questions until the four cops had finished.

"You're convinced the Longwood mansion is evil?"

"I am," Lani said. "I can't speak for Leo."

Anna looked at Leo. His only reply was a shrug of his shoulders. She looked first at Brenda, then at Ted.

"We haven't been to the mansion," Brenda said.

Anna stood up. "I need to visit the ruins of the country home that blew up."

"There's nothing there except rubble," Brenda told her.

"Oh, yes, there is," Anna said mysteriously. "It isn't visible. But it's there."

Sitting inside the rusting hulk of an ancient vehicle he was now calling home, Dick Hale cleaned his shotgun and then carefully brushed his cape. He had chosen the next person to bring to justice.

The story of the subliminal messages had leaked out, and the DJs at KSIN were understandably edgy, knowing they were all under suspicion. To a person, they maintained a high visibility when not on the air. It was an unnecessary move on their part, for the police had taken them off the suspect list—all but one of them. And Stacy Ryan was being very careful in everything she did. However, she did smile a lot. Cathy Young had taken over Stacy's slot on the air and was doing a good job.

A judge had taken under advisement a motion for the cops to provide around-the-clock protection for those young people arrested in connection with the killing-club murders and released to the custody of their parents. The whole idea was very repugnant to the judge.

Citizens of La Barca and Hancock County had extra locks put on their doors, many had armed themselves, and nearly everybody had become very cautious when outside their homes. Armed citizens stood guard around the city's parks and playgrounds, and the police were under orders not to attempt to seize privately owned weapons. That, of course, did not set too well with those who belonged to groups whose main focus in life was to disarm American citizens. But after the second person got his jaw broken by the butt of a rifle (it's called being butt-stroked), those types wisely decided to keep their mouths shut and stay faraway from those men and women who had armed themselves solely to protect their kids.

And Agnes Peters's ass was healing nicely.

"Monumental evil," Anna Kokalis finally spoke, standing amid the rubble of the blown-apart country home. She turned and walked quickly back to the road, the investigators right behind her.

"Well?" Lani asked.

"I . . . don't know," the psychic admitted. "I've never experienced a feeling quite like it. All murderers and rapists and kidnappers and others of that ilk are evil to some degree. But the evil I experienced here is . . . different. It's . . . indescribable. I don't know what to say."

"Pure?" Lani prompted.

Anna looked at her. "Yes," she said slowly. "That

would describe it. Pure evil. But supernatural?" She shook her head. "I don't know. I have tried all my life to not venture into that area. People like myself . . . we have to be careful. So many times we stand so close to the edge. I don't know how to put it any other way."

"Anna," Brenda said. "You don't have to do this. You can turn right around and go back home."

The woman shook her head. "No. I'll help. But I want to speak with a priest this evening. I must. It's important that I do."

"I'll be happy to escort you," Ted said quickly.

She smiled at him. "Thank you. I accept your offer."

As they walked to the cars, Ted gave Brenda a very dirty look. She was whistling, off-key, music from South Pacific: "Some Enchanting Evening."

Cecil Harrison sat in the backyard of his parents' home and stared out at the gathering darkness. His thoughts were darker than the growing night. He missed the weekly meetings of the killing club. He missed the screaming of the tortured. He missed the heady feeling of power, when he raped and sodomized the screaming unwilling victim of perversion . . . male or female; it hadn't made a bit of difference to Cecil. He missed the smell of blood. The sixteen-year-old grew conscious of someone staring at him from over a security fence. Pat Judson, the turdy next-door neighbor who had started a petition to get Cecil placed in a mental institution, a boys' home, back in jail, some-where, *anywhere* other than this neighborhood.

"What are you starin' at, you puke-faced son of a bitch?" Cecil snarled at the man.

"A rotten, evil punk," Pat bluntly told the young man.

Cecil's father rushed out of the house. "Hey, Judson!" he shouted. "You don't talk to my boy that way."

"I'll talk to that piece of shit anyway I like, Harrison," the neighbor stood his ground. "And I've got a right to do just that."

"Goddamnit, Judson, the boy apologized for killing your stupid dog! Goddamn mutt barked too much anyway."

"It's what he did to my son that gives me the right, Harrison."

The father had no comeback for that. Although it had never been conclusively proven that his son forced the little boy next door to have oral sex with him—it was one kid's word against the other—the father knew in his heart it was true. But how do you not stand up for your kid? "The courts will sort all this out, Judson."

"How does that repair the mental scars that my boy will carry for the rest of his life, Harrison?"

"Give it a rest, Judson," the father said wearily. "Just get off my boy's back."

"I want that worthless piece of garbage in prison, and I'll not rest until I see him there," Judson vowed.

"Come on in the house, boy," the father urged.

"I like it here," the punk said. "Fuck-face over there don't bother me none."

"Dinner's ready, honey," Judson's wife called from the back door.

Cecil Harrison's father looked at his son, shook his head, and walked back into his own house, his back stiff with anger. He stopped for a moment, staring at the Judson home. It had been a very nice dog; didn't bark any more than other dogs. He sighed. Hell, Pat was a nice guy. He closed the sliding-glass door and shut the world out.

"And pull the drapes!" Cecil told his father. "I like the night."

"Right," the father said, holding back his own anger. He fought away the urge to pick up a poker from the fireplace and beat his son's head in with it. He pulled the drapes closed, thinking: where did the wife and I go wrong? Cecil's older brother and sister turned out great. The last chick in the nest turned out . . . shit sorry, the father concluded. Boy, the grief that you have brought your mother and me. But you don't care about that, you miserable, selfish, evil, little bastard. He locked the sliding-glass doors. "Get your coat, Helen," he called to his wife. "Let's go see a movie."

"What about Cecil?" she asked.

"Fuck Cecil!" the disgusted father said.

Cecil heard his parents leave the house and drive off. Just as the sound of the car faded, his eyes caught the movement of a dark shape, slipping silently outside the fence. A strange-looking figure, almost comical, the cape billowing out behind him. But the shotgun made the scene very real and menacing. Cecil stared at the funny-looking shape and knew instantly what it represented. Cecil felt fear clutch at him. This time Cecil didn't have the upper hand. He jumped for the sliding-glass doors. Locked.

"Shit!" the punk whispered.

"Justice," the dark figure behind the fence called.

"Hey, man!" Cecil called, panic in his voice. "I got rights."

Pat Judson heard the commotion and stepped out onto his patio. He saw the man in the cape and mask outside the Harrisons' fence. He smiled. He could practically feel the panic welling up in Cecil.

"Hey, man!" Cecil called to his neighbor, standing in the light from his den. "Call the cops, man! That nut's here with a gun!"

"There is justice in this world after all," Pat Judson said, then turned and walked back into his house, closing the doors and pulling the drapes.

Cecil ran to the edge of the house and tried the gate. Locked. "Goddamnit!" he shouted. He looked up, the man and wife living in the house on the other side were staring out of the kitchen window at him. They were smiling. Cecil had poisoned their cats and dogs, too. "Call the cops, damn you!" he screamed. The man reached up and lowered the kitchen blind.

Cecil turned and had just a few seconds in which to ask the Lord's forgiveness for all the hurt and degradation he had caused in his years. He chose not to do that. "Fuck you!" he screamed at the masked and caped man.

Dick leveled the twelve-gauge shotgun, loaded with three-inch double-ought buckshot, and pulled the trigger. Cecil's head exploded in a gush of blood and brains and bits of bone.

"What was that?" Pat Judson's wife asked.

"Justice," her husband replied. "Pass the mashed potatoes, please."

CAPED AVENGER STRIKES AGAIN, the morning headlines silently screamed.

"Caped avenger," Leo said. "Good god."

"If none of the neighbors saw anything," Ted said, "how does this reporter know it's the same person?"

"They don't," Lani said. "But it sells newspapers."

"You can bet several of the neighbors saw something," Brenda said. "I pulled Cecil's file. He's poisoned dogs and cats all up and down that block; and that's just for starters."

"We know all about Cecil Harrison," Leo said. "Just like that punk Tommy Williams, Cecil Harrison was well known to every cop in the city and county."

Sheriff Brownwood stuck his head into the room. "The judge just ruled, boys and girls. We have to provide around-the-clock protection for the remainder of those out on bail and/or in the custody of their parents."

Lani hurled her coffee cup against the wall. "Goddamnit!" she yelled, summing up the feelings of every cop in the county and every cop in the country who had been following the case.

Leo asked Ted to work with Anna Kokalis and naturally Ted accepted. Since Leo still wasn't sure exactly what Anna was going to do, if anything, that left him and Lani and Brenda to do some more old-fashioned police work. Like wearing out shoe leather.

Of the fifty-odd teenagers arrested at the warehouses, about half of them had been released to their parents. Guarding twenty or so people, around-the-clock, was going to put a terrible strain on the manpower of the PD and the sheriff's department. Brownie laid it on the line to the judge.

"We just don't have the people to do it. It's going to take over sixty officers to do it. We can't do it and still give law-abiding citizens the protection they're paying for."

"You'll find a way."

Brownie smiled, sort of, at the judge. It was very similar to the smile a mongoose gives a cobra. "Now, Brownie," the judge said.

"The public is not going to like this decision of yours, Homer. And if you think I'm going to take the heat for pulling all those officers off the street to guard a bunch of goddamn, sorry-assed, worthless punks, you'd better think again."

"You don't threaten me, Brownie!" the judge warned.

"Oh, I'm not threatening you, Judge. I'm just telling you the way it is."

"Brownie, those kids have not yet been convicted of anything. They still deserve protection, just like any other citizen. I shouldn't have to tell you that."

"Oh, I know the law, Homer. Look, ask the governor to call out the National Guard. Ask him to send the Highway Patrol in here. Do something . . . *anything!* But don't lay all this strain on us. Even if we *could* do it, it would bankrupt the city and county in overtime pay."

The judge held up a hand. "All right, Brownie. All right. We'll work it out. I'll hold this order until I can get you some help. *If* I can get you some help. And there are no guarantees of that."

"Thank you, Homer."

"You're welcome, Brownie." The judge smiled. "You can be a real horse's ass at times, you know that?"

"Homer, you don't have any idea just how much of a horse's ass I can be." Brownie walked to the door of the judge's chambers. The judge's voice stopped him.

"Brownie, did you really bring in a psychic?"

"One of the CBI people did, yes."

"So it's come to that?"

"Homer, I'd solicit the help of the devil, if I thought it would help bring this case to an end."

Brownie had no way of knowing just how close he was to doing just that.

Chapter 26

A massive manhunt was undertaken to find Dick Hale. But after the second punk was shotgunned, Dick had anticipated that and shifted his base of operations. With a smile, he moved back into his home, located in the most exclusive neighborhood in La Barca. With his kids dead and his wife a babbling idiot and not likely to ever recover, the police had sealed the house. But Dick knew where the hide-out key to the basement was located, and entry was easy. Once he gathered up food, clothes, underwear, and toilet articles from upstairs, he never went back to the main part of the house again. The windowless basement had been turned into a game room and office, with toilet and shower, so Dick had all the amenities of home . . . so to speak. He showered and trimmed his beard and ate a quiet meal. Then he cleaned his shotgun, while his cape and longhandles were in the washing machine. He had his next victim all picked out. He would strike that night. And this time he wouldn't botch the job.

The airlines had no record of Stacy, Carla, and Patricia ever flying off to Mexico. The trio had obviously booked seats under assumed names. Another lead that fizzled out.

Agnes Peters ended her silence about the cops with a blistering article in the morning paper, reducing the capability of the La Barca PD and the Hancock County Sheriff's Department to the level of the Keystone Cops, Abbot and Costello, and Larry, Curly, and Moe. She had learned about Anna Kokalis and wondered if the cops were going to bring in a witch doctor next. They might as well, she concluded, since all the cops seem to be capable of doing was stumbling around and tripping over their big, flat feet.

"She's such a lovely person," Leo said, carefully folding the paper.

"She is in grave danger," Anna said somberly.

"Good," Lani said.

"I'm serious," Anna said.

"So am I," Lani replied, just as seriously.

"She's going to be killed," Anna said.

That got everybody's attention. "How do you know that, Anna?" Ted asked.

"I can't explain it in a way that you would understand. But the woman is in terrible danger."

"I have this mental picture of us going to Agnes and telling her our resident psychic feels that she is in danger," Leo said. "With all due respect to you, Anna."

Anna smiled. "I know. And I'm not right all the time. But this time the thrust was very strong."

"The thrust?" Ted asked.

Lani pushed back her chair and stood up. "I'll go see the bitch and warn her. But I won't mention Anna."

"I'll go with you," Brenda said.

"Good luck," Leo said.

* * *

"And just how do you know this?" Agnes said, leaning back in her chair and glaring at the women.

"Dick tried once before," Brenda said. "And you've been writing about him in your articles. It just adds up, Ms. Peters."

"I have a legal firearm now," Agnes said. "And a permit to carry it. I've been taking shooting lessons out at the range. If there is a next time, I'll be ready. And I'll plug that silly son of a bitch."

"I thought you were opposed to handguns, Agnes?" Lani just had to say it.

"Get out of my office!"

"With pleasure," Lani said.

"You did warn her about the possible danger?" Brownie asked the women.

"Oh, yes," Lani told her. "And we made sure the door to her office was open and coworkers heard it."

"Then we're clear. If Agnes chooses to ignore our warnings, that's her business. I just want to be sure we don't have any comebacks on this thing."

"How about the guarding of the dip-shits?" Brenda asked.

"Highway Patrol is sending some people in, along with personnel from other city and county departments. I'll still have to pull some people off the road, but not enough to cripple the department. How's the tie-in with Pat Sessions going?"

"It isn't. We're at another dead-end."

"What else is new?" Brownie said drily. "I've got a meeting with the tourist board this afternoon. They're bitching about all the money the town is losing because of the Ripper."

"Have fun," Lani told him.

Lani and Leo, Brenda and Ted, and Bill Bourne spent the rest of that day going over the statements taken from the young people in the hopes that they had missed something, *anything,* that might bring them a step closer to the identity, or identities, of the Ripper. But any clues they did not already have had died with Dick's kids.

Weeks back, the investigators had been given their own private office. Now that office was filled with boxes of files. There was scarcely room for them to move around.

A car had been provided for Anna to drive around in . . . alone. That was her request, even though the cops had tried to dissuade her from doing that, since she had been publicly named in Agnes Peters's column. Bill Bourne was tagging along behind Anna.

"She's a wonderful person," Ted said. "But my, she certainly is headstrong. It really surprised me when she said she was very proficient in the martial arts."

"Did she say what form of martial art?" Lani asked.

Ted shook his head. "I didn't ask." He cut his eyes to Leo. "You haven't said a word in quite awhile, Leo. What are you thinking?"

"Just wondering when the Ripper is going to strike again."

"Or Dick Hale," Brenda said. "AKA the Caped Avenger."

"Dick is concentrating on the released little monsters . . . and Agnes Peters. Now that the darling, little sweethearts are under around-the-clock protection, I figure Dick will go after Agnes again. Then go after the kids."

Lani looked at him. "Leo, you're not thinking of *us* protecting Ms. Liberal Cop Hater, are you?"

He shook his head. "No. Not at all. She was offered

protection; she turned it down. If she wants to trust her .44 mag to do the job, that's fine with me."

"Something's eating at you," his partner persisted.

"I don't like to be played with," Leo said, his eyes narrowing. "The Ripper is playing with us. He, she, or it, threatens my family. Then nothing happens. And it isn't the security around them that's stopping him, them. The Longwood boys are wealthy enough to be able to buy any sort of weaponry or to hire killers. All they had to do was order some of those kids to attack and they would have, even knowing it would be suicide. They're playing with us. The Ripper calls in a little poem challenging us to stop them, then he does nothing. The whole thing is an evil, perverted game to him, them. The Ripper knows we're all running around, banging our heads against brick walls, getting more frustrated every day. And the Longwood boys are loving every minute of it."

"Finish it, Leo," Lani said, a flatness to her voice.

"I was in the service with a guy who went to work for the CIA right after he got out. Operations. He was station chief and then promoted and now works out of Langley. We keep in touch. I saved his life in Vietnam. Twice. He owes me. The Longwood boys went to court to get a new name. I want that name. Vince can get it. He knows the right buttons to push in Washington."

Ted shook his head. "I don't even want to know about this. Any time the CIA gets involved, you can bet they're going to want something in return."

Leo grinned. "Friend, that's another way that Vince owes me. I've been helping the Agency in various ways for years."

Ted's mouth dropped open. "But the CIA can't work inside the borders of the United States. That's the law! If your friend did find out what name the

Longwood boys are now using, it would not be admissible in court, because it was obtained illegally."

Leo laughed. "Ted, you don't really think this case is going to court, do you? The Longwood boys are not going to be taken alive. They'll die right here in Hancock County. They've played out their string, and they know it. And what's worse, when they die, not a damn one of those young monsters we arrested will ever be convicted. They'll walk. Every goddamn one of them. Unless Dick gets them."

"But they're guarded twenty-four hours a day now," Ted said. Ted really believed in the judicial system. He still had enough naivete in him to think it worked. Sometimes it does. But not often enough.

Lani smiled. "That won't stop Dick. Ted, you don't really believe those cops are going to risk their lives protecting that pack of perverted, evil horrors, do you? Many of them probably helped torture and mutilate Tony Moreno. They're going to be on guard . . . loosely speaking."

Ted rose from his chair and walked to a window. He stared out for a moment. Without turning around, he said, "Brenda, do you agree with what Lani just said?"

"Yes," the woman replied.

Ted whirled around. "Then God help us all. For if we all believed that, then the judicial system would be nothing but an ugly, profane joke."

"That's exactly what it is, Ted," Lani said. "Haven't you figured that out yet?"

"You can't believe that!"

"Ted," Leo said softly. "Wake up and smell the coffee. Punks toss concrete blocks off of overpasses and kill and injure people. If they go to prison at all, they're out in a few years. Rapists spend a couple of years in the bucket on an average. Murderers spend about seven years. If a citizen uses a gun to defend life, loved ones, or personal property, there is a good chance that citizen will go to jail and/or face civil trial. A lot of states allow their officers to put people in jail for minor traffic violations, while allowing known drug dealers and others of their ilk to walk free. A person with an expired driver's license or expired inspection sticker sometimes gets harsher treatment in the courts than a mugger. Money talks and bullshit walks, Ted." Leo smiled. "You know why, after all the years on this force, I'm not a lieutenant? I'll tell you: I'll nail anybody, Ted. I don't care who they are or what their social standing is in the community. I gave one of Dennis Potter's kids a ticket, while I was uniform. Unknown to Dennis, the kid went to the DA and the DA fixed it. When Dennis learned about it, he took the kid's car away and sold it. The son of one of the richest men in California walked for a year. But that's the exception, not the rule. I've stepped on toes all over this county, and I'll continue to do it as long as I wear a badge. I've made a lot of enemies, Ted, and I'll retire a sergeant. Brownie's a good man, but he's still a politician." Leo chuckled. "You know why Brownie assigned me to this case? Because he knows that I'll bend the law to solve it. And so will Lani. I'm not nearly so keen on law and order, Ted, as I am in justice. You keep a cold gun, Ted?"

"Certainly not!" Ted said, indignantly.

"I do. I have a whole box of them at home, very carefully hidden. I always keep one in my unit. There are at least six people in this county walking free and working and paying taxes and obeying the law and being productive citizens right now, who owe it all to me . . . and my cold pistols. You see, I'm flawed, Ted. I believe strongly in the right of a person to be safe and secure in their homes and papers and possessions. And Brownie knows this."

Ted was astonished. "Are you saying that you've planted cold guns on dead suspects?"

Leo and Lani would only smile.

Ted looked at Lani. "And you? You go along with that?"

"I believe in justice," she replied.

Ted turned around and once more stared out of the window. "What you both are saying is that you will do anything, *anything,* to close this case. You have no plans to bring the Longwood boys into custody, do you? You plan to hunt them down and kill them, don't you?"

Ted didn't really expect an answer, and that is exactly what he got. After a long moment of silence, he turned to look at Brenda. "You go along with them, don't you?"

She met his eyes with an unwavering stare.

"My God!" Ted said. "What happened to honor and decency in this country?"

"What happened to justice for all the innocent?" Brenda challenged.

Ted's shoulders sagged as hard reality settled heavily on him. The blindfolded lady holding the scales of justice lifted her robes and shit all over him.

"You're a good investigator, Ted," Brenda said. "But you'd better put all that prep school crap out of your head. Welcome to the real world."

"I feel dirty," Ted said softly.

"Sure, you do," Lani told him. "We all do. Every cop does. For Christ's sake, Ted, we deal with the scum of the earth. We wallow and wade in the gore left behind by people who are walking advertisements for the justification of abortion. Nobody can play with shit without getting some on them. And you never really wash it all off, Ted. It clings to you."

Ted nodded his head. "I should have guessed it;

should have put it all together long before this. I've
read your files. Both of you. Both of you have been
involved in some pretty damn dubious shootings, yet
you always come out smelling like a room full of roses.
Dirty Harry and Dirty Harriet. Boy, was I stupid!" He
looked at Brenda. "And you, you jumped at the
chance to work with these . . . hired guns. You practically tore down the boss's door to get assigned to this
case. You *knew* about these two. You knew all along,
didn't you?"

"I knew they were rated as two of the best investigators in the state, Ted. The top team for the past three
years."

"You want out, Ted?" Lani asked. "Just say the
word."

He shook his head. "If I did that, my career would
be on hold for the next twenty years."

"Then hang on and let's wrap up this case," Brenda
said.

"Hang on to shooting stars?" Ted said sarcastically.
"No play on words intended, of course."

Chapter 27

Agnes Peters slowed her car to a crawl and carefully eyeballed her street as she rolled along. No dogs were barking in alarm. Everything appeared normal. Except for the house across the street with the ruined front porch, clear plastic was hanging all over the place. That had been a wild night. The homeowner had popped the preacher on the snoot, and the preacher had then proceeded to beat the shit out of the homeowner before the cops could separate them. For a preacher, he sure knew some fancy cuss words. To Agnes's delight, the homeowner had kicked that pig sergeant, Gene Clark, right in the nuts.

Agnes pulled into her drive and hit the automatic garage door opener she'd had installed. The garage door slowly swung open and the lights came on. All clear. Agnes pulled into the garage and the door closed behind her.

"The door closed," Agnes muttered. "The door *closed!*" It wasn't programmed to do that. Agnes looked toward the door that led into the kitchen. It was open, ajar just a bit. "Oh, shit!" Agnes said. She jerked the gearshift lever to *R* and floorboarded the newly repaired BMW. Tires squealing and smoking on the concrete, she blasted through the garage door just as Dick, dressed in mask and cape and boots and longhandles, stepped out of the kitchen and leveled his shotgun.

Buckshot blew a very large hole in the windshield, showering Agnes with glass. The BMW careened out of the driveway and collided with a car that was passing by, knocking the second car up onto the sidewalk, taking a fire hydrant with it. The air was suddenly filled with water.

"You crazy, goddamn bitch!" the driver of the second car yelled at Agnes, whose own car engine had died upon impact.

"Fuck you!" Agnes yelled, grinding the starter.

The homeowner across the street, expecting any moment to see another car come crashing into his house, shooed his wife and kids into the backyard.

"I wouldn't fuck you with Godzilla's dick, you ugly bitch!" the irate motorist screamed.

The Caped Avenger stepped out of the garage and leveled his shotgun just as Agnes got her car started and floored the gas pedal. The stunned motorist ducked just in time, as the load meant for Agnes blew out his rear window. Dick pumped another round in and Agnes lost part of her trunk. The trunk lid banged open and Dick shot out a back tire. She lost control of the car, and it went up onto the sidewalk and into the front lawn of a man who had just paid a small fortune to have the front porch closed in and turned into a day room. Agnes reopened it. She not only reopened the porch, she drove right through the living room and into the dining room. But this time Agnes was mad clear through. She grabbed her .44 mag and two speed loaders and struggled out of the car, paying no attention to the screaming of the homeowner's wife and the homeowner's cussing. She ran stumbling and mumbling through the rubble, and stood on the now-open

porch and leveled the .44 mag at Dick, about a block
away. She didn't come within five feet of Dick, but she
sure raised hell with her next-door neighbor's house,
who, fortunately, had taken his family to see a movie.
When the family returned, they would find that Agnes
had plugged the TV set, the CD player, the answering
machine, the fax machine in the study, and gave the
family's cat the shits.

Dick gave her the finger and vanished, his cape
flowing behind him.

The first officer on the scene arrived about thirty
seconds after the echoes of the shooting had died
away. Sgt. Gene Clark.

"You!" Agnes hollered.

"Oh, Jesus!" Gene muttered. "Not again! Lady, you
are a goddamn menace with that hogleg, you know
that?"

"He went that way, you big ape!" Agnes squalled,
pointing. "Go catch him!"

"Look at my house!" the homeowner yelled, stumbling out of the rubble.

"What about my car?" the irate motorist screamed
from up the block.

"To hell with your house and your car!" Agnes
bellowed, reloading and snapping the cylinder closed
with a menacing click. Gene ducked behind his unit,
knowing full well that if Agnes had the right kind of
ammo, that slug could punch right through his car.

Gene grabbed his mike and called in, radioing a
Code 108, which means officer needs assistance—
LIFE IN DANGER!

Several of the cops guarding the punks heard the
call and responded, figuring (rightly) that the life of
one of their own was worth a hell of a lot more than
all the punks combined.

Dick was close to Billy Fetterson's house when the

unit out front suddenly roared away. Smiling and slobbering and grunting like the madman he was, he ran across the street and jumped up onto the porch just as Billy's mother was walking out. Becky Fetterson took one look at Dick and passed out. Billy Fetterson also caught a glimpse of the Caped Avenger and ran hollering out the back door. Dick figured his luck was about shot for that night, and disappeared into the darkness.

Meanwhile, the Ripper had chosen another victim.

Lani picked up the in-office line. "Stacy Ryan just called," Brownie said. "Jennifer Lomax was supposed to be in this morning to cut some commercials. She didn't show, and there is no answer at her home. You people check it out. I got a cop's bad feeling about this."

Jennifer Lomax, known as Jenny Caesar (just like the salad, good to eat), had signed off the air at 2:00 A.M., as usual, and had not been seen since. Leo jimmied the lock on her door and found that her bed had not been slept in. She was not at home. There were no signs of a struggle. Lani was putting out an APB on her vehicle. Anna had said that when the vehicle was found, don't touch it until she did. Anna picked up a scarf of Jenny's and put it in her pocket. The scarf was very lightly scented with Jenny's favorite cologne.

"Pick up something for the dogs, too," Ted said.

Everybody thought the worst. But the Ripper's luck was slipping by like grains of sand in an hourglass. The Ripper had had a long run; had left a trail of bodies from one coast to the other. It was nearing the end.

* * *

"Goddamn you!" Jim Longwood said. "You stupid oaf! How could you let her escape?"

"It wasn't my fault," the simpering voice replied. "You're just as much to blame as I am. Besides, there is nothing to worry your pretty head about. She's probably dead by now."

"Yes. Hopefully. Well, we're in the clear, and the house is rigged. The young people should be on the move in a few hours. Look, I've got to go to work."

"I'll be listening, sweets."

Jennifer Lomax had pulled herself along the last few yards by sheer willpower. Her strength was almost gone. She knew she was badly hurt, probably dying, but was determined not to slip into that long sleep until she told somebody, *anybody,* what she had learned during the long, hideously perverted and painful hours of her captivity. But she didn't know how much longer she could hold out. Then she saw the lights of the lonely mom-and-pop store by the side of the road. She almost made it. She came to within a few hundred yards of the store, before the blackness took her. Jenny cried out once, then slipped into unconsciousness.

An All Points Bulletin had been issued for Jenny, and the cops were mounting a massive hunt for her, aided by dozens of civilians who had come forward. But it was a dog that some uncaring and worthless turd had abandoned who found Jennifer Lomax.

The dog's incessant barking finally drew the attention of the elderly couple who owned and operated the small convenience store. At his wife's urging, the man walked over to see why the dog was making such a fuss.

He stood for a moment, gazing in horror at the

sight. Then he turned and shuffled back to the store as fast as his old legs would permit, and called the police. His wife gathered up water and clean cloths and went to see what aid she could give to the tortured woman. The dog, a mixed breed, refused to leave Jenny's side.

"I don't see how she's lived this long," the EMT said. "She's lost so much blood."

The four investigators and the psychic, Anna Kokalis, looked at the tortured body with the strange markings cut deep into the flesh.

"Satanic markings?" Lani asked.

"Probably," Anna replied. "But they are nothing like anything I'm familiar with."

"Brown!" Jenny suddenly gasped. She opened pain-filled eyes. "Brown!"

Lani knelt down beside her. "Brown what, Jenny? Talk to me, Jenny."

"Brown and woman," Jenny pushed out the words. "Evil. The devil."

"A brown woman?" Ted mused aloud.

"Gil Brown," Leo said. "The Windjammer."

"Yes!" Jenny said, then closed her eyes and allowed death to relieve her of the pain.

"Son of a bitch!" Brenda said. "He was right under our noses all the time."

"My god!" the Windjammer said, when the cops showed up at the station and confronted Gil Brown with a warrant for his arrest. "I'm not the Ripper. My sister and I had friends over last evening. Frenchy and Cal Denning were there."

"That's right, Leo," the engineer said. "The party started at seven and broke up around midnight. Jenny was probably just calling out for Gil. They used to have quite a thing going."

Lani stared at the Windjammer. The man was the right age, the right size, somewhat effeminate in his manner. But after talking with a dozen people, Gil Brown had an unshakable alibi. Gil and his sister, who worked at home as a computer programmer, lived in a small but very comfortable and secluded home. A judge signed the search warrant allowing the cops to enter and search the apartment. They found nothing that would implicate Gil or his sister, who was confined to a wheelchair.

Leo and team were back to square one.

"It's them," Anna insisted hotly. "That home was filled with evil. Malevolence oozed out of every pore of that woman."

"We can't take that to court, Anna," Brenda said.

"Dogs are backtracking her movements," Leo said. He had taken the abandoned dog to a vet to have him checked out and brought up to date on shots. Leo was going to take the dog home for his kids. He looked at the team. They had all changed into jeans and hiking boots. "Let's go."

About an hour of daylight remained when the dogs stopped at a country home.

"Find out who owns this property," Leo said. "And get the explosives team out here to check it. Remember what happened last time."

It was dark when the explosives experts finished. "It's wired to blow, Leo. It's been booby-trapped all over the place. By someone who knows what they're doing. Front and back doors. Windows. The outbuildings. Everything is wired to blow. I—"

"Get out here!" one of the explosives team shouted from the rear of the home. "Back up. Get out of here.

Move, goddamnit, move!" He was running as he shouted.

The cops just had time to hit the ground when the house exploded. Just like the other country home, massive amounts of explosives went up, hurling lethal chunks of brick and timber all over the place. The concussion picked up the man who had shouted the warning and tossed him about ten feet. He landed heavily, but unhurt except for having the wind knocked out of him.

Leo picked himself up and brushed off his clothing. "Seal the place off and post guards here," he said wearily. "We'll start picking through the rubble at first light. No sense in trying to do anything tonight. There might be more unpleasant surprises waiting for us." He looked at Lani. "You got a blanket around Gil and his sister?"

"Zipped up tight," she said.

"Let's go home and get some rest."

Chapter 28

Brenda had been staying with Lani, and she shook the county detective out of a very deep sleep just before dawn. "Get up, Lani. Leo just called. A half a dozen of those punk kids have hit the road."

As the women dressed and took a couple of brush swipes at their hair, Brenda shared what she knew from Leo's call. "The kids stole some guns from their parents and took off."

"Damnit, there weren't supposed to be any guns in those homes! That was the judge's orders."

"The parents lied. What else is new?"

Leo took one look at Lani's hair and said, "You girls forget your brooms?"

Lani told him what he could do with that comment and how to insert it.

Ted wisely and tactfully said nothing about Brenda's hair or lack of makeup.

The radio squawked and the cops froze as they listened. The half-dozen hard-core members of the killing club had gone on a rampage. They hadn't just run off from home. They had killed their parents first, bludgeoning them to death before taking off. The homes looked like slaughterhouses at closing time.

Gene Clark and two other city patrolmen had one

other kid in custody at the hospital. "You have to see this to believe it," Gene told Leo at the hospital. This kid's a real basket case. It took all three of us to subdue him."

The young man, age fifteen, was in a straitjacket, screaming and bouncing off the walls. "I must obey!" he screamed. "I have to obey. They're calling me!"

"Posthypnotic suggestions?" Lani asked a doctor.

"That's what the head of our psychiatric department thinks."

"He is possessed," Anna Kokalis said.

"That's what a priest said," the doctor acknowledged.

"Can't you shoot him with something and calm him down?" Leo asked.

"He's got enough tranquilizer in him now to fell a horse," the doctor said. "It doesn't seem to have any effect."

"You can't tranquilize the devil," Anna said. "He's under the spell of demonic possession."

The doctor sighed.

"Let's check out the homes," Leo suggested.

Carnage. At the Fetterson home, Billy Fetterson had used an axe on his parents, chopping them to death while they slept. Even the ceiling was blood-splattered.

"Does this remind you of something?" Lani asked her partner.

"Yeah. The Longwood mansion."

"Do you think the boys *planned* this?"

Leo shrugged. "I've given up trying to predict what those loonies are up to, or what they'll do next. Let Homicide handle this. Let's get out to the house and start digging through the rubble."

A man and woman were waiting for them at their cars. Both young. Both very earnest-looking. The man wore a conservative suit, the woman wore a conservative pants-suit.

"You want to guess who they are?" Brenda whispered to Lani, then giggled.

"FBI. Right out of the academy. Sent in to assist us poor ol' ignorant country cops."

"Bingo!"

Both the man and woman held up their IDs. "Agents Miller and Lange," the man said. "We've been sent in here to assist you."

"You have first names?" Leo asked.

"I'm Connie and he's Frank," Agent Lange said, without cracking a smile.

"I would certainly hope so," Brenda said.

"That reminds me of a joke about two old maids," Lani said. "They were going to be frank with each other. One said, 'Oh, good. You be Frank tonight and I'll be Frank tomorrow night.'"

The two Bureau people exchanged disapproving looks. Agent Lange said, "How you can joke at a time like this?"

"Oh, you'll get the knack of it," Leo assured her. "Or you'll come unglued. How long have you two been out of the academy?"

Frank cleared his throat. "Not long."

"First assignment out on your own, hey?"

"Ah . . . yes. The first one of any great importance."

"Wonderful. Come on. I want you both to see something, and then we'll drive out to the house."

Leo walked them through the Fetterson house and watched as the two young agents fought to maintain their stoic Bureau composure. At the morgue, Leo flipped back the sheet covering Jenny Lomax. The young agents didn't lose their breakfasts, because neither of them had as yet eaten. But they did turn a tad pale.

"Now let's go visit the arches and get some food to go," Brenda suggested, a wicked look in her eyes. "We can eat on the way out to the house."

Outside the morgue, Frank and Connie paused and held up their hands. "Okay," Frank said. "You've made your point. You're the seasoned cops, we're the new kids on the block. Is this the last object lesson for the day?"

"Yep," Leo said. "Now let's go get something to eat. I'm hungry."

Lani rode with the Bureau people and wolfed down two Egg McMuffins and two cartons of milk before opening her cup of coffee. Frank and Connie declined breakfast. Lani lit up a Parliament.

"We don't smoke," Connie said quickly.

"I do," Lani said, puffing away. "Have you two been briefed on this case?"

"Very perfunctorily," Frank said.

"Good word," Lani muttered. "I'll have to spring that on Leo."

It took the rest of the trip for Lani to bring the two young agents up-to-date. They both were sober, quiet, and reflective as they pulled into the drive of the rubbled house. They got even more sober and reflective at Leo's words.

"Forensic just found some faces in what used to be the basement."

"Faces?" Connie asked. She was looking at the half-eaten sweet roll in Leo's hand.

"Yeah," Leo said, taking a big bite of the jelly roll. Part of it oozed out onto his fingers. He licked it off while offering the rest of the roll to Lani. She ate it. "More over there in the sack on the fender. Better get one while they last. Faces. Yeah. But we can't identify this one. They probably brought this one with them when they came West. They save faces. Put them in some sort of clear preservative in a big jar. They like faces."

"They were briefed only perfunctorily," Lani said, walking up eating a jelly roll. "I unperfunctorized them on the way out."

Frank's expression turned very grave at that, while Connie had to duck her head to hide a quick grin. She had picked up immediately that these highly experienced, seasoned, and very capable cops were going to rib them for a time; she was ready for it. Frank, on the other hand, did not take kidding well. They had gone through the academy together and while she liked the serious young man, he didn't have much of a sense of humor.

Leo stuffed another jelly roll into his mouth and spoke around it. "This is it," he said, holding up a clear evidence bag which contained what appeared to be a female human face, complete with long blond hair, darkened now by the exposure to air.

That did it. Frank trotted off to the bushes.

Brenda took the bag. "I'll get this back to the lab and have a description drawn up and sent out."

"No, you stay with us," Leo said. "Give it to a uniform. Jimmy over there looks like he could use a break. He's been down in that basement for over two hours, stepping over and on rotting arms and legs and faceless heads."

Connie headed for the bushes at that.

"Did I say something to offend her?" Leo questioned.

It didn't take long for the two young agents to get their sea legs, so to speak, and soon they were both changed into jeans and work shirts from out of their luggage, and right in the middle of the basement of horrors. When Leo called a halt for lunch—sandwiches and soft drinks sent out from town—they both had a healthy appetite and Frank was loosening up.

"I needed you guys," he admitted, after wiping a bit of mustard from his chin. "I've been strutting around like a peacock ever since I graduated."

"And so have I," Connie admitted. "To a lesser degree." She smiled at Frank and they both laughed.

"So how much do you guys have that you don't want to tell us about, because it was obtained illegally?" Frank asked.

Leo chuckled. Frank was stiff as a board, but sharp as a tack. "Quite a bit of the earlier stuff." He told the agents about the illegally obtained material.

Surprisingly, Frank just shrugged. "Sometimes I guess you have to do that. I wouldn't be adverse to doing it in a case like this."

"Frank!" Connie said, feigning great shock at such a revelation. "You?"

Frank took a swig of Coke. "This nation is in deep, deep trouble. So many of the people seem to have no morals, no honor, no values. We're awash in drugs and sexual perversion. I would have never dared breathed this aloud back at the Academy, but it's my belief that if we're ever to win the war against crime, we've got to get down to the level of behavior of the criminals."

"Then we'd be no better than those we're fighting," Ted said.

That conversation got nipped as the investigators watched Bill Bourne drive up and get out.

"He's got something for us," Lani said. "And he's not happy about it."

"You look like a thundercloud, Bill," Leo said. "What's the matter?"

"All the test results finally came back about an hour

ago. Fingerprints, blood samples, hair samples, DNA. Stacy Ryan had absolutely nothing to do with any of the killings we've investigated.''

Leo, Lani, Brenda, and Ted were stunned into silence, then Lani started cussing. She went through her vocabulary of profanity, which was lengthy, and finally paused for breath. Ted was stunned. Brenda was impressed.

"Stacy volunteered for blood testing?'' Frank asked.

"No,'' Leo said. "We took hair from several of her brushes, and blood from where she'd cut herself on broken glass.''

"You took this with her knowledge?'' Connie asked.

"No,'' Lani said. "We jimmied the lock on her back door, while she was at work.''

"Well, there is another theory right out the goddamn window!'' Leo said.

"But she is their sister,'' Bill said. "She is definitely a Longwood.''

Lani threw up her hands in exasperation.

"That kid that Gene and the others brought in?'' Bill said. "The wild one? He just killed a city uniform and escaped. He ate the cop's throat before he left the hospital.''

It was madness. Every kid who had been released into the custody of their parents, turned on them. Those in jail went wild and began attacking fellow inmates and guards. Two guards and half a dozen inmates were killed by the sudden and vicious attacks, before those who did not escape in the bloody confusion were shot dead. The events of that day were so bizarre, it brought the anchors of all major network news flying into the city to report directly from the scene.

Now the pressure was really on the police. Leo said to hell with it and pulled in Stacy Ryan. He pointed a blunt finger at her and said, "Stacy, you level with me. I want the truth, and I want it now."

The woman sighed deeply and nodded her head. "I had made up my mind to come to you anyway. To try to explain. I know you all believe I'm a part of this . . . horror that's been taking place. But I'm not. My brother and sister are responsible. Yes, my blood parents are the New York Longwoods. I was told I was adopted when I was just a child. It didn't make any difference to me at the time. It was only after I got into college that I began having some curiosity about it. I had some money of my own; some I worked and saved, and the rest came from the checks my adopted parents received from back East. I hired a private detective firm to investigate. What they found scared me half to death. My real parents were ruthless and cruel and evil. They were devil worshippers. You're taping this? Good. I don't want to repeat it. You want to know why they kept Jim and Jack, and put me up for adoption? So do I. My only guess is that they saw something in me that frightened them. The investigator learned that I was born with veil over my face. It's not uncommon, but it must have really shook up my blood parents. I didn't know what was happening in this county, until the news finally leaked out that it might be two twins named Longwood behind all the killings. I freaked out. I told Carla the whole story. She told me not to worry; that the twins could have no way of knowing I was their sister. I guess she was right. I was never contacted by either of them. But I knew, I felt, they were here. But I don't think that either of them work at the station. Wouldn't I know my own brothers? Wouldn't I sense it somehow? I think so. Gil Brown, my brother? There is no resemblance there. None at all. And that poor sister of his, she lost the use of her legs years ago! There's no resemblance in any way."

"Do you have a half brother and sister?" Lani asked.

"Not that the private investigator ever found. And he was pretty good. Ex-CIA with a lot of contacts and leverage." She wrote out his name and firm in Los Angeles and gave it to Leo.

"When I was being interviewed by you people, I had a hunch I was being somehow polygraphed using some new technique. When the question was thrown at me about the Longwood family, I just about lost it. As long as you people used the word Ripper, I felt I could beat the test. But when you used Longwood, I felt sure you had seen the needle jump or the graph move or whatever it does."

"We did."

"I knew about Carla's will. But I was getting desperate at that point. I knew I had nothing to do with her disappearance, but it seems to me that everything was pointing toward me as a murderer."

"What about Patricia Sessions?" Leo asked.

Stacy shrugged her shoulders. "What about her?"

"Why did you and Carla and Patricia use false names when you flew to Mexico?"

"We didn't. You can check that. Carla chartered a private plane. A Lear jet. We used the same boarding gate as a commercial flight. You can check with Carla's bank. She wrote the company a personal check for the charter fee there and back. The pilot's name is Bob Rossini. I've dated him several times since then." She smiled at Leo's expression. "I'm bi."

"Glad to hear it," Leo muttered. He cleared his

throat. "Don't leave town without checking with us first, Stacy. Not until we check out all that you've told us."

"You'll find I've told you the truth."

"I hope so," Leo said.

After Stacy had gone, Lani asked, "You believe her, Leo?"

"Yeah, I do."

"So another lead dead-ends. Where does this leave us now?" Frank asked.

"Standing knee deep in shit and slowly sinking."

Chapter 29

The city police and county deputies had no more time to devote solely to the Ripper. When the young people broke jail and/or left home, they went on a wild, bloody, senseless killing rampage that was unequalled in modern California history—or when it finally ended, in modern American history. No one was safe, especially cops—or really, anyone in any type of uniform, anywhere. For it was as if someone had pulled a cork, and let a wicked genie out of a bottle thrown up from Hell. Gangs of wild-eyed young people sprang up in cities and towns all over the nation, as if on cue, and for the next few days the police—and the National Guard in some states—fought a life-and-death struggle every waking moment of their lives.

Police stations were firebombed and fired at. Police cars, ambulances, and fire trucks were easy targets. The actual numbers of young people involved were not that many—no more than about fifteen hundred nationwide. But what they lacked in numbers, they more than made up for in sheer savagery and viciousness.

The wife of the Vice President of the United States said that the music the young people listened to had something to do with the uprising, and she was probably right to some small degree. One self-appointed guardian of everybody's morality, headquartered in Mississippi, said it was not just the music and those terrible videos on TV, it was TV itself and Hollywood in particular, and he might have been correct to a smaller degree. A TV preacher proclaimed that the end of the world was near, and urged all his followers to send him a hundred dollars just as fast as they could—in cash, preferably, so he could continue to do Jesus' work in the time we had left. He would accept checks, just make them out to him, not Jesus. The President went on nationwide TV (on the one network that would preempt regular programming for him) and urged calm. But to be on the slap-dab safe side, in case all this civil disobedience didn't stop pretty durned quick, he had ordered the Navy to ready a whole bunch of Tomahawk missiles. It was unclear to all involved just exactly where he would have ordered the missiles to be targeted. Fortunately, the Secretary of Defense told him that it would be very unwise to launch a rocket attack against any American city, so the Prez ordered the Navy to stand down, completely unaware that they had never stood up.

One citizen that was interviewed in Chicago pretty much summed up the situation. "I just don't know what in the hell is going on!"

Lani and Leo did, for the moment at least. They were pinned down in an alley by at least two and probably more deranged punks holed up on the second floor of an old building, and the punks were using automatic weapons. They were really letting the lead fly.

Leo looked through disgusted eyes at his Colt .45 autoloader. Lani was toting a 9 mm. Both fine weapons. But not in this sort of situation. There was no point in calling for backup. Every cop in the city and county had emergency calls backed up. Response time was about an hour and a half. Only a skeleton crew was manning city and county HQs, everyone else had been pulled away from desks and into the streets. Even Brownie and the chief of police were in units, answering calls.

Leo and Lani kept their heads down as rapid-fire lead chipped brick and mortar from around the shattered window of the building in which they had taken refuge.

"Keep your head down, Lani," Leo said. "I'm going to the car for some heavier weapons." He returned a couple of minutes later with two Colt AR–15's—the semi-automatic versions—and a sack filled with thirty-round magazines. The .223 caliber weapons were not exactly heavy weapons, but they would give the two cops a lot more firepower.

To prove that point, Leo and Lani waited until a brief lull in the firing, and gave the punks 60 rounds of rapid-fire .223's. They got lucky, probably from a ricochet. A scream of pain ripped from the second floor, following by wild cursing and chanting.

Leo and Lani changed magazines, and then looked at each other as the chanting grew louder.

"What the hell are they saying?" Leo asked. "Sounds like kill."

"It is," Lani replied. "The same chanting that is being heard from New York to California."

"Those damn Longwood boys set up cells to program young people. A very carefully thought-out and executed plan."

"You were right, Leo. They intend to end it right here. Go out in a blaze of glory."

Then conversation became impossible as the air was

filled with lead, and all the pair of cops could do was huddle against the wall and wait it out. Then they heard the welcome *pop* of someone firing a tear-gas canister. Two more canisters were fired, and all three sailed through the broken windows of the second floor.

"You two all right in there?" Sgt. Gene Clark of the La Barca PD called from the mouth of the littered alley.

"We are now!" Lani hollered.

There was a hard burst of gunfire and then silence. No coughing, no gasping. Nothing.

"What the hell?" Gene called.

"I don't know," Leo returned the shout. "But I'm not going to stick my head out there to find out."

"Leo?" came a shout. "It's Frank and Connie. We've got the east end of the alley covered! Brenda and Ted are swinging around to beef up Gene Clark."

"That's ten-four," Leo called. "Any sign of the punks?"

"Nothing. It's quiet."

Leo chanced a quick look. No gunfire greeted him. The tear gas was quickly leaving the building across the alleyway. Leo stole a longer look, then keyed his walkie-talkie. "I'm going in. Lani will be right behind me."

"She will?" Lani questioned.

"I wouldn't want your feelings hurt by not inviting you along."

"Thanks so very much."

"That's what friends are for."

It was talk to cover the nervousness and tension both cops were experiencing. Something to sooth jangled nerves. Adrenaline was pumping in both of them.

"You ready?" Leo asked.

"As I'll ever be."

"Now!"

The cops darted across the alley and into the building. Their eyes began to sting from the lingering but quickly fading gas.

"Don't rub your eyes," Leo said.

"Yes, Daddy."

There was no sound of life on the floor above them. The building was eerily silent. Their AR-15's at the ready, the cops moved across the floor to the stairs at the far end of the room. Leo held up a hand and pointed to himself, then up the stairs. Lani nodded, and when Leo was on the stairs, she positioned herself at the foot of the stairs, back to a wall.

She almost shot Frank Miller as the Bureau man suddenly appeared in the doorway leading to the alley. She expelled breath, calmed jumpy nerves, and nodded her head at him.

Leo slipped up the steps, then rushed the landing, rolling as he hit it. Lani heard him say, "What the hell?" She took the stairs two at a time to stand beside her partner.

The big room was filled with the bodies of young people.

"They killed each other," Lani said. "They shot each other! That was the last burst of gunfire we heard."

The FBI and the CBI and Gene Clark rushed up the stairs to stand in shocked silence at the carnage.

"They were programmed to do it," Brenda said. "The master programmer thought of everything."

"Is that possible?" Ted asked, his eyes taking in the bloody scene that sprawled before him.

"I can't think of any other explanation," Lani said. "Can you?"

The CBI man shook his head.

"I'll call it in," Leo said, his voice tired. "But it's

gonna be an hour or more before the wagons arrive. Probably more. We'll have to do some of the lab work; they're all over on the other side of the county. Somebody get a camera and evidence bags. Get the kit and let's chalk out the bodies."

"Should we be doing that?" Frank asked. "I think we should follow department procedure as closely as possible on this. There will be lawsuits for years to come."

"He may be right," Brenda said.

"Hell, Leo," Lani said. "Let's seal off the place and leave it for the lab boys and girls."

One of the punks farted in death.

"I'll stay for security," Gene volunteered. "Just somebody please bring me back a cup of coffee and a sandwich. I haven't eaten since breakfast. One sugar, no cream," he added.

Lani and Leo, the FBI, and the CBI drove about the city in separate vehicles and took in the devastation. That just a very small handful of young people could do so much damage in such a short time boggled their minds. Hulks of burned-out and/or wrecked cars and pickups were in evidence. Dozens of stores had been looted by those types of human vermin who crawl out of their stinking lairs whenever disaster strikes a community. But this time Brownie and the chief of police issued orders to their people to shoot looters on the spot.

The governor intervened an hour later, under pressure from various civil rights groups, and ordered that proclamation rescinded.

"Asshole!" Leo muttered. "He caved in."

But the governor did order out units of the National

Guard to assist the cops. Later that night, down the coast, Los Angeles blew up . . . to no one's surprise.

The Longwood boys watched it all on TV and were highly amused.

Morning dawned smoky, and with just a hint of the many canisters of tear gas that had been fired. Weary cops drank more bitter coffee and hoped to God it was all over.

It wasn't.

Two La Barca city uniforms responded to a call, and were cut to bloody shards of flesh and bone by sawed-off shotguns as they walked up to the house.

A deputy stopped to check on a car parked by the side of the road and was shot and then hacked to death by young people wielding machetes and axes. When he was found, his head was missing.

At a public housing project, a La Barca city uniform killed a young black man who was advancing upon the cop, making wild threats refusing to drop the knife he was waving around. A riot broke out, soon spilling into the downtown area.

And Dick Hale figured that come the night, it would be a dandy time to see if he could finish off Agnes Peters.

Leo and his team had gone to their homes (the Bureau back to their motel) for a quick shower, change of clothing, and a bite to eat. The mayor of the city had asked cafes and restaurants to close voluntarily, and for the hotels and motels to serve meals only to those registered there. Nearly everyone had complied. Only a few die-hards remained open. And they were about to be closed—permanently.

One small cafe (whose owner was foolhardy enough to stay open in the middle of city-wide riots) took a firebomb through the front window. Nobody was seriously hurt, but the cafe was gutted. Another owner decided to close after some passing punks pumped about a hundred rounds of 9 mm lead through the windows and door. Another small convenience store was closed after the owner was pistol-whipped into unconsciousness and robbed. When he woke up, he found his store had been completely looted.

The rioting and looting was brought under control by late afternoon, and an uneasy peace reigned for a few hours. But the cops knew that when full darkness fell, the odds of peace being maintained were slim to none. The police had taken catnaps whenever they could, and most were in pretty good shape for the long night ahead.

Dennis Potter had insisted upon keeping his people guarding Leo's family, even though no attempts had yet been made on their lives, and in view of everything that was taking place, Leo was more than happy to have the professional bodyguards in place around his wife and kids.

Every cop on the streets and patrolling the county roads was in body armor. Kevlar helmets were on the seat beside them, ready to be put on. All of them had a terrible gut feeling that this night was going to wrap it all up, and before they got it under control, it was going to be a real son of a bitch.

Lani was riding with Leo, Brenda with Ted, and the Bureau people were together. Leo had put the psychic, Anna Kokalis, at his house for safekeeping. The kids liked her.

"This would be a dandy time for Dick to surface," Lani remarked.

"Yeah. I was thinking the same thing." He cut his

eyes to her. "Surely he wouldn't go after Agnes again?"

"Don't bet on it. He hates that woman."

"He's not alone," Leo muttered.

Lani smiled and consulted a briefing paper. "Six of the punks are still unaccounted for. We've taken none alive," she added softly. "The sight of that fifteen-year-old girl with half her head blown off got to me, Leo."

"It wasn't pretty," Leo acknowledged. "But that's the master plan of the Longwood boys. Dead people don't talk." He hit the steering wheel with his palm. "Goddamnit, Lani. I've got a very bad feeling in my guts, that when we *do* wind up this mess, we're still going to be in the dark about a lot of things."

"I don't care. I just want it over."

"Wind's picking up. It's going to rain."

"Wonderful."

They responded to a call from an hysterical woman who claimed she was under attack. It was a tree limb banging against the rear of her house.

Dark clouds whipped in and further blackened the night; sudden rain squalls slicked the roads and obscured vision. Cops all over the city felt their guts tighten. It was just too damn quiet. Leo pulled into a parking lot of a supermarket and parked close to the building, cutting the lights.

"It's gonna blow, Leo," Lani said.

"Yeah. Any second now."

Then the radio went wild, as dispatchers attempted to answer dozens of calls that flooded communications of both the city and county.

"Betcha a hundred bucks it's a ruse," Leo said, still parked by the side of the building.

"No bet."

Cops began calling in that the emergency signals

were false. The problem was, so many of them were out in the county. But every call had to be responded to. If only one was real, lives might be in danger.

"I hate those goddamn Longwood boys," Leo said, considerable heat behind his words. "I've never worked a case that I took so personal."

"Are we going to respond to any of those calls?"

"No. We're going to sit right here. I got a hunch."

"You want to share?"

"There is nothing to share. I just feel that we'll do more good by waiting, than by driving all over the county." He glanced at the rearview mirror. "Car coming up behind us. No lights."

Both cops pulled pistols from leather, then breathed a bit easier when they saw it was Ted and Brenda. Brenda lowered her window, and Leo cranked down his. Both cars were dark and blended in with the night. The rain had slowed to a drizzle.

"You think it's going to pop downtown, too, hey?" she asked.

"I do. But don't ask me why I feel that. I just do. You two got your AR's out of the trunk?"

"They're on the backseat. And my thumb is sore from filling up spare magazines."

The sounds of racing engines and loud mufflers reached them. Then gunshots blasted the night.

"Here we go," Leo said. The four of them left their cars and grabbed up AR-15's. They waited in the darkness, crouched beside their vehicles.

None of them saw the shapes moving silently up behind them.

Chapter 30

The racing, roaring cars drew nearer, and the shots louder. It was drive-bys, and the shooters were having fun, blowing out streetlights, shattering windows, and shooting stray dogs and cats and any person they might see. The wild sounds of heavy metal music could be heard over it all.

"Goddamn punk assholes!" Leo said, and lifted his AR-15 as the lead car came into view. He blew the windshield out and put two .223 rounds into the driver's head. The car began spinning around and around in the wet street. The drivers of the cars behind the out-of-control vehicle slammed on their brakes and immediately began fishtailing all over the place. The lead car jumped the curb and crashed into a building. The music stopped.

"That's something to be thankful for," Lani muttered. She turned around just in time to see a half-dozen young men and women slipping up behind them, all of them carrying rifles. "Behind us!" she shouted, and started letting the lead fly from her AR-15.

Once the drivers of the spinning cars got them under control, instead of driving off, seeking safety, young men and women jumped out, wild-eyed and screaming and shooting.

Lani and Brenda concentrated on those still standing behind them, while Leo and Ted directed their fire at those in the street. It was a bizarre scene in the night. None of the attackers, front or back, seemed to care that they were being chopped down by the police fire, and Leo was going to find out why. He took careful aim and put a .223 round into the knee of a young man. The young man screamed in pain and dropped his rifle. When he tried to crawl to it, Leo put a round into his outstretched arm. The young man passed out from the searing pain.

Lani had cut her eyes, saw what her partner had done, and did the same to a young woman not fifteen yards from her. Lani had to shoot her three times, once in each leg and then in the arm, before she stopped trying to reach her weapon and lay on the wet parking, moaning and screaming out words that made no sense to any of the cops. By now the wet night was filled with flashing red and blue lights, as other cops sealed off the bloody block and quickly brought the shoot-out to a conclusion. Actually, the cops had little to do with the ending of the brief firefight: those wounded took their own lives. All except for the two that Leo and Lani had wounded.

At the hospital, Leo and several doctors got into a shouting match in the hall.

"I don't give a goddamn for their rights!" Leo yelled, nose to nose with a doctor. "I don't care if they die tomorrow. Tonight, goddamnit, I'm going to talk to them."

"Over my dead body!" the doctor yelled.

"That can be arranged!" Leo shouted.

"Are you threatening me, you—you—flatfoot?"

"Yeah, you quack!"

"Those young people are seriously wounded," another doctor stepped in.

"Yeah, I know!" Leo yelled. "Me and my partner seriously wounded them."

"Well, you should be ashamed of yourselves," another doctor said.

"Who the hell asked for your opinion?" Leo shouted. "Goddamn liberal son of a bitch!"

"I've got a right to my opinion, you trigger-happy gun freak!" the doctor responded.

Lani got between Leo and the doctors, just as Leo was balling his fists, and managed, with much pushing and shoving, to back Leo up a few yards and get him calmed down. "It's all moot now, Leo," she said. "The punks have been taken into surgery. They're going to be out for hours."

The doctor with a bias against guns gave Leo the bird, and Leo gave him two in return.

"Go pay your dues to the NRA, Wyatt," the doctor said.

It took Lani, Ted, and Brenda to keep Leo from jacking the doctor's jaw. Big Gene Clark showed up, and between the four of them they managed to push and pull Leo down the corridor and outside the lobby of the hospital. For a man his size, Leo was as strong as a young bull.

Sheriff Brownwood pulled up in a unit and stared in disbelief as Big Gene Clark stood with his massive arms wrapped around Leo's chest. Leo's feet were completely off the sidewalk. A young doctor was standing just inside the glass doors to the lobby, shooting Leo the bird, and Leo was returning the gesture twofold. Brownie wanted very badly to ask what in the hell was going on. Then he thought better of it and drove off, knowing that cops sometimes got rid of stress in very peculiar ways.

* * *

Agnes Peters sat in her den, ready for the return of Dick Hale. She was wearing a flak jacket she'd bought at an Army/Navy surplus store and a football helmet. She was dressed in camouflage BDUs and combat boots. To hell with the newspaper, her column, and the book she was working on. This was personal now. And somehow she knew that Dick felt the same way. Agnes had bought a twelve-gauge shotgun and several boxes of double-ought buckshot. Her neighbors, upon seeing her tote the gun in, had immediately bought all the three-quarter-inch plywood they could and boarded up windows. All of the neighbors felt that Agnes had gone completely around the bend.

Agnes sat in the darkened den, the shotgun across her knees, and muttered, "Come on, you nutty bastard. I'm ready this time."

Jack and Jim Longwood sat mesmerized by the footage of the riots shown on TV. They loved every second of it. Everything was working out exactly as they had planned.

KSIN radio was off the air. Someone had tossed a bomb into the studios and another bomb into the transmitter building. Blew everything all to hell. The plan was working out beautifully. It was just delightful.

Frank Miller and Connie Lange had gotten tickled at Lani's recounting of the events that had taken place in the lobby of the hospital, and were cracking up with laughter. Leo had calmed down and was taking the good-natured ribbing well. The riot, for the most part, was over. Cops and national guardsmen were now mopping up. The hospitals and the jails were equally full. All the escaped young members of the killing club had been accounted for. All but two were dead, and those two were under heavy police guard.

Across town, Dick Hale slipped up to the rear of Agnes's house. Dick was retreating further and further into total madness with each day. He no longer even thought of the members of the killing club. His sole purpose in life was to rid the world of Agnes Peters. And it would have come as a great surprise to Agnes to learn that a great many people hoped Dick would succeed.

Dick no longer wore his Caped Avenger costume. He couldn't remember what he had done with it. No matter. He still had his shotgun and plenty of shells for it. Dick's mind was more animal than human now, and those new senses were warning him that this could be a trap. Something was wrong with the scene that lay before his eyes. It was just . . . too neat. Too easy.

Dick paused, enjoying the feel of the light drizzle on his flesh. Dick Hale was stark naked except for the bandolier of shotgun shells across his chest. A naturally dark-complexioned man, Dick tanned easily and blended in rather well with the night.

Then Dick realized that he had an erection. He'd been thinking about Agnes and had gotten hard. The more he thought about making it with Agnes—and then shooting her—the better he liked it. She really wasn't a bad-looking woman. He could put a bag over her head, he supposed. Or a flag, and fuck her for Old Glory. It was a dirty job, but somebody had to do it.

Then Dick realized he was chuckling. Standing

there in the rain, a shotgun in one hand and his cock in the other. Thinking about pronging Agnes Peters.

Dick slipped up to the house and chanced a peek into the kitchen. Nobody there. He padded silently over the brick patio and peeped into the den through a crack in the drapes. There she was! What was that getup she had on? Looked stupid. But that shotgun was real enough. No matter. Once Agnes got a look at his boner, she'd fall over on her back and spread her legs. Dick had always fancied himself as a great lover.

He couldn't believe his luck when he tried the back door and it opened. Careless of her. What Dick didn't know was that the door had been left unlocked deliberately. But what Agnes didn't know was that Dick could move so silently. Their confrontation was to be a great shock to both of them.

Dick leaned his shotgun against a wall and took a one-handed grip on his erect pecker. Two hands would have hidden it with four fingers to spare. And part of a thumb. Dick took a deep breath and leaped under the archway to the den.

"Yahoo!" he hollered. He waved his pecker at Agnes. The head of it.

"Great god!" Agnes screamed. Scared her so bad she pulled the trigger of the shotgun and blew a hole in the sliding-glass door. The heavy recoil turned her chair over. Dick lost his erection and ran to his own shotgun. Agnes was crawling to her knees and grabbed up the twelve gauge. Guessing where Dick might be in her house, she leveled the muzzle and boomed off a round. The buckshot tore through the paneling and punched out the other side, narrowly missing Dick's head.

"You bitch!" he yelled, and stuck his shotgun around the corner, without exposing himself, so to speak, and pulled the trigger. Killed the TV.

Agnes fired off another round, and this time she scored. Part of the paneling blew into Dick's right buttocks. He bellowed like a bull and jumped right into the fray, firing the shotgun as fast as he could pump and pull.

Agnes wisely took cover, flattening out on the carpet behind a sofa. When she heard the firing pin strike nothing, she jumped up just in time to see Dick's big ass. She fired. Dick screamed like a panther and went out the back door as fast as he could, which was a pretty respectable rate of speed for a man his age. With some buckshot in his ass.

Agnes jumped up and ran to the back door just in time to see Dick jump over the fence. She fired again and again Dick squalled. All the neighbors had taken cover at the sound of the first shot.

"You bitch!" Dick shouted.

"Come back and fight like a man, you perverted son of a bitch!" Agnes shrieked. "You goddamn coward!"

That stopped Dick cold. His ass felt like it was on fire, but no one called him a coward. He turned around and started running toward the fence. He cleared it and was snorting and grunting like a cape buffalo, running directly at Agnes.

She jerked the shotgun to her shoulder and pulled the trigger. Nothing happened. She was out of shells. Dick impacted with Agnes at a dead run, and both of them were knocked through the stationary side of the sliding-glass door. A heavy brass drape rod came down and conked Dick on the head, knocking him out cold. Agnes's head had impacted against the heavy glass of the door, and she was unconscious before she hit the floor, also on her head.

And that was the way the cops found them.

*   *   *

304 William W. Johnstone

"You gotta see this, Leo" he was informed by radio. "I mean, you *gotta* see this!"

They were only a few blocks away and rolled up to Agnes's home within a minute, Brenda and Ted right behind them. Sheriff Brownwood came behind the CBI team.

Brownie stood over the unconscious pair and shook his head. "I have seen some sights over the years, but this takes the prize." He smiled. "Of course, we have to have pictures."

Six cameras were whipped out, and the flashes captured the bizarre scene for all time. Agnes had landed on her back, her arms around Dick's bare back. Agnes's legs were spread, Dick's lower torso perfectly placed.

"One thing puzzles me about this," Brownie said.

"Just *one* thing?" Lani questioned.

Brownie looked at her. "Why was Agnes wearing a football helmet?"

"Where are Dick's clothes?" Bill Bourne questioned.

"I like those combat boots she's wearing," Brenda said.

"I haven't seen a flak jacket like that one since Nam," Leo said.

The EMTs arrived and rolled Dick off of Agnes and checked them both. "Dick's got a concussion, and he's shot in the ass. But other than that, their signs are good. This helmet probably prevented Agnes from sustaining a fractured skull. But the impact was enough to knock her out. She's going to be badly bruised, but she'll be all right."

"Get Dick in restraints before he wakes up," Brownie said. "I strongly advise you do that."

Agnes opened her eyes and groaned. She blinked a

couple of times and focused on the group standing around her. "It figures," she said, predictably Agnes. "There never is a goddamn cop around when you really need one."

Chapter 31

The doctors removed the bits of paneling and the buckshot from Dick's ass, and then placed him in the nut ward of the hospital. Dick would never stand trial for anything. He was hopelessly lost forever in the dark, twisted world of madness. Agnes was kept in the hospital for twenty-four hours, for observation. Leo and Lani could get nothing out of the wounded young man and young woman. They hissed and spat at the cops until the doctors ordered the cops out. This time Leo did not argue. He was too pissed-off for that. Wisely, the young doctor stayed out of Leo's way.

KSIN radio was going to be off the air for several more days, maybe longer than that. But the city had calmed down, and the streets were more or less safe for law-abiding citizens. But people were being advised to conduct their business during daylight hours.

Anna got permission to visit the young man and young woman in the hospital, and emerged from their rooms badly shaken. "They are possessed," she said to Leo and Lani.

"Nonsense!" said the young doctor who had ex-changed birds with Leo. "Only a fool believes in that rubbish."

"You, sir," Anna replied, "are the fool!"

Leo certainly agreed with that assessment. He nodded his head, but kept his mouth shut. The doctor glared at him, but kept any comments to himself. Lani was tensed, ready to jump between the streetwise cop and the young doctor. But Leo just turned his back to the man and walked out of the building. He had more to worry about than one out-of-touch-with-reality, smart-assed doctor.

Outside, in the parking lot, Lani asked, "Now what?"

"We put an end to the Longwood boys," Leo said.

"Just like that, hey?" Brenda said with a smile.

"I got an idea."

"You want to share with us?" Connie asked.

"Sure. Maybe we can make them come to us."

"Oh?" Lani said. "Pray tell us your plan."

"Well . . . I haven't got that worked out yet."

"Does it have to be legal?" Brenda asked.

"Hell, no," Leo told her.

"Well," she smiled the words. "In that case, let's kick it around."

"Please excuse us," Connie said quickly, and Frank nodded his head in agreement. Connie added, "We've got an awful lot of paperwork to do."

"Right," Frank said. "We're literally overwhelmed with paperwork. So, we'll see you guys later."

With the Bureau momentarily out of it, Lani faced the woman from the CBI. "Do you have a plan?"

Brenda shook her head. "I don't even have a clue. But what I do have is a gut feeling that when we end this thing, it's not going to be done legally."

Slowly, almost reluctantly, Ted nodded his head. "I concur. Whatever it takes to bring this horrible chain of events to a close, let's do it."

"Where do we start?" Lani asked, looking at her partner.

Leo arched one eyebrow, and that gesture always irritated Lani. She'd been trying for years to copy it, and hadn't been able to master it yet. "I'm not going to sit around and wait for the Ripper to strike again. I want those young people out of the hospital, and shot up with pentothal or whatever kind of drug the experts use to deepen hypnosis."

Ted whistled softly. "Man, those doctors won't allow that. Not as long as those punks are under their care."

"They won't be under their care very much longer," Leo stated.

"And just how do you propose to swing that, ol' partner of mine?" Lani asked.

"Simple. We kidnap them."

It turned out that Anna Kokalis was close friends with a man who was an expert in the field of hypnosis. Leo had no trouble at all convincing her that this was the right thing to do. She had no qualms at all about being a party to breaking the law in order to catch the Ripper.

"But you must be prepared to face some horrible things," the psychic warned the investigators. "We're dealing with the devil here. I am firmly convinced of that."

Connie and Frank were approached and did not want to hear of the plan, in any way, shape, form, or fashion. Not just no, but *hell, no!*

Leo had busted one of the EMTs at the hospital some years back—before the man became an EMT—and because the guy was basically a decent sort, Leo had withheld the evidence which would have changed the charge to a felony. The guy owed Leo, and Leo did not hesitate to call in his markers. The EMT was pretty shaken up by his part in the plan, but Leo had him between a rock and a hard place, and he could not refuse.

It was going down that night.

"You understand that these people run the risk of dying under the amount of drugs I'll be forced to use," the expert warned.

"I don't care," Leo replied. "We've directly tied both of them to more than a dozen torture/murders. They're both scum. They want to worship Satan, we'll send them to Hell with my compliments."

The man, a professor at a nearby university who refused to give his real name, smiled. "I would not want you for an enemy, Leo."

"That's probably a wise decision, Doc," Leo said.

It's been said that money talks and bullshit walks. In this case, that proved out. Dennis Potter owned the hospital where the young killers were being treated. It took only one phone call from Dennis to clear the way for Leo and his team to make their move. A little rescheduling of personnel, and the way was clear.

At midnight, a fire suddenly sprang up at the far end of the corridor where the young killers were housed. In the ensuing confusion and thick swirling smoke— from smoke canisters—they vanished. The cops guarding the young punks saw nothing. The nurses observed no unauthorized personnel on the prison ward. Nobody saw nothin'. It was leaked to the press that probably members of the killing club had broken in and rescued their fellow partners in crime.

Several of the doctors thought that was a pile of crap, but they were urged by older colleagues to keep their mouths shut and their opinions to themselves.

They were quietly reminded about talking and walking.

Neither of the young people died, or even experienced any lasting ill effects after the hours-long ordeal under heavy doses of mind-freeing drugs. But they did talk. And what they had to say brought the investigators to the door of the Ripper. The young man and woman were "found" by a Hancock County Deputy Sheriff on his way to work the next morning. They had no idea where they had been, who took them where, or what had transpired while they were gone. Several of the doctors who worked the psychiatric ward suspected what had happened—once they observed the needle marks in their arms—but they kept their mouths shut. In their opinion, the young man and woman were utterly loathsome, unredeemable, and totally lacking in any quality that would ever make them socially acceptable, and that was being kind about it.

Agnes was still suffering from her ordeal at the hands of Dick Hale, and could not write about the strange disappearance of the wounded prisoners, even if she had wanted to, which she didn't. Besides, Agnes was rapidly undergoing a change of philosophy concerning crime and criminals and what should be done about it and them. The liberal left was about to lose a valuable ally in Agnes. She asked one of the doctors to get her an application to join the National Rifle Association.

It usually takes only one violent encounter to change a liberal to a conservative. It's called coming face-to-face with reality. Something most liberals have yet to grasp.

A description of the Ripper and accomplice was handed over to a police artist, and soon a composite was drawn up.

Gil Brown and sister. But when they got to Windjammer's home, the man and his "sister" were gone.

But Gil's crippled sister had left behind her wheelchair.

On one wall of the den, written in what was later determined to be human blood, was a message:

MARY HAD A LITTLE LAMB
LITTLE LAMB, LITTLE LAMB.
ITS FLEECE WAS WHITE AS SNOW.
EVERYWHERE THAT MARY WENT,
THE LAMB WAS SURE TO GO.
FUCK YOU, LEO!

Chapter 32

The detectives went over the house, and forensics came in and fine-toothed the home. They could find nothing to tie in Gil Brown and his sister to the killings.

"Then why did they run?" Connie asked. The Bureau had rejoined the hunt now that it had once more become legal. Sort of.

"They've tired of the game," Leo said. "They want it to end. I guess. Hell, I don't know."

"But we checked out Gil Brown and his sister," Brenda bitched. "All the way back to birth."

"Sure we did," Lani said. "But we checked out the *real* Gil Brown and sister. I'll bet you a month's pay, they've been dead for a long time. The Longwood boys took their identity. They found a brother and sister whose parents are deceased and with no close relatives. Will you backtrack that, Frank?"

"I'll get on it right now."

The Bureau found a cousin and flew him into La Barca that afternoon on private jet. He was shown recent snapshots of the Browns. He shook his head. "The resemblance is startling. But that is not Gil and Gayle."

"You're sure?"

"I'm positive."

After the cousin had left, Stacy said, "Well, I know damn well that Gayle is female. I've been to the *rest room* with her dozens of times over the years." Stacy returned to the KSIN studios to prepare to resume broadcasting. The stations were due to hit the air the following morning.

"Female," Brenda said softly.

"Oh, she's female, all right," Leo said. "But she didn't start out female."

"I think I'm going to be sick," Ted said.

"Talk about a twisted case," Connie said. "This one is going down in the annals of crime. You can bet this one will be reviewed at the Academy . . . over and over for years to come."

"Let's hope it's reviewed favorably," Lani said. "And the only way we can insure that, is to catch the killers." She snubbed out her cigarette. "But so far, they've made fools of us." She stood up and paced the room, talking as she walked. "We all agree they're still in the county. We all agree they've decided—for reasons we'll probably never know—to play out the last act right here. We all agree they have probably kept many of their . . . souvenirs from past killings." She grimaced. "Faces, skins, etc. And we all agree that we have not, as yet, found their central location."

"A massive search, Lani?" Ted questioned.

"Has to be," Leo answered it. "House-to-house. Let's work up the grids and get to it."

Sheriff Brownwood and the chief of police left only a skeleton crew to work the calls, and put everybody else going house-to-house in La Barca. At first, they demanded to see proof of where the residents worked. They had to stop asking that when civil rights and civil libertarian organizations stepped in and threatened to go to court, claiming the question was unconstitutional . . . a violation of privacy. The newspapers ran pictures of Gil and Gayle, and begged the public's help in finding the demented brother and sister before they could kill again. The broadcast news media cooperated and ran pictures of Gil and Gayle. After four days of exhausting searches, the cops had zip. Nothing.

On a Friday morning, the fifth day of the house-to-house searching, the investigators met at the office before they hit the streets.

Leo punched the flashing button and lifted the phone.

"You having fun, poopsie-whoopsie?" the voice asked.

Leo gave Lani the signal to start the trace. "Oh, it's been just one great, big laugh after another."

"I'm so happy for you," the voice said. Leo could not tell if the voice was male or female. It was being electronically altered.

"I suppose I have to say that I wish you and your brother, or sister, whoever you are, would turn yourselves in."

"I'm Jack, Leo baby. Jim is right beside me. I'm sorry that we don't have time for you to speak with my brother. But I know you're tracing this call. I'll save you the trouble. It's a pay phone on Chestnut. Well, suffice it to say, there will be a surprise for you later on this afternoon. Have fun, pig. Ta-ta." The connection was broken.

Uniforms raced to throw up a loose circle around the suspect area, but turned up nothing. Leo had anticipated that. None of the team had to ask what kind of surprise lay in store for them. They all felt they knew: another body.

* * *

The uniform assigned to guard Stacy Ryan escorted her home for lunch and checked the front rooms before waving her inside. Stacy smiled at the female officer and stepped into her home.

"Stay here while I check the other rooms," the uniform said.

Stacy waited in the den. And waited. She thought she heard a thump, but couldn't be sure. She called out for the police officer. Silence greeted her.

"Denise!" she called again, raising her voice.

Giggling drifted to her. Denise was definitely not the giggling type. Stacy quickly walked to the front door and threw it open. She ran to her car and locked the door, then jerked up her phone and frantically punched out 911. A unit was on the scene in three minutes. The longest three minutes of Stacy's life. A second, then a third marked unit pulled up. By the time Leo and Lani and their team reached the building, a cordon had been thrown up around the place.

There had been no sign of Denise.

Forty-five in hand, Leo was the first to enter the home. The smell of blood was immediately strong in his nostrils, thick and heavy. He waved the others in. Connie and Frank took the area right off the den, Brenda and Ted stayed in the central part of the home, and Leo and Lani slowly made their way down the hall to the bedrooms. In Stacy's bedroom, they found the body of Denise, sprawled on the king-sized bed. The walls and carpet were spattered with blood. Denise's head was missing. They both stood in silence for a few heartbeats.

"She was getting married next month," Lani said. "CHP guy. Nice fellow."

Leo studied the body. It looked like the head had

been removed with one blow. Probably with a very
sharp and very heavy machete, with a lot of force
behind it. There were no signs of any hacking. Leo
backed away from the bed. Lani had stepped out into
the hall.

A loud bang from the far end of the house set them
running. Another bang followed the first one. Connie
and Frank stepped into the den, embarrassed and
angry expressions on their faces.

"Goddamn perimeter bangers," Connie said, hol-
stering her pistol. "Attached to the doors. These people have a real sense of humor. Denise?"

"Dead. Her head is missing," Lani replied.

The team from the ME's office came in and Leo
pointed down the hall. The investigators stood in silence. Nobody seemed to want to say anything.

In the back rooms of a warehouse located near the
edge of town, Jim and Jack Longwood sat and
planned for their final hours of glory. The years behind them had been wonderful ones. They had suc-
ceeded beyond their wildest expectations. Now it was
time to think about and savor in anticipation that hot
moment they had been born to face.

Jim and Jack owned the warehouse, purchased by
one of their attorneys through a corporation that was
very real and making money. When Jim and Jack had
realized the game was about to end, they had closed
the warehouse for repairs and moved all their momen-
tos into the back rooms. Mirrors were placed in strate-
gic locations all about the rooms. Dozens of small
tables had been set up, and jars placed on the tables.
Faces floated in the clear liquid. Lovely faces, the hair
fanning out about them. They were so pleasureable to
gaze upon. It almost made the boys weep to think all

these lovely faces would soon be destroyed. Jim and Jack loved them all. Some more than others, of course. That was only natural.

And that was about the only thing natural when it came to the Longwood boys.

Leo and Lani and the rest of the team were not that many hours away from finding out just how unnatural the Longwood boys really were. And how prophetic Anna and Karl Muller's words would be.

"How the hell do they move around?" Sheriff Brownwood asked the team. "Their pictures are plastered everywhere. We've got roadblocks all over the goddamn county. How the hell do they do it?"

Leo had a theory about that, but he wasn't ready to share it with anybody besides Anna. Not even Lani. It was too wild, too bizarre. Leo wasn't really sure he believed it himself. Anna believed it, as Leo had known she would. But for now, that theory would stay with the two of them.

No more death pits had been uncovered around the nation, but no cop believed they had discovered them all. Many would lie uncovered for all time. The death toll was staggering, the highest in American history, numbering in the hundreds. Dozens of people were in jail, and dozens more on the run. Anna had said it was her belief that the horror would end with the deaths of Jim and Jack Longwood.

"That can't be soon enough for me," Leo had replied. He could not remember ever wanting to put lead in someone as strongly as he did now.

But Anna had cautioned, "Don't be surprised if your bullets have little effect on these two." She stared at the two cops. "Believe it. Believe it and you can stop this twin evil. I mean that."

Lani had experienced chill bumps on her flesh at that. She was silent for a moment, then said, "Have you told the others that, Anna?"

The woman shook her head. "They don't believe. And because they don't believe, they are in the most danger. Do I have to explain that?"

Leo and Lani exchanged glances. Neither would admit it, but both were a little fearful to hear more from the psychic.

Anna cupped Leo's face in her hands and looked deeply into his eyes. Then she did the same with Lani. She smiled and stepped back. "You both believe. You don't want to, but you do. Just be careful when the final encounter arrives." She turned and walked out of the room. Two uniforms had been assigned to Anna. One was a driver, the other rode shotgun. Anna was being driven slowly up and down every street in La Barca, and crisscrossing the highways in the county. Anna believed she would find the Longwood boys. It was just a matter of time and patience.

Lani and Leo were riding together when the call came over their radio. "See the man," dispatch said. "Watson's garage. Riverside Drive."

Lani always got a large kick out of that address, since there wasn't a river within fifty miles of La Barca. She acknowledged the call and Leo turned the unit around. They met with a very badly shaken Mr. Watson. He tried to light his pipe, but his hands were trembling so he finally gave it up and put the pipe in his coverall pocket. He pointed to the rear of his garage.

"In the back. In that old green Olds. The junked one. I hope you have strong stomachs. And don't ask me to go back there, 'cause I ain't gonna do it."

Sitting on the driver's side, skinned hands on the wheel at ten and two, was the headless body of what appeared to be a young man in his late teens. He had been sexually mutilated. There was a note on the dash.

HERE I GO DRIVING, IN MY MERRY OLDS-MOBILE. CATCH US IF YOU CAN, LEO & LANI.

Leo cursed and then said, "Call it in, Lani. Use the phone in the garage. Let's keep the press away from this as long as we can."

But some members of the press had been following Leo and Lani, staying back a block, and they were soon hard on the story like white on rice. While uniforms prevented them from actually seeing the horribly mutilated body, and none of the cops would have anything to say about the body, they quickly found that Mr. Watson was all too eager to talk to them.

"Here we go again," Lani muttered.

Agnes was back in full swing, but it was a very different Agnes than before. She was not hostile to the police, not nearly so sarcastic in her questioning, and seemed to actually be on the side of the cops.

"It's a miracle," Lani remarked.

Leo smiled. "No. Just a person who has finally come face-to-face with reality. We owe Dick a favor."

A uniform walked up and whispered in Lani's ear. She sighed and thanked him.

"What?" Leo asked.

"Another body. This one clear on the other side of town. The Longwood boys have been busy. Brenda and Ted are over there now, and asking that we join them as quickly as possible."

"Bad one?"

"The worst yet."

"You mean the worst that they've seen?"

"No. The worst yet. Period."

"That would be going some."

"Gene Clark tossed his cookies."

Leo shuddered. If Big Gene had lost it, it was bad.

The pair of cops walked to the car, shaking their heads at the dozens of questions being thrown at them from the huge knot of reporters.

The second body found that day was what was left of Paula Darling, Dick's secretary. At least that's who they thought it was. The ME's people were going to have to reassemble all the body parts, right down to the fingers and toes. And this time the Longwood boys had left behind what the press would soon be referring to as their calling card: the nameless face of a woman, long dark hair fanning out, floating in a jar of clear preservative. With Paula's skinned head sitting on the lid of the jar. The penis of the teenager found in the Olds just moments before was sticking out of Paula's mouth. The testicles were found in Paula's left hand.

Big Gene Clark was sitting in an old chair in front of the long-abandoned wreck of the building, when Lani and Leo drove up. "I've had it," the huge cop told them. "I've never felt so murderous in all my years on the force."

"We do know the feeling, Gene," Lani said.

"I think that's Paula Darling. I coach one of her kids in Little League. Who the hell is going to tell her kids? Her husband split several years ago. I hate this goddamn fuckin' job. I'm gonna pull the pin after this is over. I'm gonna go live in the mountains. I mean it. I'm gonna make friends with the bears and the birds and all the other animals. Animals don't do things like this. Only man does things like this."

They left Gene sitting in the chair, muttering to himself. It was getting to them all.

It was about to get worse.

Chapter 33

Stacy Ryan came wide awake. But she had the presence of mind not to open her eyes more than a crack, and to control her breathing. She could do nothing about the racing of her heart.

The police had insisted upon moving her to a safe location. It hadn't taken her brothers long to find out where that was; and she was certain it was Jack and Jim, or Jackie and June, whatever.

A strong odor assailed her nostrils. She couldn't figure out what it was. Smelled sort of like . . . copper, she thought. Then it came to her. Blood. It was the smell of blood. So the cops guarding her were dead. Had to be. All three of them. Dear God! she thought. I'm next!

She watched as shadowy forms slipped into her bedroom. Three of them. *Three* of them! Three of them? That third shape looked very familiar to her. Then it dawned on her who it was. One of the cops assigned to guard her. Her darling brothers really got around.

She watched through slitted eyes as the renegade cop unbuckled his belt and let his trousers fall. He stepped out of his trousers and then his underwear shorts hit the floor. She could see that he had a huge erection. The thought crossed her mind that the guy must be related to a horse.

Then Stacy got mad, the anger quickly overriding her fear. The turncoat son of a bitch might rape her, but it would be after a fight.

She was dressed in PJ's, lying on top of the covers. There was faint light seeping in from down the hall, and she could see that one of her brothers was now most definitely a female, and a rather shapely female at that. Dear Lord, what kind of a family tree lay behind her?

The trio moved closer, close enough for Stacy to smell the musky odor of maleness at full erection. She tensed and spun on the bed, grabbing the cop's dick with one strong hand and giving it a brutal twist and yank. With her other hand, she grabbed his balls and squeezed with every ounce of strength in her.

The cop screamed in pain, and Stacy shoved the man hard against Jim and Jack, knocking them to one side. Stacy was off and running up the hallway before her brothers could react. She reached the den and paused at the side of a dead policeman, jerking up his pistol, a 9 mm autoloader. Stacy knew something about firearms, and she thumbed the pistol off safety and sent a wall of lead howling down the hall. She quickly ejected the clip and slammed home another one. She crouched behind a couch and waited. She heard the sounds of breaking glass and a groan of pain that probably came from the renegade cop.

Stacy jerked up the dead cop's walkie-talkie and keyed it. "This is Stacy Ryan. Two of your cops are dead, and the third one is with Jack and Jim Longwood. He's helping them. Get over here!"

"Units are on the way," dispatch said. "Are you hurt, Stacy?"

"No."

"Stay calm."

"Calm's ass! I've got one of your officer's pistols, and I'm going to blow someone's shit away if I can get a shot at him or her."

"Her?"

"Yeah. One of my brothers is now my sister."

"Ah . . . 10–9 on that. No. 10–22 that. I understand. I think."

In the distance, Stacy could hear the sounds of sirens getting louder. The house was filled with both city cops and county deputies. Leo and Lani arrived about five minutes after the first unit.

After making sure that Stacy was all right, Leo phoned Brownie and told him what had taken place.

"Starting tomorrow, we polygraph every field deputy and every employee," Brownie said. "Since that isn't worth a shit in court, Leo, why don't you let slip tonight that we plan on doing that. Let's see how many run."

Leo's smile was hard. "And if we spot them taking off?"

"I think you know what to do. First share our plan with Bill Bourne, Gene Clark, and a few others you know are clean."

Leo chuckled. "I'll do that, Brownie. Good night."

He pulled Lani to one side and told her of the Sheriff's plan. Big Gene Clark was just walking in the door, dressed in street clothes. Leo told him of the Sheriff's plan, and the huge Black cop smiled, his eyes hard as flint. "Bill's outside talking with a civilian. I'll pull him away and tell him. Then I'll get my shotgun."

The press praised the courage of Stacy Ryan in the face of rape and death, and blamed the shotgun deaths—which occurred the same night—of six La

Barca city patrolmen and two deputies on the remaining members of the killing club. Spokespersons for the two departments blandly stated that it was a real tragedy, and had no more to say on the matter.

Cops, like many of the military's elite special operations groups, prefer to take care of their own. Oftentimes in a very final way. It's just neater.

Cops began working double shifts, voluntarily and without pay. Both departments were smarting from a comment made by the governor when he thought the press weren't listening. Dumb move, for the press is always listening. The governor had said to an aide that perhaps the entire hierarchy of the Hancock County Sheriff's Department and the La Barca City Police Department should be replaced—and a lot of the detectives, too—since they seemed to be unable to bring this case to an end.

The gov lost a lot of votes with that remark.

The citizens of La Barca and Hancock County grew very cautious. At dusk, the city took on all the excitement of a ghost town. A few frat boys from the local university thought it would be fun to prowl the streets and see if they could scare some people. Stupid move, but then, frat boys are famous for doing some extremely stupid things.

One frat boy got his head blown off by an elderly lady with a twelve-gauge shotgun, and another took a .357 mag slug in the guts from a homeowner. The three other frat boys were tossed in jail and told by Sheriff Brownwood, "Stay there, goddamnit, until you get some sense." One street-hardened deputy drily commented that it would bankrupt the county waiting for that to happen. No charges were filed against either citizen.

A few of the local rednecks thought that, by God, since the cops seemed unable to catch the killers, they

would. They loaded up their rifles and single-action
.44's and .45's, put a case of iced-down beer in their
high-tired pickup trucks, made sure they had plenty of
country music tapes to listen to, and set out to catch
the killers.

About an hour later, Jim Bob shot Harry Lee in the
knee, Billy Joe blasted a road sign, and Linda Lou,
who was riding with Virginia Mae, blew a hole in a
California Highway Patrolman's car; he had driven
out to see what all the shooting was about. The rednecks were put in the same holding tank with the frat
boys. One deputy was heard to mutter that perhaps
they would all kill each other, and thereby do the
world a great favor.

If there could be found some way to isolate and
lobotomize a certain segment of smart-assed college
kids (usually referred to as frat crap) and dumb-assed
rednecks (usually referred to as white trash), and a
certain segment of minorities (put whatever fits here),
a cop's life would be immeasurably simplified.

The final hours of the long nightmare came the
afternoon after the killing of Stacy's guards. A young-
sounding person, who said he'd been bicycling, called
in to say that he'd seen three people, two men and a
woman, one of the men walking in a strange manner,
enter the rear of that big warehouse on Indian Drive.

The phone tip was put with hundreds of others in a
huge overflowing basket. Lani just happened to walk
through that area and paused for a moment to go
through some of the called-in tips. She felt a tremendous surge of adrenaline flow through her. The man
seen "walking in a strange manner" just might be the
man that Stacy had put the pressure on the night
before.

Lani called Brenda and Ted. They were out of
pocket. She called Connie and Frank. They were

working the other end of the county, chasing down tips. She caught Leo just as he was preparing to leave for the day. Leo noted the time the phone tip was logged in, and stared at Lani.

"What do you think?"

"I think we should check it out."

"Let's go."

In the car, Leo called in according to routine, and told dispatch where they were going. Dispatch logged it in and asked, "Are you requesting back up?"

"Ten-fifty. Not at this time."

"That's 10–4." But due to the heavy air traffic, dispatch had logged it in as Indiana Drive. By the time the tape was replayed and checked, Leo and Lani would be involved in a situation unlike any they had ever faced.

Or ever would again.

Chapter 34

The sign stated that the huge warehouse was being remodeled by the Woodson Company. The company was very real, making a profit, and owned by the Longwood boys.

Leo and Lani sat for a time in their unit. Lani called in and said they were 10–8 at the location. Dispatch acknowledged and again logged them in as being on Indiana Drive.

Both Lani and Leo checked their guns. They each carried their personal choice of pistols. Leo a .45, Lani a 9 mm. Lani had a Ladysmith .38 snub in an ankle holster, and Leo carried a two-shot 410 derringer in an ankle holster. Lani had a .38 Chief's Special in her purse, and Leo had a Beretta .25 in his right back pocket. Cops very quickly become not the most trusting folks in the world. In many instances they are outgunned, and nearly always hampered by laws that work against law enforcement.

"Shotguns?" Lani asked.

"You bet."

They each shucked a round into their riot guns and stuffed extra shells into pockets. They stood looking at the warehouse. It was huge, thousands of square feet.

They had no idea what might be stored inside the building, if anything.

"Do we call for a search warrant?" Lani asked.

Leo smiled and pulled several sheets of paper from the inside pocket of his jacket and handed them to Lani. They were search warrants, presigned by a judge. Lani put them in her purse.

"Let's do it, Lani."

The cops walked to the rear of the building. Leo tried the door. It was unlocked.

"This is supposed to be a high-security building, I don't like this," Lani muttered.

"Me, neither. But as long as we're here . . . " He let that trail off, shoved the door wide open, and stepped in, quickly moving to his right.

Lani followed, stepping into the dusty gloom of the building and moved to her left, her sawed-off pump shotgun held in a combat stance.

The heavy steel door swung closed behind them on well-oiled hinges and locked with a very audible click.

"Shit!" Leo whispered hoarsely. "We've been had, Lani. It's a goddamn setup."

"How right you are, Leo pig," the voice came out of the gloom.

Both Lani and Leo had instinctively and very quietly changed locations and were in a crouch. Neither one of them spoke, not wanting to give away their position.

"Pig bastard!" a distinctly female voice called.

"How do you like the game now, you cunt!" a heavy male voice called.

Lani cut her eyes to Leo. The turncoat city cop, Greg Stern.

"I've always wanted to butt-fuck you, Lani," Stern called. "Now I'm going to do it. I want to hear you scream."

The female voice called out what she was going to do with Leo's butt, and Leo's asshole tightened.

"No way out, little pigs," the first voice shouted. "Steel doors all the way around. Those high-security windows are very nearly soundproof. The nearest building is a quarter of a mile away, and there are no residents living out here. Didn't we pick a perfect place to butcher pigs?"

Both Lani and Leo had to silently and reluctantly agree with that.

"For a couple of hick-town California pigs, you're both pretty smart," the female voice sprang out of the gloom. "I always felt it would be the Feds who would finally catch on to our little game. Not a couple of local yokels. By the way, I'm Jimmi Lee now." A giggle followed that.

When neither Lani nor Leo would reply, Jimmi Lee screamed, "Answer me, you pig bastard and bitch!"

Leo smiled grimly and then jumped to his feet, pumping off five rounds of double-ought buckshot pushed by magnum loads just as fast as he could pump and pull. Then he dropped to the dirty floor and rolled to a new position. The booming was enormous in the cavernous warehouse.

"You ruined Sunflower, you rotten son of a bitch!" Jack yelled. "Oh, God, she was so pretty. I hate you, hate you, hate you for that!"

Lani and Leo heard the smacking sounds of heavy kissing, then, "Goodbye, my darling. Go kiss a pig's snout!"

Something pale and dark and wet came sailing through the hot still air of the warehouse. The thing landed at Lani's feet. It was a human face. A female human face, with long, dark, wet hair. Lani almost lost what remained of her lunch.

"Sunflower was a redneck chick from North Louisiana," Jack explained, calling from somewhere in the warehouse. "But she had the tightest pussy I ever fucked."

"You filthy beast!" Jimmi Lee shrieked.

"With the exception of yours, my dear," Jack pacified his brother/sister.

Lani caught Leo's eye in the gloom, and both of them grimaced in disgust and revulsion.

Lani picked up a short wooden stake and showed it to Leo. He nodded his approval. She hurled the stake in the general direction of the voices. The stake smashed into something, the sounds of broken glass loud as it tinkled to the floor.

"Oh, you evil, evil destroyer of lovely things!" Jimmi wailed. "That was Butch. A surfer boy from down at Malibu." Kissing sounds drifted to Lani and Leo, followed by sucking sounds.

"I hate to think what's coming our way next," Lani whispered.

"I have a pretty good idea," Leo returned the whisper. "I just hope it doesn't land on *me!*"

It didn't. The penis landed between the cops, and they both glanced at it in the dim light.

"Ol' boy was heavy hung, wasn't he?" Leo whispered. "That's what we used to call a corncob dick back on the farm."

"I just can't wait to have you explain that to me." She looked at him. "Farm? You? The closest you ever came to a farm was when we had to help round up all those cows on the Interstate."

"They were bulls, Lani."

Then there was no more time for whispers, for Jack and Jimmi Lee and Greg started hurling heavy nuts and bolts and washers at them, laughing as they pelted the two detectives.

Lani and Leo separated on signal. They could not

use their walkie-talkies to call for assistance because of all the steel in the building. They were on their own.

"Have Leo and Lani checked in?" Sheriff Brownwood radioed to dispatch.

"That's 10–50, Sheriff. They went 10–97 at the warehouse on Indiana Drive. Haven't heard from them since."

Brownie thought about that for a moment. He keyed his mike. "There is no warehouse on Indiana Drive. That's all residential."

"That's where they said they were, Sheriff."

"I'm heading that way. Have a unit back me up."

"That's 10–4." There was a short pause. "HC–17 will join you at Madison and 67th."

La Barca city police were monitoring all the calls, and Gene Clark bumped the sheriff. "There is no warehouse out there, HC-1. I *live* on Indiana Drive."

"That's 10–4, Gene. Dispatch, why did Leo and Lani roll on this call?"

"Anonymous phone-in tip, HC-1."

"They've been suckered!" Brenda broke in. "It was a setup."

Brownie said, "Dispatch, unless they are working a life-threatening situation, I want all available units out looking for Lani and Leo. I want this as a silent code three. Do you copy?"

"That's 10–4, Sheriff."

"HC–17."

"Go, Sheriff."

"Check out Indiana Drive."

"Ten-four."

"Gene?"

"Go, Sheriff."

"What is your 20?"

"Park and 27th."

"I'm at Elm and Diamond Drive. I'll wait for you."

"Ten-four."

Gene pulled up behind Brownie and both men got out. "Where the hell could they be, Gene?"

"I don't know. I've been thinking. I don't know those streets in all those subdivisions just outside of town, because we don't work them. Hell, they could be anywhere."

"Wherever they are, they're in trouble," Brownie said, a numbness to his voice.

"They're inside someplace," Gene said. "A place with lots of steel that's preventing the use of their handsets."

"Or they're dead," Brownie spoke the words softly. "Or if the Longwood boys have them, wishing they were dead."

New voices had been added. Lani and Leo now knew they were up against at least six people, and both believed there were more who had yet to be heard from.

Leo and Lani were both in good defensive positions—their backs to a wall and plenty of cover in front. But none of those things offered them a way out. Neither could understand why no backup had rolled to assist them. It was department policy that if a unit who answered a trouble call didn't check in fifteen minutes after going 10–97, backup would roll.

"It's over, boys," Leo called into the gloom. "You're trapped in here. There are cops all around this place."

"Liar, liar, pants on fire!" Jimmi Lee yelled. "If there were pigs outside, they'd be trying to break down the doors." Truth was, she/he/it and his/her/its cohorts couldn't understand why the cops hadn't shown up. Contrary to what the city and county cops believed, this had not been a setup, just a screwup. The teenager who called had seen three people entering the warehouse. The cyclist just did not want to get involved.

"Hell with taking them alive for fun and games," Greg Stern said. "Let's kill them and split."

"The game must end here," Jimmi Lee said. "It's over, Greg. It was written that way."

"I don't read the rules that way," the turncoat cop said, and jumped to his feet, running toward a side door, the Uzi in his hand spitting out lead.

Lani and Leo fired as one, the buckshot tearing great holes in Stern. The renegade cop flopped to the dusty floor, dying.

A teenager, who should have been interested in girls and cars, not the devil, jumped up, screaming obscenities at the pair of cops. He also had an Uzi in his hands and knew how to use it.

Lani silenced both the kid and the Uzi.

The quiet seemed loud after the gunfire.

"Well, now," Jack spoke. "You pigs seem to be doing a good job of holding your own. We'll have to do something about that, I suppose."

Lani and Leo had again changed locations, working closer to the Longwood boys . . . or the brother and sister. Whatever. They both knew that by now, dispatch had ordered a code three search for them. Surely help was on the way. Neither could understand why backup had not already arrived. What they did not know was that as soon as they had entered the warehouse, their car had been moved by one of the teenagers; simple matter to hot-wire it. He had learned how to do that by watching TV.

Every cop in the county, including a dozen units of

the CHP, were frantically searching for the missing detectives. Two units had actually driven past the warehouse, and one had circled the huge building. But it looked so deserted, no vehicles in sight and no sign of human life; the latter being something that would be debated for years to come.

"I'm out of here!" a teenage girl said, and took off for a side door.

She was not firing, and Leo and Lani let her go, hoping she would throw open a door and give them at least a small chance of getting out of this death trap filled with loonies.

Jack Longwood fired a long burst from his Uzi, just as the girl flung open the side door. The impact of the lead threw the girl outside, her back bloody. She managed to stagger to the front of the warehouse, before collapsing on the parking area. She lay in plain sight.

But this area had already been searched by several units. It would be several more minutes before Indian Drive and Indiana Drive would be compared.

Leo took careful aim with his .45 and blew the lock out of the side door, before gunfire from the other side forced him down. The door might close, but it would no longer be able to lock. Leo did not know what had happened to the teenage girl.

Jack and Jimmi Lee and the two who remained loyal to them began hurling jars at the two cops. Human faces flopped out as the glass jars burst upon impact with the concrete floor. Breasts and penises and other parts of the human anatomy lay quivering and glistening wetly all around the two cops.

By now, it had reached the point where Lani and Leo had seen it all. Their minds just turned off and tuned out to the horrible sight. They were drenched from feet to knees, and the odor of dead flesh now exposed to air insulted their nostrils with a putrid stench. They could not take a step without the soles of their shoes landing on some piece of human flesh. There was no way for them to avoid it.

"Isn't this great fun?" Jimmi Lee shouted, then giggled. "Here is your evidence, pigs. Have some more with my compliments." She flung a jar at the cops. "This is Violet from Omaha. Here's what I saved of Stud from Dallas, Lani baby. Suck on this dick, you *dick!*"

"You want to see something beautiful, Leo pig?" Jack yelled. "Here, see this."

A thrown eyeball struck Leo on the cheek. He recoiled in horror.

"See it, pig!" Jack laughed. "You get it? See it!"

"I've had it!" Leo said. He stood up and leveled his shotgun. He shot Jack in the center of the chest, the buckshot knocking the man to the floor.

Jimmi Lee laughed.

Jack rose from the floor, the front of his shirt soaked with blood. He smiled at Leo.

Leo was numb. Dumbfounded. He stood almost rooted to the spot, listening to Jimmi Lee's taunting laughter. No, Leo thought. Nobody took a magnum load of buckshot in the chest at close range and lived. Nobody . . . *human,* that is. Was his theory correct? Had to be.

"Poor Leo," Jimmi Lee said, a sneer in her voice. She spoke from the shadows, and neither Lani nor Leo could get a good look at her. "He doesn't get it, brother dearest. He's simply not as smart as we first thought."

"Perhaps he never will, darling," Jack replied.

"Perhaps you're right."

"Such a pity," Jimmi Lee said. "But it must be him."

"Bad grammar, dear. But don't belabor the obvious. Shall we resume play, Leo?" Jack asked, as he lifted his Uzi. Leo hit the floor as the lead howled and bounced all around him.

Lani crawled over to Leo. "That's not possible . . . What you did. I saw it. He's *dead!*"

"No. But bullets won't kill either one of them."

"What? What are you talking about? What do you mean?"

"Later."

"Fuck later! They're not trying to kill us. I get the impression they want us to kill *them!*"

"Again."

"*Again?* Again what?"

"Oh, my, sister dear!" Jack said. "I was right. He really is a bright boy. Just listen to them."

"But the cunt is stupid as shit."

Lani narrowed her eyes at that.

"It's time, Leo. You must know what to do," Jimmi Lee said.

"I don't know what to do!" Leo yelled.

"Yes, you do, darling," Jimmi Lee said. "You were born to do it."

"Where were you born, Leo?" Lani suddenly asked. "You've never said."

Jack and Jimmi Lee both laughed.

Leo stood up then, and faced the pair of loonies. Lani slowly rose to stand beside him.

"Yes, Leo," Jack said. "Do tell us where you were born."

"I don't know," Leo spoke to the buckshot-mangled and bloody man. "I'm adopted."

"Yes," Jimmi Lee said. "We know."

"How could you possibly know that?"

"We know many things that you don't know." Jack smiled. "You bastard whelp out of a priest and a nun!"

Chapter 35

Leo did not lose his composure. "None of us have the option of choosing our parents."

Jimmi Lee giggled. She coyly covered her mouth with one dainty-looking hand. But Leo was of the opinion that hand was much stronger than it appeared. "Stop playing with him, brother. Tell him the truth. We don't have time for games."

"Oh, very well. Our parents, whom you two got to know quite well during your snooping around back in New York—not as well as you think, but well enough—had four children. The firstborn was not marked to carry on. He was given up for adoption. Of the triplets, who were born some years later, only two were suitable to carry on the family tradition. One of them was given up for adoption. You see, Leo, you and Stacy Ryan are brother and sister." His smile was grotesque.

"Hello, big brother," Jimmi Lee said with a giggle.

"I don't believe you," Leo said.

"Oh, it's true," Jack said. "What reason would we have to lie? Do you think our coming here to La Barca was mere coincidence? Why not Los Angeles instead? It's much larger, and it would have been so much more difficult for the pigs to catch us. No, Leo. We have to use you and Lani in order to live."

"Now, wait just a damn minute!" Lani said. "You're saying, I think, that you both are some sort of . . . immortals?"

"Ummm," Jack mused. "Well, yes. If you wish to put it that way."

Leo had been looking for the two remaining locals who had joined the Longwood boys. His eyes finally found them, sprawled in pools of blood behind a crate. His last blasts of buckshot must have caught them. He shifted his gaze back to Jack. "If you two are immortals, why weren't your parents?"

"Oh, they were," Jimmi said.

"But you killed them!" Lani blurted.

"No, we didn't. They're alive and doing quite well, thank you."

"But the police positively ID'd them," Leo said.

"They ID'd them as best they could. It's rather difficult to identify someone without hands or a head."

"Who were the man and woman you killed?"

"Transients we found on the road and brought to the house," Jack said. "Throwaway people. They were of no significance."

"Where are your parents?" Lani asked.

But Jack and Jimmi Lee would only smile at that.

Lani suddenly burst out in a fit of giggling as a wild thought hit her.

Leo looked at her as if she had taken leave of her senses. "You find this funny?"

"I keep looking around for John Carradine and Boris Karloff to stroll in."

"Oh, that's funny!" Jimmi Lee said, and laughed. Then she waved a hand effeminately and all humor left her. "Get on with it, Jack," she said harshly. "We're running out of time."

Jack's eyes turned cruel and evil as he stared at Leo. "Are you both ready?"

"Well, goddamn, man . . . whatever you are," Leo flared. "Ready for *what?*"

"They're crazy," Lani said.

"Hardly," Jimmi Lee said, adding, "you stupid bitch!"

Lani jerked her 9 mm from leather and emptied it into the woman's chest. The force of the many hollow-nosed slugs knocked Jimmi Lee off her feet and to the dirty and bloodstained floor.

Jack stood unmoved by the sight. He smiled at Lani. "That, dear, was a very futile act."

Jimmi Lee crawled to her feet. Her blouse was bullet-pocked and wet with blood. She smiled at Lani. "You really are quite proficient with that weapon, aren't you?"

Lani ejected the empty magazine and tried to insert a full one. Her hands were shaking so badly, that Leo had to take the weapon and click the full mag into the butt. The slide slammed home. He handed the weapon back to Lani. "Put it away. It's useless." He looked at Jack. "We're good and you're evil. Is that it?"

"That's part of it. But you're not all good. You're a team. A combination of good and evil. We need that."

"I'm evil?" Lani found her voice.

"Your grandfather was, back in Louisiana," Jimmi Lee said, a disgusted look on her face as she held out her ruined blouse with her fingertips. "I paid a hundred dollars for this."

"My *grandpere* was a kind, gentle man," Lani said, slipping into a word of Cajun.

"Your grandfather was a *loup-garou,*" Jack said.

"That's a goddamn lie!" Lani flared. "My *grandpere* was no damn werewolf."

"Oh, yes, he was. He prowled the bayous at nights,

when the moon was full and blood-red. We know all about you. Your blood is dark and tainted."

Before Lani could once more deny the charge, Leo said, "You don't want us to kill you. You could have killed us a dozen times over. But we're no good to you dead. You want to become *us.*"

"Oh, my!" Jimmi Lee said. "He is a bright boy, isn't he?"

"Well, now," Jack said with a smile. "You almost completed the puzzle, Leo. You win the cigar."

"How in the hell do you plan to *become* us?" Lani questioned.

"Well . . . I will admit that it is rather an awkward procedure, quite pleasurable for us. But the both of you will have some slight discomfort. However, we'll try to make this as painless as possible."

"Fuck you both!" Leo said.

"Really!" Jimmi Lee said brightly. "Oh, goody. That can certainly be arranged." She started to peel out of her bloody blouse.

"Figuratively speaking," Leo quickly added.

"Shit!" Jimmi Lee said.

"That's how it's done," Lani slipped the final piece of the puzzle into place. "Got to be. She was too damn eager to oblige, Leo."

Jimmi turned mean eyes to Lani. "You're not quite as stupid as you first appeared, dear."

"Hell with you, lady—Jim—whatever the hell you are," Lani told her.

"No, dear. Not yet, for us. Hell is where you and your partner are going."

Jack smiled. "Slipping into the vernacular of your relatives down yonder on the bayou, dear—why don't you just shuck out of them drawers and let's fuck!"

Leo jerked up his shotgun and blew Jack's face into a bloody mask of blood and shredded tissue, the force knocking the man to the floor. "Run, Lani! Go, damnit, go!"

But Lani wasn't about to desert her partner of so many years. She grabbed her shotgun and turned Jimmi's face into the twin of Jack's. "Now, we run!" she yelled, and the both of them took off for the open side door.

Jimmi Lee jumped to her feet and looked wildly around her. One eyeball was hanging down on her cheek. She paused long enough to jam the eye back into the socket and locate the running cops. She screamed and took off after them. Leo paused in his dash for the door and leveled his shotgun, shooting the woman four times in the stomach, chest, neck, and face; the shotgun jerked upward with each boom. She staggered and stumbled, but kept right on coming, covered with blood.

"She won't go down for me, Lani!" Leo yelled.

"This is no time to be thinking of sex, Leo!"

Street-hardened cops often develop a very wild and weird sense of humor.

Leo watched Lani make the door, just as Jimmi Lee came within swinging range of him. He reversed the shotgun and, using all his strength, hit her in the face with the butt of it. He hit her so hard the stock broke off. Jimmi's feet flew out from under her, and she hit the floor. Leo turned and jumped out into the welcome but waning daylight.

A dozen vehicles from the local PD, Sheriff's Department, and CHP were wailing up, as Lani and Leo ran to the front of the building.

"Circle the building!" Lani yelled, frantically shoving loads into her 12-gauge "Shoot anything that comes out. Use your shotguns and keep pumping the buckshot at them. Drive them back inside."

Brownie and Gene Clark jumped out of their cars

just as Anna was driven up, riding with Brenda and Ted; Connie and Frank were right behind them. "What the hell is going on?" Brownie yelled, just as Jimmi Lee came screaming out of the warehouse, the flesh of her face hanging down in bloody shreds and her throat and chest shot full of holes. Still, she kept on coming. "Good God in Heaven!" the sheriff yelled. "What the hell is *that?*"

Lani put five loads of buckshot into the woman, knocking her to the ground.

"Keep the press out!" Leo shouted. "Shoot them if you have to, but keep them out of here. Don't let them film this."

Jack staggered out of the side door and looked all around him. Half his head was missing, and he could only see out of his right eye. He spotted Lani and laughed.

Leo picked up a length of steel concrete reinforcing rod, about five feet long, and walked toward Jack Longwood.

"What the hell are you doing, Leo!" Ted yelled. "For God's sake, man, get back, get back!"

Lani dropped her shotgun to the ground and picked up a length of steel rod about the same size as Leo's. She joined him in his slow walk toward Jack and Jimmi Lee, who was rising to her feet. The brother and sister stood like some bloody monsters from out of a terrible nightmare.

Jack and Jimmi Lee both laughed and then charged the cops, screaming in some language that had been unused for thousands of years and was understood only by the undead.

Dozens of cops stood in silence and watched the unthinkable events play out before them.

As if they had been rehearsing for this moment all their lives—and they probably, unknowingly, had—

Lani and Leo sidestepped the charge of the brother and sister and drove the steel rods into the chests of Jim and Jack Longwood, piercing the hearts. The brother and sister fell to the ground. They did not move. They were dead. It was over.

As much as it would ever be over for Lani and Leo.

Chapter 36

Brownie was issuing no statements on the case other than that it was over. He would have an official statement after reading the reports from Leo Franks and Lani Prejean. When a network reporter insisted on a statement, Brownie walked out of the room, after having come perilously close to telling the reporter (Brownie couldn't stand the guy anyway) to go screw himself . . . with a Roto-Rooter.

About thirty minutes later, after Brownie read the preliminary workup sheets, he seriously thought he might be suffering a massive heart attack. When he had recovered, he shouted, "Leaping Jesus Christ!"

"He read the prelim workup," Lani said.

"Holy Joseph fucking Mary!" Brownie squalled, his voice carrying all over the huge building.

"I do believe you're right," Leo said.

"Great God Almighty!" Brownie screamed. "Werewolves!"

"I wonder if my granddaddy *was* a *loup-garou?*" Lani mused aloud.

"Ask your parents."

"I believe I will."

"Immortals!" Brownie shouted. "Demonic shape-changers!"

"At least you have parents to ask," Leo said.

Lani touched his hand. "We just might both have bad blood in of us, Leo."

"Holy shit!" Brownie finished the report. The volume of his shouting had not lessened.

Leo looked at his watch. "Thirty seconds to go."

They both heard a door slam.

"Twenty," Lani said.

"Get out of my way, goddamnit! Move that chair. Clear the aisle!"

"Ten," Leo said.

"I want everybody out of the room adjacent to Leo's office! Move, goddamnit!"

"Now," Lani said.

The door was flung open, then slammed closed. Brownie leaned over the table.

"Watch your blood pressure, Brownie," Leo said.

"Yeah, boss, you look really terrible," Lani said. "You want me to make you some chicken soup, maybe?"

Brownie glared at her. "You're a Cajun from Louisiana, for Christ sake. What the hell do you know about making chicken soup?"

Lani looked hurt. "I can make a gumbo."

"The last time I ate a bowl of your gumbo, I squirted fire for three days. And don't change the subject."

"What subject might that be, Brownie?" Leo asked.

"What subject?" Brownie shook the papers in front of the two cops. "This goddamn subject. Werewolves? Immortals? Stakes through the heart. I mean, come on now. You can't expect me to stand up on a nationwide TV and radio hookup and read this. Can you?"

"It's what happened, Brownie," Lani said. "It's the truth. You were there the last few minutes. You saw enough to know we weren't dealing with mere human beings."

Brownie relaxed and sat down. Leo got him a cup of coffee. He took a sip and sighed. "Jesus, what am I going to say to the press?"

"Brownie, you want us to falsify a report?" Leo asked. "All you have to do is say the word."

"I won't order you to do that. I would never order a cop to do that."

Lani looked at her copy of the prelim. "We can rewrite it and still tell the truth; we'll just leave a few facts out. But everything else will be the truth. As far as we know it. Sheriff, I . . . " She shrugged her shoulders and closed her mouth.

"I know, Lani. I inspected the warehouse. What else is there to say?"

"Nothing," Leo finished it.

Lani and Leo worked up their reports and Brownie was satisfied and so was the press. The reign of terror was over. Now the cops could get back to the everyday routine of child abuse, elderly abuse, animal abuse, murder, rape, kidnapping, domestic disturbances, holdups, prostitution, gambling, gangs, hit and run, DWI, and drugs . . . all pretty mundane stuff.

Jack and Jim Longwood had been correct about at least one thing: their trail of blood set records in America that surpassed even that of Vlad the Impaler.

Connie and Frank turned the classified information about the elder Longwoods still being alive over to their superiors in the Bureau. If anything was ever done about it, that news never reached Lani and Leo.

Lani called her parents and inquired about her grandfather's background. Her mother told her never to ask again and hung up on her.

Stacy Ryan and Leo Franks could have sued for their share of the Longwood monies. They did not. Stacy continued to run KSIN, and Leo was promoted to the rank of lieutenant on the Hancock County Sheriff's Department, and Lani was promoted to sergeant.

At the insistence of Lani and Leo, the bodies of Jack and Jim Longwood were cremated and the ashes sealed in a concrete and steel tomb.

On the afternoon following the cremation and burial of Jack and Jim Longwood, Leo got a call at his office. Father Daniel from his flower shop back in New York State. Leo listened, said goodbye, and hung up.

"What?" Lani asked, after looking at the strange expression on her partner's face.

"The old Longwood mansion in Albany."

"What about it?"

"It collapsed about an hour ago."

HAUTALA'S HORROR AND
SUPERNATURAL SUSPENSE

GHOST LIGHT (4320, $4.99)
Alex Harris is searching for his kidnapped children, but
only the ghost of their dead mother can save them from his
murderous rage.

DARK SILENCE (3923, $5.99)
Dianne Fraser is trying desperately to keep her family —
and her own sanity — from being pulled apart by the malev-
olent forces that haunt the abandoned mill on their
property.

COLD WHISPER (3464, $5.95)
Tully can make Sarah's every wish come true, but Sarah
lives in teror because Tully doesn't understand that some
wishes aren't meant to come true.

LITTLE BROTHERS (4020, $4.50)
The "little brothers" have returned, and this time there will
be no escape for the boy who saw them kill his mother.

NIGHT STONE (3681, $4.99)
Their new house was a place of darkness, shadows, long-
buried secrets, and a force of unspeakable evil.

MOONBOG (3356, $4.95)
Someone — or something — is killing the children in the
little town of Holland, Maine.

MOONDEATH (1844, $3.95)
When the full moon rises in Cooper Falls, a beast driven by
bloodlust and savage evil stalks the night.

*Available wherever paperbacks are sold, or order direct from the
Publisher. Send cover price plus 50¢ per copy for mailing and
handling to Penguin USA, P.O. Box 999, c/o Dept. 17109,
Bergenfield, NJ 07621. Residents of New York and Tennessee
must include sales tax. DO NOT SEND CASH.*

YOU'D BETTER SLEEP WITH THE LIGHTS TURNED ON!
BONE CHILLING HORROR BY

RUBY JEAN JENSEN

ANNABELLE	(2011-2, $3.95/$4.95)
BABY DOLLY	(3598-5, $4.99/$5.99)
CELIA	(3446-6, $4.50/$5.50)
CHAIN LETTER	(2162-3, $3.95/$4.95)
DEATH STONE	(2785-0, $3.95/$4.95)
HOUSE OF ILLUSIONS	(2324-3, $4.95/$5.95)
LOST AND FOUND	(3040-1, $3.95/$4.95)
MAMA	(2950-0, $3.95/$4.95)
PENDULUM	(2621-8, $3.95/$4.95)
VAMPIRE CHILD	(2867-9, $3.95/$4.95)
VICTORIA	(3235-8, $4.50/$5.50)

*Available wherever paperbacks are sold, or order direct from the
Publisher. Send cover price plus 50¢ per copy for mailing and
handling to Penguin USA, P.O. Box 999, c/o Dept. 17109,
Bergenfield, NJ 07621. Residents of New York and Tennessee
must include sales tax. DO NOT SEND CASH.*